GORDON DICK

Opportunititty Knockers

First edition

ISBN: 978-1-7352513-0-1

Cover art by Adam Rudd

This book was professionally typeset on Reedsy.
Find out more at reedsy.com

Contents

II   The Fall

I

The Rise

1

The Sleepwalker Awakes

"You're not happy," the siren exhales, pressing herself into my side.

"No," I agree, staring out at the sun slipping into the sea like a suicidal Christmas bauble bound to a brick, coloring the clouds like period blood in a cream pie. "I'm not."

"Then run away."

"With you?" I whisper, turning my head to behold her unbearable beauty.

"You must cut your own chains," she replies, empathy oozing from her almond eyes. "I have to go," she sighs, craning in to kiss me goodbye before rising to walk towards the water.

"Please stay," I implore.

Surf lapping her legs, she turns her sultry self to me, the hint of a headshake bringing a bittersweetness to her ephemeral full bloom. "You must free yourself," she shouts.

I struggle up to stop her, but my legs lock as if mired in mud.

"Cut your chains and you'll be free," she yells, flapping her arms and soaring towards the sunset.

Fluttering furiously, I hover hardly a foot from the sand, looking like a chained parakeet pulling towards a painting of a palm tree.

Sinking back into my blues, a lightning bolt of bliss spirals from my spelunker up my spine, and I look down to see a lass's lips locked to my lion.

Monday, November 18, 2013, 12:17 p.m.

Sarah looks up with oddly innocent eyes, as if turning her attention from a lollipop to an airplane.

"Dreaming about me?" she asks, sitting up astraddle my stiffy.

"Mm hmm," I mumble, wishing she were mute so I could imagine my phantasmic temptress on top of me.

"You were hard as a rock when I came in," she coos, come hither eyes casting their serpent spell on my spitter. "Were they good dreams?"

"Uh huh."

12:23 p.m.

"Pull out!" Sarah snarks. "I don't want your cum oozing out me all day."

Is she so snooty as to snub her sweet's seed inside her? Is the pill not preventing her withering womb from bearing my bambino?

Pulling out is a pain. A burden we men bear to give the gift of our gloveless glory. When reasons aren't so wanting, we also live with the liability. Hit one egg with your little army and you're either forking out a fortune or the father of a murdered fetus, all at the whimsy of a woman whose rationality ranges from naught to negative with the march of the moon.

My ploinker pulls out, splashing his sploodge in the bowl of her belly button.

"You're so gross!"

So sentimental.

"Here, let me clean it up."

I clutch the closest soiled clothing, my work apron. Whatever, it's laundry day and I don't work til five. With a southward swipe, I leave a lacquer of love all the way to her woo.

"Did you use your *work* apron? You're so *gross!*"

1:07 p.m.

That's twice in a week Her Cuntliness came home to lunch on my lion. The trend wouldn't be troubling if those weren't the *only* times we porked in that period.

Is she burning to bone her boss? Is that it? Alleviating her lust with my loins?

I'm quaffing my coffee, getting up the gumption to endure all the drudgery between now and tonight when I cut loose at karaoke.

My cellphone rings. My boss. Against better judgment, I answer.

Can I come in early? Brandy's brats are sick or some shit.

6:45 p.m.

The father on table two is flailing his ham hands and shouting "waiter," as if his agitation alone wouldn't have obtained my attention. His corn-fed features support the supposition that Homo Sapiens and Neanderthals swapped sploodge, just not the part about Homo Sapiens being the primary providers of pedigree. My hypothesis is proved by his porcine progeny, busy making a mess of their bread for the busboy as mom's fat face remains fixed to her Iphone's Facebook feed.

Remind me to stop by the drug store for a home vasectomy kit.

Against all odds, I fail to notice the missing link's melodramatics and move on to the cuckly couple at table three.

"Waiter? Excuse me, *waiter?*" the pantywaist appeals. "Do you know how much *longer* it will be?"

"Very soon," I reply, not about to bring up the burst pipe or backed up dish-pit drain, the cooks mopping madly at the lahar of sudsy food scraps flooding the kitchen. If their pizza *was* on its way, then I dare say I may detect the bouquet of its burning amidst the melange.

"You said that last time."

"And it's even sooner now."

"That was twenty minutes ago."

"Perhaps you and the lady would like another round while you're waiting?"

"Alright… but our pizza *is* coming soon?"

"Quite. Another round of the same?"

"Actually, could I have my martini a bit *less* dry? That last one was *too* dry. And maybe just a *tiny* bit dirty this time. Oh, and could I switch to Tan*queray?*"

"Of course sir. Another lemon drop for you madam?"

"Oh… I don't *know,*" she sighs, feeling the hard won weight of her agency and hoping a man might deal with the details. "I want something *citrusy,* but not a *lemon drop.* What do *you* recommend?"

"Another vodka drink? Or a different liquor?"

"Oh I don't *know!*" she flusters. "What do *you* like to drink?"

I like bourbon, neat, or rye on the rocks.

I'll take a beer in the bottle, or ten if they're on tap.

Almost anything with alcohol is acceptable.

Except tequila. That shit is poison.

"How about a tequila sunrise?"

"Oh, why not. Sounds festive."

"It is madam, like waking up in your lawn to the sprinklers going off."

"You sure you want that hon?" the idiot interjects. "Remember the *last* time you had tequila?"

"Can you let it *go?*" she snaps. Reassuming her pseudo-classy composure, she squeezes my forearm, smiling like a trophy wife offering the pool boy a cookie. "Don't mind *him, I'll* have the tequila sunrise." The justice is not lost on me. Something stirs down deep.

A smirk. She's earned it. "Of course madam."

I move on. The port commissioner is requesting me to come and kowtow to his commands. Lucky enough to have noshed before our culinary Krakatoa, the curmudgeon might care to pay for his repast.

No, he will *deign* to pay the damage, as the dickhead will deign to tip me ten percent whilst acting as if his chump change is charity.

"Would you care for some dessert sir? Perhaps an after dinner drink?"

6

"No thank you," he grumbles.

"Shall I grab your check then?"

"That chicken made my hands sticky. I need a moist towel."

Really? Does the dirty old dickhole even *know* what need means? "But of course sir."

Containing my contempt as I set forth for the server station, I grab a soup bowl and a bleach white bar rag, wetting it with hot water. Inspired by the spunk adhered to my apron, I clean up the crust with the fucktwat's towelette, getting a gust of giddy from the moment's magic, but not lingering long, lest my little gift grow cold.

"Your moist towel sir," I announce, setting it forth with a flourish.

"*Thank* you!" he patronizes, rubbing the towel around, taking extra time to wipe the webbing between his fingers. I detest few things more than a disingenuous 'thank you,' an indignity I endure daily. It's especially insulting when I've gone so far for the sake of service.

I must... I can't... I shouldn't... fuck it. My face slips into a psychotic smile like a clown on a coke binge. "You're so very welcome sir!" I say, super sickly-sweet like frosted sugar on a shiv. "It's such a pleasure serving such a pillar of the community! Perhaps I may have the pleasure of cupping your balls while you wipe the grease off your hands?"

Jaw dropping at my daring, terror fills his face, his towelette falling to the floor as he clutches his heart.

As I stare at him stupefied, sympathetic citizens hurry to help. Shit! Fuck! Fucking motherfucking shitballs what the fuck! Okay, okay, okay, okay, calm your clams and riddle this rationally, as dire straits deserve at least poorly plotted plans. Of paramount importance is the moribund commissioner, but since my princely presence would only up the odds of the attack being terminal, his plight must be purged from the program, leaving first and foremost the fact that I've never been fired before and must resign immediately to maintain my track record.

Offing my apron as the manager materializes, I offer it unasked. "Best of luck," I say, holding my hand out for a shake which he is too stunned not to take.

Glad to be leaving on good terms, I walk off into the wet northwestern night, the sound of sirens echoing my anguish.

Fuck! What if the coroner finds my cum on his fingers?

A primal scream lets loose from my lips, an eruption of suppressed suffering commanding the clouds to turn their tap from drizzle to downpour.

Proactively protecting my ego from the evening, I place the blame for my breakdown upon my parents for having not properly prepared me for the drudgery of adulthood. Between my mother, a canine acupuncturist, my father, the outlaw organic farmer infamous for inventing the log cabin composting outhouse and feeding the fruits of his family's feces to clueless farmers market frequenters, and a homeschooling spent blowing through banned books in our garden's gazebo, I'd no notion how soul numbing the working world would be.

When fate found our farm defending its composting in court, we lost our land to a class action lawsuit. As our formerly faithful customers symbolically bleached their bellies with store bought foodstuffs, I turned 18 in a tricked out school bus, all that was left of our old life. Doing what any whiz kid would when running from the roost to find his fortune, I picked up employment too dull to distract me from destiny's designs. Reputations ruined, my parents packed up what was left of their livelihoods and moved with my little sis to the San Juans.

Eight winters I've wasted since first washing dishes by the waterfront, and though time has trampled my dreams into dust, perhaps the flakes are still fertile.

7:15 p.m.

I belly up to the bar dripping rain and restlessness, a pit stop in the progression from breakdown to rebuilding.

"Holy smokes!" exclaims bartender Jay, overplaying his impression of my manic mood with a shiver of shock. "You look like you need a drink!"

"Jim Beam neat, double," I reply.

"Tough night? I don't usually see you this early."

"I got off early."

"How'd you manage that?" he asks, grabbing the bottle off the shelf.

"I walked off."

"Just left?" he enquires, pouring a compassionately topfull tumbler. "Just like that?"

"Like the building was burning."

"Huh. Got another job lined up?" he asks, setting the bourbon before my fidgeting fingers.

"Nope," I reply, drinking it desperately down to half full. "I'm a free agent."

"Doing what?"

"I dunno," I shrug. "Life I guess."

Jay sucks a lime wedge and shakes his head, as if the fruit had failed to embody life's bitterness. "You *always* have another lined up. Jobs are like women, they only want you if you're taken."

"Yeah," I mutter. "If jobs are what you're into. What do I owe you?"

"This one's on me bud. You'll need your money for your premature retirement."

"Thanks Jay."

"Sure thing bud, you've always taken care of me."

"Gotta please the tip gods," I reply, pulling out a five for a tip. "Though I'm not sure I believe in them after tonight."

"You gonna tell me what happened?"

I tell him my tale, divulging every indignity but the scuz scrubbed from my man skirt.

"You asked him if he wanted his *balls* cupped?"

"Yeah."

"And he had a *heart attack?*"

"I think so."

"What were you *thinking?*"

"Why you gotta bring thinking into it?" I ask, downing the last drops and slipping from my seat. "I'll be back for karaoke later. Gonna go see if Sarah's finally seen a dermatologist about her resting bitch face. If not I'll be back sooner than later, probably single. Pray for me."

"Who to?"

"I dunno," I shrug. "Dion*ysus?*"

7:42 p.m.

Sarah looks up from the chick lit held between her hands, her empty green eyes giving me a glower. "You're home early."

"I got off early."

"How'd you manage *that?*" she snarks, resentful for her romancesturbation's interruption. "I thought you were closing?"

"I just left."

"Just left? You *just left?* What the fuck you mean you *just left?*"

"I don't think using unladylike language and patronizingly repeating yourself will make me say it any simpler Sarah. I didn't feel like being there, so I left."

"So you're unem*ployed* now?"

"You could say that, but I think free is more fitting for my current condition."

"*Free?* Are you fucking *kidding* me? What the fuck is *wrong* with you?"

"Depends who you ask. *Personally,* I feel *great.*"

"Oh *do you?* Well *we* need to talk."

"No Sarah, *you* need to talk," I correct, cruising to the cupboard for a jigger of Jack. "The word *we* implies that *we both* share this need, when *I* would much prefer sweet sweet silence to your nagging nastiness."

"What the *fuck* John? Why can't we have a *rational conversation?*"

"Because a *rational conversation* requires *two rational individuals.*" I reply, sipping my spirits and sighing exaggerated satisfaction. "Would you care for a *rational monologue?*"

"What the fuck's *that* supposed to mean?"

"It means the only rational bone you've ever had in your body is *mine.*"

"*Ha! Ha!*" she scoffs, in calculated career cunt disbelief of my daring. "And I suppose *you're* rational? Quitting your job and getting drunk? Sounds like

10

you're the one with problems."

"Which problems would *those* be Sarah?" I enquire, shlucking my shot and pouring another to temper my tension. *"You're* the one whose after work whine fest drags on til bedtime, at which point if I'm lucky you'll let me pump you while you parrot porn lines in a tepid parody of passion. Sounds like it's *you* I'm drowning out."

"At least I have a job, a *real* job!"

"Ha! *Real job?* What? Paralegal for a di*vorce* lawyer? If facilitating the fracturing of families is more real than helping people who can't cook eat a meal that wasn't microwaved then I don't want a *real job.*"

"At least I have *money!* At least I don't live paycheck to paycheck like *you!*"

"Fuck you and your obsession with money! *You're* not good with money. Your *family* is. You only have a savings because of those checks your grandma sends you. At least my money is *my own fucking money!*"

"Now John-"

"Don't *do* that! Don't tell me I'm out of line cause I'm just getting *started.* I've had one shit show of a shift, but your act takes the cake. One day – and it won't be *long* sugartits, it won't be *long* – your princess tiara will have no one to admire it but a herd of cats. Every Ben and Jerry's pint will have a bottom, a bottom as hollow as your heart." I bound about as I berate her, filling my backpack with what I'd least like deposited in the dumpster. "But hey, at least you'll have your sisters in self-delusion, with their Facebook likes and mimosa brunches to cheer for you on your cock-carousel cruise to cat ladyhood. Oh don't be dramatic about it. Some milquetoast might marry you despite the rash of red flags. But it won't be *me* Sarah, it won't be *me.*"

"I hate you! I *hate* you!" she fumes, flailing her arms in frustration, a quaking choler bringing her body to the brink of blowup.

"Now that's a start-"

"Fuck *you!*"

"I'll return tomorrow for the rest of my shit-"

"You're a fucking *ass*hole!"

"I'll leave my keys then."

"I hope I *never* fucking see you again!"

"I saw a cat in the alley if you're ready to start your collection." If looks could kill… well, too bad sugartits. "Good*night*."

Shit! My Jack Daniels. As I chug the last shlug she quivers on the couch in a sorrow I'd assumed her constitutionally unequipped. "*Wait!*" she wails. "*John!*"

Shit! I must flee before this simulacrum of sentiment coaxes my cock to console her. "This had better be important princess, cause the clock's ticking and I've got a big wide world to see."

"I love you."

"Me too."

8:21 p.m.

When frustration forces you to cast off constrictions, the cosmos does not kindly supply surrogate circumstances, but leaves holes to highlight your failure of foresight. Thankfully, there are professionals prepared to talk you through the transition.

"Everything alright?" Jay asks. "I hope you're not having deep thoughts. You shouldn't mix those with alcohol."

"No," I reply, washing down some whiskey in search of salvation. "Shallow thoughts, wide problems."

"What the fuck's that mean? You cheat on Sarah with a fat chick?"

"No. We broke up."

"Shit bud, I'm sorry."

"No, it's good."

"You got another lined up?"

"No… not really."

"Not *really?*"

"There's one girl I could probably plow. But girlfriend wise? No."

Jay shakes his head at my hopelessness. "You *always* have another lined up. Girls *love* taking men away from each other. They probably get more pleasure from it than the relationship itself."

"Think so?"

"For sure! They're twisted creatures. I just do my best to fulfill their fantasies." Though beer-gutted and balding, Jay heroically helps a revolving door of damsels with their daddy issues. The man is a role model for the era of eroding morality, king of the cultural decline. "Oh well, you didn't seem happy anyway."

"I wasn't, but the problems were bigger than just her."

"Apparently."

"It's all connected."

"You aren't getting new-agey on me, are you?"

"No," I reply, slamming my shot.

"More whiskey?"

"Please."

"This one's on me bud," he says, pouring til only surface tension keeps it contained.

"Thanks," I say, holding my head above my bourbon and letting the whiskey warm my suffering soul. "It's all connected. We couldn't just be free together, living lives of mutual discovery like birds freed from their migrations by global warming. She wanted to trap me in suburban purgatory. She probably would've made me stay home changing diapers. Every day the same, Ground Huggies day. I felt like the dick cake she wanted to stuff in her freezer after her trip around the cock carousel licking cum frosting."

"You make it sound like a carnival," Jay jests, piqued by my portrayal of American matrimony.

"What the hell *else* is it?"

"A buffet. Most men are passive, never putting in a good argument on their own behalf. These men get eaten alive like dishes in hotel pans. The clever men, in contrast, think like diners and strut around heaping their plates."

"With the passive men in the hotel pans?"

"*No,*" Jay replies with a face palm. "With *women.*"

This rouses the resident old timer Ed from his televisional trance. "Cheers brothers!" he cries, raising his glass to the glory of unmanacled manhood. "To the unpleasant truth, and to women! May we drink the milk but never buy the cow."

Clinking glasses and going for a gulp, I take a tick to weigh Ed's wisdom. As long as I'm drinking the milk, why not go where the grass isn't making the maidens mad cows? Why not take that final step to a fresh start?

"Do you have WIFI?" I enquire, lifting my laptop from my bag to the bar.

"Yeah, the password's up there," he replies, pointing at a sign above the pint glasses, 'WiFi password: 2Drunk2Cyberfuck.' "Don't spill any booze on your laptop," he says, eyeing me oddly.

"Don't worry. It's just a thing, and things aren't really my thing, so what's it matter? Besides, the road to opportunititty knockers."

"You going somewhere?" Ed asks.

"Off the deep end sounds like," Jay jeers.

"The land of opportunititty!" I reply

"Where's that?" Jay asks.

"I dunno," I shrug. "But I'm leaving tomorrow."

"I've been there," Ed says between sips, wonder in his wide eyes, gaga in his gruff voice. "Southeast Asia."

That's it! The dream siren's decree suddenly makes sense. I may have cut my cords as was her wisdom, but to fly I must find a big metal bird. "They like karaoke over there, right?" I enquire.

"Sure do."

"And the girls?"

"Heaven."

"Watch out for ladyboys bud," Jay warns.

"Whatever. I'll be able to tell."

"I wouldn't be too certain," Ed snickers. "You know, I had a buddy went to Bangkok back in the eighties. Meets a girl on Khao San Road. Now, that's the manic neon heart of Bangkok's tourist scene. If you've ever been curious about the athletic abilities of a vagina then Khao San is your place. Anyways, my buddy says this girl's the prettiest thing he's ever laid his eyes on. Real tall for an Asian broad but my friend's a pretty tall feller himself. After flirting awhile she drags him back to his hotel room. She goes just about straight to sucking him off, but anytime he tries to travel south of her equator she swats his hand away. Now, my buddy's horny, got a stiffy so hard you could dig to China with it…" He pauses ponderously, bunching his brows as he strokes his stubble. "Or America, I guess, since he was already on that side of the Pacific…"

"So he had a hard on. What's the point?" Jay asks.

"The point is that at this moment he looks down at her skirt and sees a tent so big you could fit the seven Dwarves and still have room for them to take turns with Snow White." At that Ed sips his whiskey wisely, as if plumbing his parable for some mysterious meaning.

"So he ran?" Jay asks.

"They do butt stuff?" I enquire.

"Nope. He paid for her transition and they bought a beach bar in Phuket."

"So he went to *Bangkok* and said *fuck it?*" Jay asks. "Who *named* these cities?"

"Dunno," Ed says. "Queer ain't it? It's as if Thailand's founding fathers saw sex tourism on the country's horizon and named the cities accordingly."

"Hmph," I snort.

"True story though. Were it a fairy tale they'd say they lived happily ever after. It was nice to see my buddy fall in love. Real nice. He didn't have much luck with the ladies back in the states."

"Doesn't sound like he had much luck over *there* either," Jay jeers.

"I wouldn't say that. Luck is, after all, as much about one's attitude as anything else. Of course *I* couldn't have found happiness in his situation, but that don't matter. Way my buddy tells the story they took it real slow, kept it strictly above the waist til the transition. As a woman, my buddy was her first and only. I never saw a happier guy. If that's not luck, then I don't know what is."

"Sounds pretty gay to me," Jay says.

"How could it be gay if he didn't touch her penis?"

"You ever find yourself with a ladyboy?" Jay asks.

"Well sure, I've met a few of them."

"That's *not* what I *meant.*"

"Say," Ed says between sips. "What you looking at on your laptop over there?"

"Flights." Over a grand to fly to Bangkok tomorrow. *"Fuck!"*

"And there he goes," Jay jests. "Off the deep end."

"Eleven hundred bucks to fly to Bangkok. One way."

"You still want to go to Bangkok after Ed's story?"

"Why not?" I shrug. "It's not gonna happen to me. I don't dig tall chicks."

"You thought about the Philippines?" Ed asks. "That flight's usually cheaper."

I check. Seven hundred bucks to fly out midnight tomorrow. More than enough time to rebuild from my breakdown, pull my possessions from the apartment, and bumble my way aboard. Perfect! "It's only 700 bucks."

"Man I had fun down there," Ed reminisces. "This one time back in '88, or was it '89? Can't be sure, memory's a muddled mess at my age. Well, let's see, it was right after my wife and I divorced, so I guess it was '89. Soon as the papers went through I hopped a flight to Manila and spent two weeks straight in Angeles, spending each night with a different bar girl."

"Fourteen whores in *two weeks?*" Jay enquires. "Isn't that ex*cessive?*"

"Not at all. You see Jay, there's a healing process when you break up after a long relationship, which I realize is something you've probably never had. Unless you want that process to drag on for months or even years, you've gotta be proactive about treatment. It just takes one woman for each year you were with your ex, and you're a new man. Tina and I were together fourteen years, so two weeks with a different woman each night and I was feeling fine again. How long were you with your ex, John?"

"Three years."

"So three girls and you'll be good as new. You could do that in a day if you needed to."

"I'm not sure I want a bar girl, let alone *three.*"

"You wouldn't pay for it? It ain't like over *here.* We're talking about regular girls that just don't have many options. Maybe they had a kid with the wrong guy and now other local guys don't want anything to do with them, so they work at the bar, going home with westerners to feed their family. By fucking them you're feeding their kids. If that ain't philanthropy, then I don't know what is. Certainly nothing worth getting compunctions about."

"Uh… I'd still rather have a nice girl."

He eyes me oddly, nods. "Well that's what I'm telling you, they're *nice girls*. You mean you want a *clean* girl, an *innocent* girl. And why not? You're young, American, and appear to have a pulse. They'll love you long time or short time, in patience or in haste. I see you got your debit card out. You buying that ticket?"

"Yep."

"You'll need an onward or return flight within thirty days of flying in. Won't let you into the country on a one-way ticket without an onward flight."

"Sounds like you know all about it," Jay jeers.

"Sure," Ed grumbles. "A man has *needs*."

2

Rebel Reborn

Tuesday, November 19, 2013, 10:05 a.m.

From the blackness I am reborn.

Fumbling for familiarity, I find it in a pyramid of Pabst cans located in the corner. Jay must have been worried about my well being and let me crash on his couch. Heaving my head to assess my suffering, I make sure my wallet and wiener are in their proper positions. You never know when you're nursing such a number.

Finding my best friend still affixed, I feel for my phone, flipping it open to find a surprisingly polite text from my ex saying my belongings are boxed and if I come by while she's working then leave the keys on the counter.

Foraging the floor's refuse for my effects, I realize I'm halfway to hell, in that limbo of meth labs and military brats between Lacey and Fort Lewis. Fishing for cab fare, I find a frumpled wad of ones, a piece of paper upon which Ed has itemized the musts of Manila, and an ATM receipt rubbing in a $100 withdrawal at 10:43 p.m.

Dammit. That would've bought me loads of liquor in the land of opportunititty.

Hell, there's one lady who'd be elated to aid in my ditching of Medusa, my faithful friend and now former coworker Annetta. When Sarah and I broke up briefly back in August, Annetta was so sweetly consoling that when I reconciled with Sarah my orgasm was as gumptious as a compressed air can's last quiff. Though Annetta may have wished me well when the witch and I worked it out, her words were weighted with the melancholy of what could be, a tenderness since tinting the sexual tension between us. So why did I settle for Sarah instead of anointing Annetta my inamorata? Because I would never be Annetta's beau. She's as loving a lass as ever lived, but you could easier catch the clouds than hold on to her heart.

"Hello*ooooo*," Annetta lilts across the line, the vibrato in her voice going straight to my stiffy.

"Hey."

"You're up early. Everything alright?"

"Uh… sort of."

"I'm not covering your shift tonight."

"Oh, you busy?"

"No, I'm taking today off from responsibility. Today is a day of whimsy. A day to clear cobwebs from childhood fantasies."

"A noble endeavor. Did any of your childhood fantasies involve being a chauffeur?"

"Why? You need me to take you to get tested?"

I inform her of my newfound freedom, tonight's flight and how close I'd come to my very first firing.

"*Jeez*, you didn't have to outdo me in the whimsy department. You really just walked off?"

"Like the building was burning. Can I ask you a favor?"

"Yeah *Jooohn*," she purrs. "But you're gonna have to put out for it."

I quest for a quip, but find myself foiled by a rush of blood to my boner. "That's fair. I need to get picked up as soon as possible, then I need to get my shit from Sarah's place and put it somewhere. My brother's place maybe. After all that I need a ride to the airport. I'm probably forgetting some things."

"Where are you?"

"On the edge of Lacey somewhere. Hold on, let me get my bearings." I step

19

outside to survey my surroundings. Out the dirt driveway and across the road to the right is the local power substation. "I'm by that power substation just past the railroad crossing on Mullen Road."

"What are you doing out *there?* I hope she hadn't lost too many teeth to meth. I like to pretend you have standards."

"She had nice gums at least. I guess bartender Jay let me crash here. The details are fuzzy."

"*Jeez* John! I'm coming to get you. Meet me in front of the power station in a half hour. Try not to die in a meth lab explosion before then!"

10:38 a.m.

A passenger might pause at all the filth on the floor, its paint job a dirt-dusted, bird-bombed once-white, its sheepskin seat covers coated in coffee stains and incense ash, but to step inside Annetta's Nissan is to be whisked to a world of whimsical wonder. Moving trinkets and tapes from the passenger seat, she'll smitten you a smile as mushy as a mute volunteering her virginity, frizzy Persian hair haloing her head while your new favorite song floats from the stereo.

"*Jesus* John! Is that *dinner* you're wearing?"

"Oh… yeah," I reply, looking down at my dishevelment as I secure my seat belt.

"You look like hell."

"No. *Hell* is what I walked away from. I *look* like *shit.*"

"You know John," she purrs, perching her paw on my pants. "I don't *mind* helping you. But you owe me! And since you and Sarah broke up…"

"Guess I'll have to give it my best," I say, my member mightening at the memory of August's frenzied fling. But then she reenters the road, and my stomach spoils the spell in a split second flat.

"Jeez John, why so excited? We're only freeing you from the wicked witch."

"Could you stop the car?"

"Here?"

"*Yes!*"

"You okay?"

"*No!*"

Annetta slams the brakes in the brink of time for the modern art of my masochism to plaster the pavement. Feeling in the brisk autumn air the freshness of my freedom fighting my infirmity, I pray to Dionysus as I settle back into my seat, promising to make him proud should I survive my suffering.

"We're not gonna make it very far at this speed. You gonna live?"

"Probably."

"Good. I just cleaned my car a couple months ago. Guess I'll have to nurse you back to health before I take advantage of you."

Whimzled by the warmth of her words, my left hand lands on her knee and flits northward. "Let's start with the nursing now," I suggest.

"You're not cute enough to crash for," she replies, pulling my paw from her panties.

11:02 a.m.

"You're not going off the deep end, are you? Because you look like you're applying to be a panhandler."

"Think I'll get the job?"

"I think you're a shoe in."

"It was a busy night," I shrug.

"*Busy?*"

"It's hard work canceling all of one's obligations. Besides, I had an epiphany."

"Is that code for nervous breakdown?"

"When Sarah wanted to fight last night I realized what it was really about."

"You drinking like a fish and sleeping around like a bunny rabbit?" She smittens me a smile as wanton as teasing. "John... my little bunnyfish."

"No... those were just physical manifestation's of my oppression." Is that not the way a wench would word it? Blaming her beau for her capricious crimes? Who can say I'm not sensitive to the hamster wheelies of women? "If one were

21

to ignore the scientifically proven fact that the majority of lovers' quarrels stem from the female's sexual frustrations, then ostensibly she wanted to fight about my escape from the tyranny of employment, but it was really more about our differing relationships with consumerism. She buys into the American mantra that a person's purpose is to plunder the planet for the sake of success, identifying with a job she despises and shit she doesn't need. She's a fucking paralegal. I mean, who gives a shit? Every night I got to hear about some suburban couple getting divorced, and nine times out of ten it's the guy getting fucked like Forrest Gump at a used car lot. And then she'd say she wanted to marry me, as if that somehow sounded like a promising proposition."

"Wasn't she about to inherit a couple million from her grandma?"

"So?"

"So I doubt you'd lose anything in the divorce."

"Yeah, just emasculated every day leading up to it."

"So you got drunk and bought a ticket to *where?*"

"Manila."

"The Philip*pines?* Why *there?*"

"It's not here."

"That's *it?*"

"That's its most thrilling feature."

"Hmm… let's see. Boobs, beers and beaches? My bunnyfish's basic needs?"

I imagine myself settled into the sand as the sun sets, boxed between a bosomy beauty and a bucket of beers.

"Such a *slut* John!" Annetta nickers, looking over at my leer. "You better give it to me good before you go away and get tropical super syphilis."

"Ugh," I moan, the mental flash of a festering phallus striking terror in my tummy.

"Just wear a condom, you'll be okay."

"Can you pull over?"

"Here?"

"*Yes!*"

"Again?"

"YES!"

We're in the capitol neighborhood, a conspicuously dignified district of Victorian homes protecting the pretensions of the state capitol campus from downtown's decay. Painting the pavement and proclaiming myself prolific for producing so much modern art in one morning, I look up at an old lady flogging her furball for flinging itself forward to examine my exhibit. Sorry lady, I can't help it if your ankle-biter's an art aficionado.

"You sure you'll live?"

"I'd bet on it," I reply, reassuming my seat belt. "But then, I don't have to pay up if I lose."

"Do me a favor," she says, slipping back through the bike lane into the tide of traffic. "Don't die over there. I might want to see you again someday."

"Yeah..." I sigh, thinking bittersweetly of the breasts I will so soon say goodbye to. "Someday." Such a whimsious word, but I say it's a slacker. Someday smokes ruby doobies and dreams of lubey boobies, but tough titty making it move in the morning.

"Who knows? Maybe you won't come back. Get yourself a little Asian wife and settle down, buy a karaoke bar by the beach. Have a dozen kids."

"Ugh."

"Yeah, it's a disturbing idea. You have enough trouble taking care of yourself."

"There's a spot over there," I say, pointing at the side road separating Sylvester park's panhandlers from the Greyhound station's grunge, across Capitol Way from the brick apartment building I'd lived in til last night.

"She's not home, is she?" she asks, parallel parking between two SUVs.

"No. She might come home for lunch at noon, but it's safe now."

"Good. I don't think she likes me."

"I'd take that as a compliment of character," I reply, stepping out and locking up, lest some riffraff rifle through her things while we're away. "She despises all the good things in life."

"Or maybe she could sense that I wanted to jump you," she speculates. "Trust me, girls have a sixth sense for that shit. Plus we did fuck that weekend you two broke up. Like, *all weekend.*"

"She never said anything about it," I say, musing over the memory as we cross Capitol Way.

"No, but subconsciously she knew."

"Spare some change man?" asks some crusty kid camped out under the Elks' awning with his mangy mongrel and skin-pocked paramour, three flees in the infestation Olympia's soycialists subsidize as a sacrifice to social justice, the new religion of the left shysterminded by globoshlomos to atomize America into identitarian tribes, lowering wages by luring women to flood the workforce in a quest for corporawhorical equality, making a mint off the cultural cancer of rap whilst blaming the nigger's beggary on the mighty white male, who must forever repent for the privilege provided by eons of ancestors weeded by northern winters, the new original sin of white guilt for which even the most ivory of zhids are exempt because six million of their make believe breed were baked in a conflict funded on both sides by themselves.

"Ask Obama."

"Aw, come on man. We haven't ate since yesterday."

"Then ask your mama."

"My mom's dead."

"You're a fucking asshole," his girlfriend informs me.

"There's a dumpster out back," I offer, unlocking the building's front door. "I think I threw some leftover pad thai out a couple nights ago."

"You're such a *jerk!*" Annetta nickers, pinching me in punishment for making her moist with my meanness.

"I'm practicing for Manila," I say, slamming the door on these derelicts lest they let themselves in. "There's probably lots of street people there." We hurry down the hallway to my, or rather to *Sarah's* apartment. It was always Sarah's apartment, even when I paid half the rent.

Roused by my arrival, Sarah's poodle presents her belly for rubbing like a proactive slut with an unsubtle approach. I want to tell her it's not her fault, that the time she barfed on my boots is kibble under the couch, but don't declare my departure lest it muddy the mood.

A brace of boxes front the refrigerator, the plurality of my possessions.

"Two boxes? Is that *it?*"

"Yeah, should be," I reply, a weight lifting as I lay my keys on the counter. "You mind if I shower real quick?"

"You're *sure* she's not coming home?"

"Not for an hour or so, if at all."

"Then maybe you should brush your teeth too."

I forage for clean clothes, but settle on the least soiled, returning in ten to Annetta browsing Sarah's bookshelf.

"She reads a lot of trashy romance."

"Yeah, it's ironic cause she wouldn't know romance if I tattooed it on my penis and smacked her on the face with it."

"It makes sense though. She fell for you, after all."

"You're admitting I'm romantic?"

"Maybe I'm saying you're trashy."

"Whatever. You fucked me."

"I was slumming it."

"You ready to go?"

"Aren't you gonna make sure it's all there?"

"Nah."

She lavishes me with a leer dripping in devilry, magnetizing me towards the lips I've so longed for. But even in her arms all the memories of Medusa permeate the apartment, and when my eyes lock with Lassie's sideways stare a gust of guilt goes through me, as if I were boinking the babysitter while the kiddo cries in the crib. "Let's go back to your place," I suggest, uncoiling from our kiss.

"I live with my parents."

"Oh, right."

"I'm not wearing panties."

Some sentences are God granted with a greatness beyond the words from which they're woven, her four words finding all reasoning rerouted to my auxiliary head. In a paroxysm of passion I cast her upon the couch, pulling my pants down posthaste.

Our fervor fired by weeks of wistfulness, our minutes of magic quickly crescendo, instinct finding my little fellas frosting a couch cushion.

"Should we clean that up?" she asks, aghast at the globs pooled upon the padding.

"The dog will get it," I reassure.

"Gross!" she exclaims, procuring a paper towel. "You really are an awful creature," she declares, dabbing up my dollops.

"It's endearing, isn't it?"

"Whatever."

"Let's blow this joint."

She flushes the refuse while I reassemble myself. Bidding Lassie goodbye, we grab a box each. Locking us out, I catch Lassie licking the leftovers.

Tonight she'll lick Sarah. It will be her last taste of me.

A surrogate goodbye.

Closure.

"Shit! I left my panties."

6:09 p.m.

Oh how tenderness torments when time is so tight, tearing your heart between telling it all and keeping lips tied. For what could words do but twist up the truth, when touch tells it all, if occasionally uncouth?

"You gonna open your fortune cookie?" Annetta asks.

"Oh... I guess," I reply, cracking it open. Is a heart not like a fortune cookie? Not telling its tale til it's been torn in two?

"What's it say?"

"Good things come in big packages."

"What's it really say?"

"'Not all who wander are lost.'"

"I think you got the wrong fortune. You're lost even when you're not wandering."

"What's yours say?"

"Lets see... it says..." Her face lights up like a Christmas tree plugged in to an electric eel. "'Your efforts to help a friend will be well repaid.' Well, you know what *that* means." So funny a female's facility at finding felicity in a fortune, as if our terrestrial trails were sponsored by spirits capable of communicating by cookie.

"You tell me."

"You'll *see*..." she alludes. "When's your flight?"

"Midnight."

"We're having an adventure first," she announces, starting her steel steed with a lusty leer.

"Where to?"

"I dunno... somewhere dark... alone."

And so we wind our way north up East Bay Drive, urgent in our ardor, electrically alive. Stopping under a maple tree on a dead end street, she looks over longingly for a bittersweet beat. What lascivity lurks behind her luscious lips? What titillations tremble in her throbbing thighs? Could this be the moment so long muddling my mind, where she casts aside free love, and makes herself mine?

"Have you ever done it in a car?" she enquires. "I bet you've done it in lots of cars."

"A few."

No more is said, as we make the backseat our bed, as words are wont to wilt, when our hearts are atingle, our bosoms atilt. For all falsehoods are foiled by the subtle signals of skin; its shudders, its shivers, its goosebumps, its quivers, all pushing us away or pulling us in. But should a clutch call for commentary, a cue for your beau, to hold to his tempo, or to hasten it anew, then a whisper would work, if its words you must use. But should fervor find your tongue in a bind, all the worries of the world removed from your mind, then feast in your triumph, for transcendence you've found, in the arms of your lover, your souls have soared from the ground.

8:46 p.m.

How less bittersweet goodbye could be, if of tomorrow it could but tell.

"I wish I was coming with you," she says, taking the airport off ramp.

"Me too."

"But I guess that would interfere with your search for a wife. You gonna be okay over there?"

"I'll be fine."

"It's too bad," she bemoans. "You're finally freed from the wicked witch and now you're going away."

"I'll be back."

"If you don't die."

"I won't."

"I might want to see you again."

"You will."

"Just wear a condom, *okay?*"

"The whole *time?*"

At the drop-off zone I clutch her close for one last kiss, fleeting yet fated to float forever in the mists of memory, perhaps to pull us together again.

"See you later John."

"See you later Annetta," I reply, slipping from my seat.

"Just wear a condom!" she calls, as I tread towards the terminal.

Foot traffic fixed on us, I turn back towards her, my signature smirk turned up to ten. "Shall I send it to you as a souvenir?"

3

Night Flight

That Night

While the wind whisks me away, I'll apprise you of the proceedings that made me almost marry Medusa.

Her Cuntliness claimed she couldn't recall our first fuck. Though we'd only pounded seven or eight pints apiece, which was nearly enough to make her amenable, a licentious lucidity belied her blackout.

Since she'd not informed me of her affliction, but merely that her apartment was proximate and I should come play with her peaches (which sounded quite sensible, as I believe it was beginning to bother the bartender), I cannot bear blame for the frenzy that followed; the headlong hurry back to her abode, our clothes coming off as quick as the door closed, her claws cutting tracks in my back as she thrashed in throes of ecstasy, eyes an emerald inferno boring into my being, thighs clamping me as we came, draining my last drop and with it my will.

When my mind motioned to let her go from my life, my johnson hung the jury, and two years of mistrials ensued. Terrified of further entrapment, I retained my financial sovereignty through a second savings account of which Her Cuntliness had no clue, carefully keeping but a pittance in my pocketbook to maintain a pretense of poverty.

I must admit, when she paid for our week in Hawaii I felt a pang of penance for my fiscal falsehood, but that was quickly cured with a plate of poke and a piña colada.

I tell this tale to cure any confusion about my ability to afford this adventure, to prove my bank balance as robust as my body and brain. You see, this flight has found me with time for reflection, and though I've tried to talk to the asshat in the aisle seat, he's one of those insufferable sorts who, wanting the wisdom of a man like myself, pegs his importance to his corporate climb, as many men do in our corpulent clime.

During these idle hours of anxious insomnia I've threshed out a theory. The theory of relativititty postulates that a titty's attractiveness is a product of comparison to previous conquests, the hedonic treadmill of trollops blunting the butterflies once aroused by a rack, necessitating ever nicer nanas to get giddy from a grope.

Might this jaunt forever jade me to American minge?

4

Manila Knights

Thursday, November 21, 2013, 11:26 a.m.

Puncturing heaven's pillows, we whoosh through their white, emerging from their mists to an immeasurable metropolis disappearing into the distance, a helter skelter sprawl scattered with skyscrapers lazing in the haze like stiffies in a steam room.

My paleness proclaiming my mighty whitey purchasing power, I clear customs quickly and wad my wallet with funny money from a cash machine. Finally freed from the intercontinental cocoon of airplanes and airports that lets us leave and land in the stately sterility of one another's exhalations, the effluvium of a million automobiles sticks to my instantly sweat soaked skin. Finding a fleet of the idling offenders awaiting my wishes, I command a cabby to convey me to Remedios Circle, where Ed has informed me I'll find a full selection of services.

If you took LA's traffic and subtracted any sense you'd have yourself a hint of the confusion that follows; the fleets of Frankensteinian junkers overlooking lane lines, the honking horns as we sit stalled in traffic, beggars bounding to the wealthy white man to cheerfully check if the lock on his door works, the colorful commuter vehicles riddling the road, looking like a jeep and a chicken bus had an illegitimate love child. (Jeepneys, I will later learn these contraptions to be called.)

Discharging my charioteer at Remedios Circle, I brave a half block of feculence on foot, checking into the first hostel I find on Adriatico Street, a neighborhood where high rise condos cast their shadows upon tin shacks, a place so progressive fecal composting is a sidewalk affair, a ward so welcoming your willy whacker's wishes will be enquired into at every corner. Should your little man's mind change between blocks, another sympathetic soul will be happy to help.

My backpack stashed, I dash across Adriatico, seating myself at an open air bar for liquid realignment.

8:06 p.m.

A boarding house for globohobos to prove the intrepidity of their travels by sharing their stink with strangers, the hostel is a world away from the meat market two blocks below, only betraying its third world whereabouts when one looks out the window or tries to flush toilet paper.

"I can't believe this fucking city man, fucking filthy," Marco says between sips. "I gotta get outta town." On walkabout, looking for the meaning of life in beer bottles and board shorts, Marco maintains an innocent inability to see the wisdom of the unwashed.

"It's not that bad," Eddy shrugs. "Just don't wear flip-flops out there." A Cambodian Canadian on a soul quest to reconnect his boots to his roots, Eddy sees the suffering with more understanding eyes.

"Easy for you to say mate, you look like them. Nobody's asking you if you need a woman, or Viagra. I mean, bloody *hell* mate! Do I look like I can't rise for the occasion? Do I look like I have to pay for it?"

"What are we doing hanging around here?" I ask. "Let's go out for the next round."

"Alright," Eddy agrees. "But can we keep it close? I've got a morning flight to Bangkok."

"You guys been across the street?" I enquire.

"That tin shack with the shirtless guy cooking food?" Marco asks.

"Yeah, Erra's."

"Man I was there last night and this fucking pregnant cat wouldn't stop begging me for scraps. What the bloody hell do I look like, some kind of animal rights activist?"

"Ah don't worry about that," Eddy encourages. "She probably just wanted her baby daddy back from your plate."

"Oh God mate! Don't say that. You'll give me nightmares."

"How did the meat taste?" I ask.

"I don't know mate, like pork."

"Exactly," Eddy says. "*Like* pork."

"It *was* pork."

"Sure, sure," Eddy dismisses.

"You ever ate cat Eddy?" I ask.

"Once, in Vietnam."

"What did it taste like?"

"You know, *like* pork."

8:39 p.m.

Marco inhales his noodles while Eddy and I sip our suds, watching two streetwalkers accost a codger as he pays his tricycle fare. (A tricycle is a motorbike with a covered sidecar painted like a 70's lunch box, and the core of this country's economy.)

"We need more of this in America," I muse, as the fight over the fella's phallus turns physical. "This would make great reality television."

"Eh. You get used to it," Eddy replies, unimpressed. "Hey Marco, you trying to finish before the cat comes back?"

"I don't think the cat's coming back," I say, leaning in to inspect Marco's almost empty plate. "Here kitty kitty kitty."

"It's not responding," Eddy says.

"I think it's dead," I declare. "Must've choked on the noodles."

"Awe come on guys!" Marco pleads.

"Hey man, you're the one eating pasta a la pussy," I say. "Actually, that doesn't sound half bad."

"What do you think they did with the babies?" Eddy asks.

"I bet they'd be good tempura battered," I reply. "As long as they weren't too far along."

Months from now, Facebook will inform me that Marco is trying out vegetarianism, or was it vegemitearianism?

9:54 p.m.

We've bounced back across Adriatico to Bedrock Bar & Grill, a cave-ish caricature of its namesake cartoon town with a doll at the door and neon lights both announcing nightly live music.

"You boys understand what the fuck she's singing about?" Marco asks, referring to the floozy singing on stage, whose accent makes her English sound as if she's testing out a tongue transplant.

"I dunno, love or something," I reply.

"I wonder if she understands the words," Eddy muses. "Or if she just memorizes the lyrics phonetically."

"I'll help her memorize them phallically if she wants," I offer philanthropically.

"She's not a bad singer," Marco declares. "The pronunciation's just funny. At least she's pretty though, eh boys?"

Keeping our attentions turned to the trollop, we nod distracted agreement to acknowledge our attraction whilst simultaneously showcasing it to prove we're not poofs.

"You boys up for shots?" Marco asks. "I'm buying."

"Sure," Eddy answers.

"Sounds good," I reply.

Marco departs, promptly reappearing with the bitty bartender behind him.

"Thanks love," Marco says, casting her a crooked grin as she lays down a tray laden with nine shots of brown booze, bouncing back to the bar ablush.

Face flushed, Eddy gapes aghast at the booze before us. Marco picks up a shot first and, like lemmings, Eddy and I follow suit. "Cheers mates!" Marco toasts. "To Manila! May we escape her with wallets and kidneys intact."

"To Manila," we parrot, facing our fate. Ugh, third world rum. I chase it with a chug of Red Horse, the local malt liquor.

"Three rounds huh?" I chide. "You trying to flush fluffy from your mouth?"

"You boys ready for the next round?" Marco asks, ignoring the question.

"You guys go ahead," Eddy croaks.

"What about you mate?"

"What about me?"

"Another shot?"

"Sure," I reply, recalling the commitment I'd delivered to Dionysus. Without his word, a man is merely a woman with a wiener.

It is wisened that in wine the truth is divined, and this proves true, as by the fourth shot of the foul shit I'm admitting my addiction to my newfound friends. "I want to sing karaoke," I blurt.

"You want to do kara*oke?*" Marco questions.

"Yeah, I'm in Asia. I want to do karaoke!"

"I saw a karaoke bar across the street," Eddy offers.

"That instinctual for your people?" Marco asks, knitting his brows suspiciously. "Knowing where the nearest karaoke bar is?"

"No more instinctual than making cat taste like pork," Eddy shrugs.

"Well fuck it," Marco declares. "Let's check it out."

Swigging our suds and slamming the bottles down decisively, we dash across Adriatico to this den of degeneracy, a ditsy doozy at the door all but bared to us as bait. Above the bimbo a reader board reveals the prices to be paid for our depravation: 300 pesos for a lady drink, 1000 pesos for a VIP room.

"What's a VIP room?" I ask.

"A private karaoke room mate," Marco answers.

"What's a lady drink?"

"It's like, you pay for her drink, and then she chats with you while she drinks it."

"Sounds seedy."

"Nah mate. It's just a little chat anyway, aye?"

Marco chats up the hostess, who returns his goofy grin with professionally feminine friendliness. "Come on guys," he cries, urging us on.

We follow her up the stairs and down a dark hallway to a private parlor with several sofas and a karaoke machine. We order a bucket of beers, which arrives with six sweeties who line up like suspects in the case of a stolen heart. Before I can ken the parade's purpose, two tarts split off to sit with Marco and Eddy, leaving the other lollipops pie-eyeing me plaintively, like a litter of puppies in a cardboard box.

"Which girl you want mate?"

"Huh?"

"Don't worry mate, it's just a chat."

"I'll take her," I say, pointing in the approximate direction of the doxies, not caring which girl I get since their affections will be fictitious, their flatteries frittered on lesser men than myself. My apathy emboldening the most ambitious of the bimbos to sit herself beside me, I tell her to set up the machine while I sift through the songbook's sorry selection, settling on the Beatles' 'Yesterday,' which turns out to be a cut-rate copy recomposed by computer.

As our group's buffest and blondest, Marco gets the most for his money, his hussy only holding back out of hope for more of it. Eddy, though a nori sheet short of a sushi roll, is content with his cutie. Though my floozy is flirtatious, when I mistake her professional friendliness for affection and lunge at her lips, I find myself flailing through empty air.

"No kissy... unless you want pay my bar fine?"

"Bar fine?"

"You want take me hotel?"

"Um..." I mumble, torn between temptation and the puritanical principal that pussy should never be paid for with less than a lifetime of misery. "No, sorry."

Friday, November 22, 2013, 10:28 a.m.

The morning buzzes with backpackers whirling under the weight of their overburdened bags, sensitizing yours truly to his shabby chattels. With their creams, pills, and convertible pants, they must savvy something I don't, must have melded these provisions' powers into an armor against the pestilent poverty simmering outside.

Marco is saying something.

"Huh?" I ask, still attuning myself to the time zone.

"What's your plan mate?"

"Oh... I dunno," I reply, stirring my coffee ineffectually. "What's yours?"

"Reckon I'll catch a bus up to Baguio. See the northern highlands."

"What's up there?"

"Rice terraces and pine trees and shit."

"Sounds nice," I reply, needing a plan in the jealous way a teenager needs a cell phone now that Eddy is Bangkok bound and Marco is off to Bagawhatever. "I dunno, I think I might catch a boat somewhere."

"Aw yeah? Where to mate?"

"I dunno," I shrug.

"I think there's a boat to Coron today."

"Where's that?"

"Southwest of here. North of Palawan."

"And where's Palawan?"

His grin overcomes his hangover. "Did you look at a map mate?"

"Sure, I mean, I've looked at the country on Google Earth a couple times."

"Palawan's in the southwest. Long skinny island reaching towards Indonesia."

"And it's nice?"

"Yeah, it's a tropical paradise full of limestone cliffs and shit. It's even got an underground river."

"Oh, sounds nice. You can get there from Coron?"

"Sure thing mate. The ferry goes on to Puerto Princessa, or you can catch a

37

little boat to El Nido."

"Guess I might check it out."

"Beats staying in this dump, aye mate?"

"Yeah."

"Well mate," he announces, tidying his trash and standing up. "It's been fun. Reckon I'll pack my bag and rock up to the bus station."

"Alright man," I say, holding my hand out for a shake. "Happy travels."

"Happy trails mate."

Staring into my instant coffee, my longing to leave grows all of a sudden urgent, the gulf between these tramps and yours truly all but unbridgeable. They assume the air of intrepid travelers taking trails never trod, as if it were an aura you could don when you depart and remove when you return. Only I here realize the rarity of actual adventure in the days of digital addiction, a world where any vapid vixen can turn the tritest of trips into the soul quest of the century by showcasing it through a series of insufferable selfies, getting herself gads of 'you-go-girl's and a thousand likes from thirsty lads.

I don't need adventure. I need beer, titties, and a nice view.

Cleaning up my crumbs with the hardened habits of hospitality, I dispose of the dishes and totter towards reception.

"May I help you?" the doxy at the desk enquires.

"Is there a boat to Coron today?" I ask.

"Yes, at five this afternoon. You want to go?"

"Yeah."

"You better buy ticket soon. Have you checked out?"

Is that a philosophical question? "No. I probably should huh?"

"Yes. Check out is 11. We have storage area if you need to leave your bag until the boat leaves."

Taking leave of the lass to prepare for departure, I enter the dorm room to find Marco throwing his bag on his back.

"Well, I'm off mate," Marco says with a friendly shoulder slap. "Best of luck. Hope you find a nice karaoke bar in Coron."

"Thanks man. Enjoy the mountains."

Shoving my shit into my pack for the pilgrimage, I return to reception for check out, stowing my bag in storage whilst I procure my passage.

Though the heavens hang heavy, the commoners are more concerned with my nuts' needs than the weather's whimsies. Warmed by the selflessness of strangers, I navigate Adriatico north to Robinson's mall, where the 2Go Travel office is located. At the mall's entrance, sharply dressed disciples line up to be led through a metal detector into this air-conditioned consumer Canaan, this bright beacon of abundance bringing the good word of wealth to the sea of suffering outside.

Wandering these hallowed halls, their breadth becomes clear. I need help, lest I amble for hours pursuing this peddler of paradise, falling prey to false prophets in search of my messiah. Questioning a cutie selling cellphones at a kiosk near the food court, I savvy my salvation to be situated beside the very entrance I'd come in, with a separate street entrance, so I retrace my steps.

The air erupts in deafening downpour as the couple before me finishes paying for their passage, a feculent flow of flotsam flooding Adriatico. I wonder if Marco's feline friend is safe and sound. That is, assuming she's not bound for Baguio in his bowels.

Filling in the facts this country's budget big brother requires to keep tabs on my travels, the repetition-worn receptionist returns my passport and takes my pesos, printing a two page ticket of rules and regulations, including the decree that the only animals allowed on the ferry are fighting cocks. As I riddle how I'll round up a last minute rooster, the storm stops, the stench of struggle scoured from the sky to settle into the sea.

5

Dolphin Safe White Meat

5:32 p.m.

Workers bound about unbinding the cobweb of cordage pinning us to port, the city's skyscrapers soaring behind them like concrete cocks, goading God to drop the soap.

Manila's feculence overflowing in a layer of bobbing litter as we leave the harbor behind, I muse you might say these bottles and bags to be on the way to their afterworld, slowly sailing to that plastic paradise in the mid Pacific, where they may photodegrade into infinitesimal fragments, melding with the massive gyre of junk and attaining enlightenment.

As the city silhouettes against the sunset, supper is served on the deck in pre-portioned Styrofoam cartons. I sip my suds and let the line shorten before procuring an insipid pittance of chicken and rice, a ration perhaps plenteous for a Lilliputian local brought up on the brink of beggary, but meager for a magnificent man like myself.

10:21 p.m.

In karaoke I connect with these provincial peasants, bridging the gap between Old Glory and my new freedom-challenged friends with my velvety voice. Wooing my worshipers with the majesty of America, I've been careful to keep the truth from intruding into their picture of the promised land. My supplicants having slowly retired to rest, only rosy-eyed Jessa remains. A Catholic cutie bubbling with the bashfulness of the romantically repressed, she sits spellbound by my speech, swallowing every syllable that slips from my lips as I tell her tales of a world without want, a wonderland where wishes flower to fruition with but a token of toil. Would it not be cruel to crush the hope of Hollywood without healing the hole in her heart the loss would leave?

What a wonder such womanhood can be packaged so petitely! It's as if God foresaw sex tourism and made them travel-sized. She's saying something.

"What's that?"

"You have girlfriend in America?"

"No. Not right now."

"What you mean?"

"I used to. We broke up."

"Broke up?"

"We're no longer together."

"Oh… why?"

"Well… lots of reasons."

"This normal?" she asks, furrowing her face in frowny confusion.

Shit, I've come too close to touching on the truth. "Um… no… couples usually stay together."

"So why *you* no longer together?"

I need to keep her in my clutches, not bore her by backpedaling. What makes these maidens amorous? Birthing a man's babies from the wedding til her womb wilts and feeding his face til his heart fails? "She never cooked for me. Not once." A white lie, as Sarah had sometimes microwaved my meals.

"*No!*"

"Yes."

"A girl should cook for her man."

"She didn't think so."

"I think you better off without her."

"I suppose so," I agree, curbing my concurrence, so as to sound neither spiteful nor spineless.

"In my country every girl want cook for her man," she states, as if any other ethic were unsuitable for sustaining civilization, which of course is correct, as it is the denial of our duality, and particularly the prejudice against the family-minded female, leading the western world to its impending implosion. Say what you will about the backwardness of the barbarians breaching our borders, but you wouldn't say their women don't care for their kin, that papooses aren't popping from their pooters far faster than from us infidels, whose birthrates are below two per trollop and inversely correlated to IQ.

Should western civilization survive, it won't be the cosmopolitans that keep our sisters safe from shariah, but the corn-fed cousin fuckers who fend off the infestation. Walk around Walmart for a taste of this tomorrow.

"What you do in America?" Jessa asks, eyes lit with lust, heart melting from the manifest destiny dripping from every pore of my person.

"I wait tables."

"What you mean?"

"I work in a restaurant."

"But how you afford to travel?"

I consider clarifying that the greenback is God's chosen legal tender for trade, and as such my sweat is worth more than her countrymen's, but realize economics, besides being hard on women's hamsters for its reliance on logic, is too serious a subject for seduction. "Well, it's rather interesting. I was given a research grant for a book I'm writing."

"Ah." Her passion perks, her peaches pert, charging the chasm between us. "You are a singer *and* a writer! So *talented!* What you write about?"

"Well... *this* and *that.* Some *fiction,* some *non*fiction. What brings me *here* is a book I'm writing about the history of karaoke at sea. You see, the Philippines are the world's epicenter for nautical karaoke."

"Oh... *really?*"

"Yes. It's rather fated that I ended up here, isn't it?"

"Fated? What you mean?"

"Written in the stars," I reply, waving my hand at the heavens.

"Mmmmm," she murmurs. "The stars."

"Are you going to Coron or Puerto Princessa?" I ask, setting my hand on hers, keen to confirm destiny with a dicking.

"Puerto Princessa," she replies, puppy lust in her almond eyes. "Where you go?"

Cursing my luck, I consider lying, so she'll have more motive to do the monster mash with my meat monkey on the poop deck, but can't commit, being too moral a man. "Coron," I reluctantly reply.

Dizzy dreams dashed, her lips pop into a pout. "Too bad, I could show you around Puerto Princessa."

"You live there?"

"I grow up there. My family live there.

Contemplating how to pluck the carnal joys of destiny from the cruel jaws of defeat, I draw a rum-rattled, jet-lagged blank.

"You come to Puerto Princessa after Coron? I there for two weeks," she says, rescuing our romance from the fickles of fate.

"Maybe after El Nido."

"Is big port. Maybe you do research there?"

"Research?"

"For your book."

"Oh... right. Actually, I nearly forgot, I'm supposed to be there next week."

"Really? When?"

"Wednesday."

"You have phone?"

"No."

"Oh... one moment. I come right back." She breezes to the bar, borrowing a pen and paper and dashing her digits. Gliding back, she sits down beside me a clutch closer than before, biting her lip as she lays the paper in my palm.

"You call me in Puerto Princessa?"

"I will."

"Promise?"

"Promise."

"I need to sleep," she sighs, as if some puritanical instinct had been triggered by my touch. "You promise you call me?"

"You bet," I say, slipping my arm around her and lunging at her lips, only to find my face in empty air as her kisser recoils.

"I have never kissed a boy," she proclaims, as if the past were somehow pertinent to the magic our mouths would make in meeting. "I don't know you well enough for that,"

"Right. I thought we could correct that."

"Good*night.*"

6

The Whore from Heaven

Monday, November 25, 2013, 5:28 p.m.

Woebegone that I cannot wallow in whimsy with the waders in the water, forsaken by my failure to find a cutie in Coron, I forget frugality and order a Maker's Mark to jazz my juice.

"Put that on my tab Marcel," requests the bloke beside me.

"Thank you kind sir," I say, heaving my head to behold my benefactor.

"My treat. Nice to see someone your age with class," he says, assessing me to see if the tribute were true. The good sir himself comes off as a man of means who has transcended high society and gone back to bohemian, Hawaiian shirt and silver hair to his shoulders, equal parts breeze and sleaze like a spring gust of chloroform. "So what's a young fella like you doing here in El Nido? And don't blather some bullshit about finding yourself."

"God no," I snicker. "If anything I'm trying to lose myself."

"Well, that's just as bad. Finding oneself and losing oneself are both just names for navel-gazing, the euphemism we use for the intellectual masturbation of human house cats. You see, that's the problem with your generation. You got no meaning cause you got no struggle. Struggle is the metaphorical egg to meaning's chicken. You can't pull a chicken from thin

45

air, nor can you pull meaning from a liberal arts degree or a job at Starbucks."

"Well… that's an interesting way to put it. Personally, I don't give a damn about meaning. Meaning can go have a threesome with the chicken and the egg as far as I care, as long as it leaves me alone to play with pleasure."

"I wish more kids your age had such a healthy attitude," he says, giving a knowing nod.

"Me too," I agree. "So what's a gentleman like you doing here?"

"Ha! Gentleman! You're mighty kind. What's your name?"

"John," I reply, holding out my hand for a shake.

"Nice to meet you John, I'm Jack."

"Likewise."

"Well," he begins, taking a tick to savor a sip before recounting his quest. "What am I doing here? Not much different from what I do anywhere else. You see, I've reached a point in life where, through a series of fortuitous events of equal parts foresight and aftershave, I've transcended employment. No longer needing to trade my precious hours for greenbacks, I indulge in life's finer pursuits: lazing on the beach, gin and tonics any hour I feel, sleeping til noon." He leans in, a worldly wink giving a glint to his grin. "Fraternizing with bar floozies."

I reappraise him. He's younger than I'd first figured, his wavy gray hair and goatee lending him the look of a budget Richard Branson, an eye twinkle telling of wisdom won in search of sin. "Sounds nice."

"Gotta live while you can kid. No number of years being browbeaten by a witch of a wife will take death away from you, but It might make you yearn for its release."

"Yeah," I reply, shivering at the vision of Sarah and myself growing into our golden years together, her hamster already huge from the endless exercise of reconciling reality to feminist fictions further fueled by an inheritance many multiples my savings, the misbelief that money adds the worth it would were she a man enabling her egotism to take her through the wilting of the wall without winning any wisdom to blunt the bitterness of beauty blighted, unable to understand that her worth as a woman has been retaken by eternity.

"I know paying for it is something guys your age get compunctions about, but I'd like to think I improve these girls' lives."

"Yeah? How's that?"

"Well, of course there's the physical side of it, and some people think it's taking advantage of their poor economic prospects to pay them for it, but the truth is that if it wasn't for guys like me, these girls wouldn't be able to feed themselves, let alone support their families. So sure, it's philandering, but it's also philanthropy, so you might call me a philantherer."

"That's cool."

"It's a noble calling," he declares, downing his drink.

"Sounds like it."

"I only tell you this cause you look lonely," he says, getting up to go and signaling to settle up. "Trust me son, it always costs you. My wife took half my money and my best years. These girls just want to feed themselves."

"Nothing wrong with that."

"Nothing at all. I apologize for my hasty departure, but a young lady is expecting me. If you feel like it, check out Haven, the karaoke bar down the street. The girls will show you a good time."

"Karaoke?" I ask, perking at the prospect of serenading the natives.

"Yeah."

"Like with the private rooms or one big room?"

"Just one room."

8:07 p.m.

Pulled inside by the sign promising a dose of my addiction, a flock of floozies betray the bar's bottom line. To the left a table of tootsies tattle and titter and fuss over phones, others scattered about with dirty old white dudes, feigning interest in anecdotes that have long since transcended truth to become personal mythology. Not caring to catch these rambling has-beens' hubris, I ruminate retreat, but can't commit, and belly up to the bar.

"How are you tonight thir?" the bow-tied bartender asks, underlining his lisp with the matching poof mannerisms.

"I'm alright," I reply, feeling dirty for descending into this den of depravity.

"Would you like thomething to drink thir?"

"Can I get a Pale Pilsen?"

"Of courth thir," he says, leaning a few inches forward with a conspiratorial twinkle. "Anything *elth* thir? Perhapth a lady drink for one of the *girlth?*" he enquires, coming off queerly committed to the cucking of his own countrymen, perhaps hoping some of the hard up will give up on girls and settle for sodomy.

"No. Just a songbook."

Deflating like a dog rebuked for his behavior, he nods towards a number of binders on the bar. "Over there on the counter thir. thixty pethoth."

Paying for my pilsner and tossing the twink a tip, I search for a song to tingle the tarts. Mere minutes later crooning a pitch perfect Johnny Cash, the girls gape at my grandeur, gabbling about the gobbling they'd greedily give His Girthiness. It's time to muster my mojo, so they may remember my melody while getting mashed by old men, perhaps making it possible to enjoy the journey if they keep their eyes closed and imagine the member to be mine.

I am, after all, a charitable chap.

Stymieing my struggle to subdue my desire til I can find it for free, one angel's eyes meet mine as if magnetically. Tearing my attention from the travel-sized trollop, my eyes return of their own agency to find her nibbling her nails nervously, her pupils popping like a deer in the headlights of an oncoming erection.

Slipping back to my barstool, my belly is all butterflies, so I slam my suds to flush the fuckers.

"Another Pale Pilthen thir?" the bartender asks, grabbing up the empty bottle as soon as I set it down.

"Yeah," I reply, pondering those peepers that had retained their tenderness through the hardships of harlotry. "And… and a lady drink for the girl in the white dress."

"*Ah,*" he says, slipping me a sly smile. "You want to talk to *Rain?*"

"Yeah," I answer, annoyed by the innuendo.

"Two hundred ten pethoth."

I pay the price and settle into a seat, watching as the Mama San summons my sweet, who gives a bashful blush as if called in the cafeteria to her crush, sitting down beside me while the girls giggle and gush.

"Hi," she swoons.

"Hey."

"How are you?"

"I'm good."

"The girls, they think you are good singer," she says, projecting her prurience upon her compatriots.

"And *you?*" I ask, smittening her my smirk. "I saw you staring."

"Because you were looking at *me!*"

"Funny how everyone sees things their own way."

"What you mean?" she asks, affecting a frown as she swabs the sweat on my neck with a napkin. "Why you so wet?"

"It's just sweat."

"My grandma say when you wet like that, it make you sick."

Awe, how cute. She's already worried about my wellbeing. "It's just the heat. I'm not used to it."

"Hmph," she snorts, unscrunching her skin, peepers imploring me not to repudiate her passion as put on merely for money. "Will you sing again?"

"I guess I could," I reply, finding it impossible to repress a boyish beam. "For *you.*"

Unlike a western lass, who's minge would cringe at such sincerity, she returns my tenderness. "You have nice voice," she purrs. "The girls all think so."

"If I sing again, will you sing for *me?*"

"Okay... but I don't sing good like *you,*" she whines, putting on a pout as she napkins my neck. "You so *wet!*"

This prance around the impending proceeds for almost an hour; Rain watching me sing with eyes so eager they'd pop if you poked them, savoring every syllable that slips from my lips while the other girls glance on, green-eyed that she should be the one graced with my grandeur. Never did I dream

I'd ever pay for poonani, but as she swipes my sweat a crescendo of cravings surges inside me like a concert conducted by Beethoven's boner.

"Rain?"

"Yes?"

"I want to take you home."

Seeing the wish in my eyes that she would want me in her thighs, she gives a negligible nod, as if I'd cast it as a question. "Yes," she whispers.

"Yes?"

"Mmm hmm. Okay."

"You'd like that?" I ask, praying her participation isn't purely professional.

"Yes," she affirms, nodding bittersweetly at the transience of our tryst, the sociogeographiconomical gap conspiring to pull us apart. "I would."

"You mean it?"

Again her nod is minute, but her wistfulness is weightier than words.

"What do I do?"

"Tell Mama San you want take me hotel and pay my bar fine at the bar."

Tummy atumble with the frivolity of a freshly emancipated morality, I make the arrangements and await her out front. Minutes drag on like days. As I begin to fear I've been fleeced, she slips out a side door in jean shorts and a T-shirt, a satchel of sundries slipped over one shoulder. It's like awaking on Christmas morning to find the presents rewrapped in newspaper. I guess her summer dress had symbolized the sweetness I'd given up as engulfed by the fires of feminism, those precious petals of flowering femininity every pubescent pud-puller projects upon his unrequited amour.

"You changed."

"Yes," she says, lighting a cigarette. "Dress only for the bar. We get tricycle?"

"It's only a few blocks. Let's walk. You want something to drink?" On the seaward side of the sandy street is what Americans call a convenience store, a store that exists to keep sloth and vice on good terms.

"Maybe just water."

"Just water?"

"I always have to drink at the bar," she bemoans.

"Okay."

Refreshments purchased, we patter past hotel reception, up a flight of stairs and down an outdoor hallway to my room. Casting off her clothes with professional efficiency, Rain Frenches me frantically, but emotionally she's missing.

"You have condom?"

"Yes." His Girthiness is engorged. Though Rain parodies passion, her dew flaps are a desert. Aching for this angel to melt into the moment, I kiss her cans with the compassion she so needs right now, in this world where tricks treat her as a toy to be purchased for their pleasure. Slipping towards her slit, I muse her muff might be marinating in another man's mojo, but when I nibble her nani her bouquet is ambrosia.

Have you ever noticed how an Oriental's cooch conjures an orchid, while an Americunt's minge looks more like the Mothman?

Though our whoopee isn't worth writing home to mom about, Rain's bitty little body and tight little twat make me finish in a flash, despite the filthy feeling of paying for the pleasure.

While I cast off the condom and toss it towards the trash, Rain rustles through her things, revealing a rainbow colored tattoo arching across her shoulders. 'Princess Rain,' reads this label of looseness, this marker of a minge that's lost count of the cocks.

"Interesting tattoo," I state, deciding it as stupid as those stamping stateside strumpets. "What's it mean?" A scrumpet's inked skin may map out the mess her mom and dad made of her, but her commentary is the key.

"I call myself Rain because rain give life. The princess is just because... because what girl don't want to be princess?"

"I see." She never grew up. That's okay, a childless maturity is rarely recovered from.

She checks her phone, frowns. "I have to go now."

"Stay," I implore, pulling her close for a kiss requited only in action.

"Mama San say after boom boom I go back to the bar."

"You have to?" I ask, deflated by the informality of this angel's exit, the weight of what I'd done dawning on a soul now saddled with the pox of one who's paid for it.

"Mm hmm."

"You like it there?"

"*No!*" she cries, scowling at the obviousness of her answer. "It always so *loud!* I can't *sleep!* Every night I have to *drink!*"

"I wish you'd stay."

"Mama San mad if I stay. Can I shower?"

"Okay... Rain?"

"Yes?"

"Would you... would you like to see me tomorrow?"

"Yes," she replies without pause.

"You would?"

Her nod is all but naught, yet in its numbness I note a bittersweet sincerity. "Mm hmm."

"You mean it?"

"Yes. May I shower?"

"Of course."

"Where is it?"

"End of the hallway outside."

"You have a towel?"

"Yeah, over there."

She slips away with her sack of soaps and lotions, powders and prophylactics, enough cunt cleansers to scrub the Jesus juice off the willy whacker of a pedophilic priest, a purse of purifiers more for her soul than her slit. After ten minutes of eternity spent sipping my suds and mulling my morals' incredible capacity for molding to their milieu, she returns twinkling with tender innocence. Infatuated with her freshness, bewitched by her ability to shrug off her shame with a shower, I stand up and seize her, cradling her cans as we kiss. If brevity is the soul of wit, then levity is the soul of a tit. While Americunts' melons swiftly succumb to the grip of gravity, hers point out pertly in defiance of destiny.

Though she doesn't deny me, I sense her sorrow and release her, struggling not to reach for her rubies as she shimmies into shirt and shorts like a Christmas present rewrapping itself.

"I go now."

"I'll see you tomorrow?"

"If you want."

"You want that?" I ask, still seeking reassurance that her motives are more than monetary.

"Yes. I go now. Mama San worry about me."

"Goodnight," I sigh, leaning in to lay on her lips my goodbye.

"Goodnight."

She slips away, but to what? More lady drinks? To have her flower defiled only to put on her panties with another petal plucked, a speck more spent with every spin til in time her heart is hollow, a plastic Easter egg with its candy consumed?

Tuesday, November 26, 2013, 8:54 p.m.

Though my doxy disengages as she doffs her duds, this time she lets a trace of trust tint her monetarily motivated submission, a faltering faith in forevermore emanating from her eyes as I thrust into her thighs. I long for our lust to last, but her melancholy is too much for my member, which quickly crams with cream that cruel cover that keeps our treasures from truly touching. Reluctant to release her, I cast away the condom with a minimum of movement.

But my minx has no mind to budge from the bed, instead clutching me close, covers cocooning us from the wicked world outside the window.

"May I stay?" she pleads.

"Of course," I reply, relieved she's not rising to shower off her shame, staying instead to marinate in our musk.

"It's so loud there."

"You're not happy there," I state, sympathetic to her serfdom, myself so freshly freed from my own confinement.

"*No!* Of course *not!* It so hard to *sleep!* I always have to *drink!* Drink and talk every *night!* And sometimes... you *know!*" she cries, her pitch pushing up

53

at every exclamation to accent her sorrows.

"How long have you been there?" I ask, craving to ken this cutie who like glittering gold no stumble could stain.

"One month." So short, no wonder the wench still oozes innocence. Might she have a notch count not so far from mine, maybe even lower? Where is a working girl's Rubicon crossed, the final cock that forever keeps her crevice from craving anything but cold hard cash?

"How often do you… how often do you leave the bar with someone?" Too direct? Too personal? No, her clutch conveys that she craves my compassion, yearns to yield her yang to my yin.

"Two or three times a week. Any more and my… you *know!* It get too *big!*"

"Rain?"

"Yes?"

"What's a sweet girl like you doing there?"

"I am not sweet."

"Yes, you are."

"No, I am *not.*"

"So then what's a sour girl like you doing there?"

"I just need the money, you *know?*"

"I guess so."

"Why a nice guy like you come to my bar?"

"What makes you think I'm nice?" Nice is a ninny's prize for pandering to a modern mollycoddled maiden, a carrot to keep him around to absorb her emotional incontinence.

"You *are* nice. I feel it in my heart. Why you come to my bar?"

"I just came to sing. You kept looking at me."

"You were looking at *me!*"

"And you looked so sweet."

"I am not *sweet!*"

"So I had to talk to you, and then I had to have you."

"Hmph."

I slip onto my side, telling her by touch she need not her heart hide. What a cruel world that herds such honeys into whoredom when Americunts are so keen to make themselves unmarriageable but can't sell themselves because the law won't let them.

"You have girlfriend?"

"No."

"Why not?"

"I did," I sigh. "But we broke up."

"Why you break up?"

"We wanted different things," I reply, praying she won't press the point. "What about you? You have a boyfriend?"

"*No!*" she cries. "How can I have boyfriend? No boy want a girl who do this."

"Why do you do it?"

"You know… for the *money.* My family so *poor.* I send them money, but if mama knew how I get it she *cry,*" Rain blubbers, eyes brimming to bursting with the sorrows of selling her fanny for her family. Is this not an angel in my arms? For what is more selfless than selling oneself so others may eat? I ache to understand this nymph's every nuance: the nitty, the gritty, and the titty.

"Did you ever have a boyfriend?"

"Yes. Once."

"And?"

"He left me."

"I'm sorry."

"It not your fault."

"Why did he leave you?"

"Because… you *really* want to know?"

"Yes. Everything."

"I was pregnant with his boy, but he die in my tummy," she replies, peepers pleading me not to hold her admittance against her, questing for our connection to be more than meaningless, even if in the morn a musk is all that's left of our love. "So he leave me. He say I no good for making babies. No good for making family. After that, every boy around know that I no longer, uh, *you know!*"

"Virgin?"

"Yes, they know I no longer virgin, and so other boys not want me. So I think, what does it matter? If no one want to love me, then at least I can help my family, so I come here."

"I'm sorry," I say, clutching her close to console her, bridging the canyon between our cultures with a kiss and a titty cup.

"It not your fault."

"I think you'd be a good girlfriend."

"You are sweet."

"So are you."

"*No!*" she cries, her minge's martyrdom aching in her eyes. "I am *not* sweet. May I sleep? Here with *you?*"

"Yes."

"It so loud there. So hard to sleep. Make me always tired."

"You're too good for that place."

"*No!* I'm no good anymore. No boy want a girl like me."

"Don't say that."

"It true."

"Don't cry."

"Why you so nice to me?"

"Cause you're a sweet girl."

"Mmmmmmmm you lie," she purrs. "Will you see me again tomorrow?"

"I have to leave tomorrow," I lament.

She melts herself into me, as if to forget in our fusion all the sorrows outside, a hint of heaven to help her through the hell of whoredom. "I'll miss you," she murmurs.

"I'll miss you too."

Isn't it unreal that so few syllables can mean so much? I long to linger, but alas, she is merely on loan from the meat market, and I must soon consult that magical machine that metes out money from someplace unseen, an amenity unavailable in El Nido. There's nothing for it but to fade into fantasy as we forget for tonight, for these few fleeting hours of intimacy, that tomorrow will tear our paths forever apart.

56

Wednesday, November 27, 2013, 12:14 a.m.

I wake to Rain's phone ringing, Rain rolling over me to rustle through her bag beside the bed, sitting up astride me as she answers, back and forth torrents of Tagalog finding her face in a frown.

"Mama San wants me come back to the bar," she sighs, setting her phone on the night stand.

"I wish you'd stay," I say, the weight of her wistfulness pulling her into my arms, my member mightening under the warmth of her womanhood.

"Mmmmm," she coos between kisses aching for evermore. "Maybe just for a minute."

"Just a minute," I repeat.

"Mmmmm," she moans, as we roll over to root in the position God planned. "Come outside of me, *okay?*"

12:26 a.m.

"I have to go," Rain rues, slipping on her shoes.

"You have to?"

"Yes."

"Okay."

"You have Facebook?"

"Yeah."

"You find yourself for me?" she asks, a hint of hope softening her sadness as she opens the app.

"Sure," I reply, accepting the phone to search for myself.

"Message me," she implores, holding the phone fast in her hand when I give it back to her, as if to capture our rapture in the bits and bytes of Facebook friendship. "Maybe one day I see you again?" she asks, eyes aching for the affirmative.

"I hope so."

"Yes, me too, but somewhere better than the bar. Some better place," she purrs, a pause finding us falling into a bittersweet embrace, two bodies begging to be together again. "Thank you," she whispers.

"For what?"

"Because you are sweet to me. Not many people so nice to me here. Some are so mean."

"I'm sorry."

"Don't be *sorry!* It not your *fault.* You message me?"

"Yes."

"I hope so."

"I will."

"Thank you for our time together. I have to go."

"Goodnight."

"Goodnight. Take care always, okay?"

"Always. You too, okay?"

"Yes, always. Goodbye."

"Goodbye."

Tears charge her cheeks as we kiss one last so long, my own falling forth as I watch her walk away.

10:02 a.m.

There are five Facebook messages for me.

The first is from Bartender Jay: **Did you make it to the land of opportunititty ok bud? Remember to check for Adams apples. You may have found the garden of Eden, but some fruits are better left unpicked.**

The second is from my brother River: **You okay? You seemed weird when you dropped your stuff off. Then again, that's no different from normal. Are you going to need me to store those boxes long?**

The third is from my mother: **Hello? John, my ever irrational child, I don't know whether to be proud of you or worried. I'm glad you quit waiting tables. It was no good for you. There was no outlet for** your passion, no room for you to grow. But maybe you could have told us what was going on with you before you ran off on a spirit quest? Anyhow, my heart tells me this journey is what you need right now, but still I wonder if you're safe. I hope you can find a good naturopath if you get sick. Be safe with the girls (I know you know what I mean!) and don't fall in love with one that only wants your money or your passport. Check up soon. I can't wait to hear what discoveries you make on this soul search of yours.

PS, I'm glad things didn't work out between you and Sarah. She was physically and spiritually malnourished. She would have made sickly babies.

The fourth is from Annetta: **Hows the trip going drunky pants? I still kinda wish I was there but I guess that would interfere with your search for a wife. The restaurant sucks without you. The port commissioner pulled through, in case you were worried (Though I doubt you were). It was only a minor heart attack. He orders salads now. Salads and mineral water. Don't get tropical super syphilis, I might want to take advantage of you when you get back...**

The fifth is from Rain: **Thank you so much for the last two nights! I hope I hope I hope I will see you again! I'm so sorry we meet like this :(I hope I see you again before you go home. :) I will always remember you. Take care always :)**

I sigh. If only I weren't leaving! But then, what's holding *her* here? Had she not hinted that every ounce of her aches to find a beau to obey before her heart is hollowed by a parade of penises?

Tummy atumble with headlong hope, I reply: **Run away with me.**

Then I message Annetta: **The trip goes well. I'm in El Nido in Palawan. No wife yet. If I find one would you like to join us in a tropical love triangle?**

Then my mom: **Don't worry mom I'm making good decisions.**

Then my brother: **Just needed a little non American air. American air has too many PPM of freedom. It's stifling. Do you mind holding those boxes for a few months?**

Finally, I message Jay: **Made it safe and unsound. Anatomical searches have come up negative for Adam's apples and positive for sexy. Must continue research.**

With every second that slips by my heart beats harder. Has my nymph not noticed my wistful words? Is she not fixed to her phone awaiting digital redemption, as damsels do these days from morning til midnight?

Consoling myself with all the minges to melt at my melody, mere seconds from setting this silliness aside with a heavy heart, the reply comes:

YES!!!!! Today?

Now

Where I meet you?

In front of the internet cafe. How soon can you be here?

20 minutes. I'm so happy!!!

7

Hearts Healed

10:37 a.m.

There are wonders in this world no con can counterfeit, mirth a movie cannot convey, joys so jazzed words wither in their wake.

"I missed you," Rain coos, coming up from our kiss, misty eyes melting the iceberg in my bosom.

"I missed you too."

"I'm sorry for last night."

"For what?"

"Because I had to leave. I wanted to stay. I *really really* wanted to stay."

"It's not your fault."

"I know… but."

"But what?"

"It is shameful, what I do here. You will forgive me?"

I hold her head to my heart, for whatever words I whisper, they will only touch on the truth without penetrating its pith. "Nothing to forgive, it's okay," I reassure, running my hand through her hair as her tears tumble onto my T-shirt. My eyes mist with mirth, a solitary tear falling forth. "As long as you're with me everything will be okay."

"Promise?"

"Promise."

"Mmmm. Will you sing for me tonight?"

"Yes."

"Every night?"

"Of course."

"Forever?"

"Mm hmm."

"Promise?"

"Promise."

"Where we go now baby ko?"

"We could go to a hotel, unless you want to leave El Nido now. Will they look for you?"

"No! I am not *slave!* Maybe tomorrow we go? I just want... I just want to be next to you. That is all I want. We go same hotel?"

"Lets get a bungalow. Down the beach."

"Okay."

"You sure they won't look for you?"

"No," she replies, putting on a pout. "I think mama San glad I gone."

"Why?"

"Because... because men complain that I not good at... you *know!*"

"Boom boom?"

"Yes. But how can it be good without love? I cannot fake that."

I clutch her close to taste of her tenderness, the world washing away as her mouth melts into mine. "Don't worry about that place, okay? It's us now."

2:15 p.m.

Love! Could it be love in our loins? What is love?

Love is a mushrooming emotion much maligned by our masters for its ability to bring women back from the brink of ideological immolation. With the infection of feminism poisoning our passions, we suck each other's spit without chewing each other's mental grit, sharing our sheets but concealing our souls. Mistaking our weariness for wisdom, we finally wed with hearts as wilted as a cat lady's womb, our bosoms too bonsaied to bear the fruits of fidelity.

As if pillaging prepares one for farming a field, promiscuity poses as perspicacity in the western world. We swear we're weary of playing games, but our seriousness is what scared love away. Love wanted to wander through the fields of our fantasies plucking daydream daisies, to slurp sleep soup with the same celestial spoon. Love wanted to wade in our wisdom's waters, but we were busy sandbagging our souls.

"I love you," she coos, reading my skin like a trashy romance written in braille.

"I love you too."

"Mahal kita."

"What's that mean?"

"I love you. Is Tagalog."

"Mahal kita."

"Promise baby ko?"

"I promise." Why does she press for me to promise my passion? But then, can I blame her? Who wouldn't cop a sloppy feel on the real deal after leaving a life where a cash flash meant a monster mash with an expat ass?

"Mmmmm! Where we go tomorrow mahal ko?"

"Puerto Princessa I guess. Then from there, anywhere in the country."

"Maybe we go my city?" she implores. "You can meet my family."

Back home a harlot would wait for her whimsies to wander before recruiting family to affirm her fella's deficiencies. What has this trip taught me if not the importance of pre-emptive impulsiveness? "You think they'll like me?"

"Of *course* they like you baby ko!" she cries. "Because you are *good* to me. I feel it right *here*." she holds my hand to her heart to assert her sincerity, her titty testifying to her truthfulness. "In my heart I feel you are true. *Yes!* But I do not care where we are if you are with me. That we are together is what matters."

"I don't care either," I declare, kissing her other can, in case it had anything to add.

"Promise?"

"Promise."

"Mmmm! Let's *go!*" she trills. "You and *me!* Tomorrow *morning! Mmmm!* You give me new *life* baby ko!"

"Is this crazy?"

"What you mean?"

"Running away like this."

"*No!*" she cries. "We not run a*way!* We run *to* love. *Life* is crazy baby ko! To hide from its *magic* is crazy! This is *right!* I *feel* it baby ko! Right *here!*" Again my hand is held to her heart, and her candor is crystal clear.

4:23 p.m.

"Thank you baby ko," Rain murmurs, plopping herself on the sand and pecking my cheek.

"What for baby ko?"

"Because you give me *hope!*"

"Me too baby ko. You give me hope," I say, placing my hand on her hip as if hope were a euphemism.

"I *do?*" she coos, poising her pout to request a kiss.

"Because you're so sweet," I reply, slipping her a sappy smile to buoy her heart's rebuilding.

"I am not sweet," she purrs, peepers pleading pardon for peddling her pooter. Apologizing, perhaps, that she could not give me that gift a girl gives only once, that gift God gave her to gift her groom in good faith of her fealty, not a trophy to be taken by the first fella to defile her.

"You must not have met many American girls. Compared to them you're pure syrup. Just a twinkle of your tenderness could turn lemon into lemonade."

Finding my floozy unstirred by my statement, I realize my lyricism to be lost on her.

"I am sweet to you because… because you are my *baby ko!* But *I* am not sweet… because… because you know what I *did!* Why you say American girls not sweet?"

I sigh. What else can one do when characterizing Americunts? To applaud their autonomy would ignore that our nation has favored its females to a fault since we made the mistake of consenting to their suffrage, their proverbial sucking of big brother's hairy bosom as he pats them patronizingly, blathering that beauty is in the boner of the beholder to make them feel better about their boyfriend's inability to find their flower between their folds. To fight with them is futile, for they have dropped dialogue from debate, substituting an arsenal of epithets designed to dehumanize you for daring to doubt their hamster's hooey. To defeat Medusa you must sap her serpents by removing your grandeur from their grasp, preferably through the propulsion of a plane and not by bunkering in the basement with a pile of porn.

"Why?" I reply. "Hard to say *why,* but to them *wholesome* is just a *sum* that fills a *hole.* Their idea of a fulfilling relationship is to nag their boyfriend until he gives in to their goading, making them lose all respect for him. What they *really* want is the man who *won't* give in, but the problem is that he's the one who'll have too much self respect to stay with *her.* Basically, they want a man that doesn't exist. A unicorn, as they say."

Pretending to picture the plight of western penis, she puts on a pout. "That true baby ko?"

"Unfortunately."

"Why they like that?

Again I sigh, having since the last sigh not riddled the reason Americunts are so cold. One can harp about the hold Hollywood has on their hearts, or their endless effort to reconcile their soul's search for a man to be their master with their corporately conspired quest for equality, but the affliction's origins are as old as monogamy itself. At this critical crossroads females found themselves not with a stake in a stud, for whose primacy their pussies were programmed to purr, but with sole rights to one man's rod. While some lucky ladies still landed powerful providers willing to womanize to improve their appeal, many more wound up mated to milksops. Needing a system to suss the studs from the duds, women found ways to test a man's mettle, proddings to provoke a cad's smirk and a cuck's submission. Even so, sometimes the system went sideways when a woman wed a weakling who'd held his nerves together long enough to repeat the provisions of his imprisonment to the priest, leading to her hen pecking her hubby in hopes of luring a Lothario from the lummox she'd mistakenly married. Though nagging was thus begat, it was only in post world war two prosperity, when survival of the fittest found itself applying for unemployment, that this dreadful disease became such a bane.

"Baby ko? Why they like that?"

I doubt that evolutionary psychology is my strumpet's strong suit. "Prosperity."

"What you mean?"

"Don't worry your pretty little head about it."

"I won't be like that baby ko, I promise," she purrs, eyes dewy with dreams being rebuilt in her bosom.

"I know you won't."

"But American girls are so *pretty!*"

You guessed it, I sigh. "Sure, on TV."

"Hmph. If you say so baby ko," she coos, hanging her head, still heavy from the humpings of oogly googly old geezers, on my shoulder. "I'm so *tired* baby ko. Maybe in Puerto Princessa we rest a few days? Just you and me. Then maybe we go see my family."

"Of course baby ko."

"Mmmmm! I love you baby ko."

"I love you too."

"You give me new life," she murmurs, closing her eyes to the world's worries. What man could remain unmoved by such meekness?

Thursday, November 28, 2013, 5:21 p.m.

Having been presently promoted from bar bimbo to love dove of my life, Rain already saddles herself with the shrewd spending of my savings. At each hotel she exchanges torrents of Tagalog with the receptionist, scowls, shakes her head and swivels it my way, saying, "It's too expensive. We try another, *okay* baby ko?"

I know I should infer her fussing over my finances as a sign of her love's sincerity, or at least her plans to suck me dry slowly, but by the fifth hotel my hard on is in such haste to break free from his bondage that anything with walls will do, budget be damned.

She's saying something, but all I hear is her voice's voodoo casting its spell on my spelunker. "What's that?" I ask.

"500 pesos is okay baby ko? Is not too much?"

"It's fine," I reply, quelling the compulsion to comment that I'd fucked her for five times that.

My ruby and the receptionist fire a few more torrents of Tagalog. "Okay baby ko, she show us room first."

The lady leads us to a cramped compartment with cockroach corpses and peeling paint crushed into the cracks of the creaky floorboards and built up beneath the bed, a gecko glued to the wall adding extra ambiance. But even a bed of hay would be heaven with my harlot to hold, as the sweetest of suites would only sour my soul without my wench to warm it. Returning to reception to rush through the paperwork, we rollick to our room in rut.

All the pent up passion from our eternity in transit finds our effects on the floor, the euphoria of our flesh coming to a sensual crescendo. But when our minutes of magic come to a close, she surrenders to her incessant search for reassurance.

"I'm sorry baby ko," my beauty blubbers, burying her pout in my pecks.

"For what?"

"Because of what I *do*," she sobs, syllables syrupy with sorrow. "How we *met*. It is *shameful*."

"It's okay." Isn't that what all fallen hearts need to hear? That to whatever depths of depravity we've wallowed in our weakness, our skin's sins on our souls need not a mark forever make?

Holding her head up to look at me longingly, a solitary tear falls forth, a pearl promising piety. "Because I really *love* you! I really really *do!* So I am *glad!* Even though we meet in such bad place, I am happy."

"Me too."

"Promise?" she implores. "You don't judge me?"

"Never."

"Because I am ashamed."

I hold her head between my hands, my face flushed with fresh faith in forever. "Don't be. The past is behind us. What matters is our future."

"Mmmmmm yes baby ko," she coos, melting into my arms. "The future. Mahal kita."

"Mahal kita."

"Mmmmmm."

Surrendering myself to the warmth of her woozy, I drift with her to dreamland.

11:11 p.m.

Perhaps never has knowing passed more purely between paramours, all the worries and what ifs that linger when we're lonely washing away in the wordless whispering of skin against skin.

"Baby ko? We go my city Davao soon? I miss my family. I want them meet you."

"Okay baby ko. We'll book a flight tomorrow."

"Mmmmm! I think my family really like you. I *do!* I have four brothers and three sisters, but one my sisters in Russia with her husband. What about your family? You have brothers and sisters?"

"One brother, one sister."

"Is small family. You think they like me? Because, you *know!* I am poor

Filipina girl, and your family American. Is o*kay?*"

"Of course baby ko."

"Thank you for accept who I am baby ko. How you tell your family we meet?"

"Um… I'll say we met at a bar, that's how we do it in America."

"In America boys meet girls in bars?"

"Some do. Others bravely show a better than life face to the internet. How do you do it here? Church? Social circles?"

"What you mean baby ko?"

You've no notion how nice it is to be with a beauty who makes no masquerade of being my intellectual equal. "Through friends."

"Yes, mostly through friends. How come you no have American girl?"

Haven't I already explained this? Does Hollywood have such a hold on her heart that their beastliness is unbelievable?

"I don't like them."

"Why not baby ko?"

"Many, *many* reasons," I reply, tired of talking of the culture of equality at all costs that hijacks the feminine fairness god made for motherhood to curdle our country's cuties into mockeries of men.

"You know baby ko, I worry cause I am Filipina girl, not American girl. I hope your family like me."

In a stateside strumpet such self-doubt would be dubious, likely a shit test to tell the supplicants from the suck my pants, but I sense her sincerity. "They will."

"Promise?"

"Promise."

"Thank you baby ko."

A pregnant peace punctuates her search for reassurance, an island of dreams in a sea of insecurity.

"Baby ko, how long you stay in my country?" she asks, tenderly twiddling the hair over my heart.

"I don't know."

"Always?"

"Eventually I'll have to make money," I reply, regretting the admittance immediately. Why must intimacy embolden honesty to take such liberties with love?

"You work here," she whines.

"You could come with me," hope replies, mending honesty's mistake.

"To America?"

"Yeah."

"I want to baby ko, but…"

"But what?"

"I scared. My English not good. What I do in America?"

Though misinformed my mistress may be, her misgivings aren't misplaced, as such a fragile flower shouldn't have to share in the amorality of America. But then, might her groping grasp of English prove propitious, preserving her purity against the cuntery of my culture? "Take care of me."

"For *always*?" she asks, walloping me with her wooziest, dooziest, mud puddliest peepers.

"Yes."

"Okay baby ko. And we have kids baby ko, five of them!" Perceiving the panic provoked by the prospect of progeny, her googly grin is replaced with a pout, her search for reassurance renewed. "You *sure* I can come with you baby ko? Cause you *know*, I am poor Filipina *girl*."

"It'll work itself out, don't worry."

"I can't *help* it."

"Be here with me now."

"I *am* here with you now baby ko!" she cries, rivers running from her eyes. "But I hope we have *always*… for*ever*."

"Don't cry baby ko."

"I am scared. If you fly home then you so far away, and if I go with you then I am so far from my family."

"Nothing a plane won't bridge."

"Yes… I know… but to me it is so far. I have never been that far."

"Don't worry mahal ko. It doesn't feel as far when you fly it."

"Okay, I try not worry mahal ko. Ikaw lang sapat na."

"What's that mean baby ko?"

"You are my one and only."

Are not all inamoratas one and onlys for their while? Or is she claiming a connection that goes deeper than a dicking, a tie that transcends eternity and links our souls supernaturally, leading two halves into a whole against all odds of ever meeting in a world so wide? "Ikaw lang sapat na."

"Mmm baby *ko!* You learn my *langu*age!"

I answer her ardor with the language of love, the wordless whispering of skin against skin.

"What you think about baby ko?"

How can one portray one's ponderings within the limits of language? Are thoughts not a synaptic synergy of senses and subconscious as ephemeral and enigmatic as the moment itself? "Nothing."

"You think about something."

A pout like my peach's seeks naught but sweet nothings, syrupy syllables to soothe the hamster in her head, not truths to translate as declarations of doubt. "About how happy you make me," I whisper warmly into my angel's ear, feeling her fear in sweet surrender disappear.

8

Family Freud

Monday, December 2, 2013, 12:02 p.m.

"Baby ko, how long it take fly your place from Philippines?"

My gaze glows from the ocean blue below to my aisle seat angel. "Twelve hours non-stop, but usually there's a layover, which makes it more like a day."

"So *long!* You will be so *far* from me." This again? I suppose women's worries are cold sores of the subconscious, never really removed, only simply sedated until triggered to return.

"Not if you're with me."

"I Facebook my friend yesterday. She say it take long time for you get me there. She say the, uh, *how* you say? For me to go there with you?"

"Visa?"

"Yes, she say visa not easy. Say it take a *year,* maybe *more* baby ko."

"We'll figure it out baby ko," I reply, rubbing my ruby reassuringly. "Don't worry."

Clasping my roaming hand between hers in a moment of modesty, she hangs her head on the shelf of my shoulder. "I hope so," she says, settling herself in for a round of reassurances.

"We will."

"Thank you baby ko."

Why is she always thanking me? Are we not traveling together on the road to redemption, rediscovering our dreams on the drive? "Why are you always thanking me?"

"Be*cause* baby ko! You give me new *life.*"

I squeeze her squiz through her skirt, smittening her a smile of proportional parts emphasized sincerity and disguised doubt. "We're giving each other a new life."

What am I renouncing? What about Rain? Would she not catch the contagion of consumerism if I moved her to America? The monkey might begin benignly with little luxuries like lip glosses and lotions, but in time the cancer would consume her. Shit! That satchel of sundries she's always clutching so close. She could've caught the contagion from a trick or the television.

Her prognosis is poor. Hooked on having the newest novelties, the afflicted is forever one frill from fulfillment, one curio from completion. Burning through baubles without care for the cost, the diseased finally dies during a late-night infomercial credit card declined stress triggered heart attack, leaving a life worth of crap for their kids to drag to the dump.

"What's wrong baby ko?"

"Oh... nothing," I reply, returning to reality. "Just thinking of home."

"You miss it?"

"Not really."

"But it is your *home!*"

"Yeah."

"What about your family? You miss them?"

That bag of mixed nuts? "A little I guess."

"But they are your *family!* You must *miss* them?"

"It's just... I don't know how to explain it baby ko," I sigh. "Americans isolate themselves from each other more than Filipinos. I worry you won't like that."

"Why you *say* that baby ko?" she gasps.

"Cause I worry you'll be unhappy."

"Baby ko, why you *say* these things? If you are *there* I am happy! You are my *life* baby ko! Never forget that, *okay?*"

"Okay baby ko."

"Ikaw lang sapat na."

"Ikaw lang sapat na."

"Mahal kita."

"Mahal kita."

Polly wanna cracker?

1:04 p.m.

Eager to feel the envy of friends and family, she grips me like a girl parading her first puppy. I pity the poor cabby, forced to follow her western woozy. Wallowing, most likely, in a well-founded feeling of inferiority.

Following fifteen minutes of kisses and coos, Rain calls the cabby to a stop. Feeling guilty for her gropings, I tip him 40 pesos to blunt his bitterness with a beer.

Rain pulls me past a parcel of peddlers and down a dusty dirt path, into a shantytown of tin-shelled shacks. Having never known such preeminence in this precinct, the inhabitants hang their gobs agape, dazzled by my dignity.

We come upon a courtyard of rollicking runts and women washing clothes for their kin. A half-pint hurries from a hovel at the far end, the first of a dozen dickens that crowd my cutie, hugging her and bugging their eyes at my boldness. Charmed by the cheer these children can pluck from poverty, I give them a grin.

"Mama!" Rain cries, running over to be riddled with rapid-fire affection.

"Mama, this my boyfriend John," Rain announces, once the fussing is finished.

"Welcome to my home John," she says, assessing my splendor with the suspiciously hopeful air one would use on a ripe avocado at a discount grocer, her face furrowed with a leathery look of sober survival, worn from the worries of feeding her family on a pittance, a prayer and her daughter's indiscretions.

"Nice to meet you... uh..."

"Call her Mama," Rain whispers.

"Nice to meet you Mama."

"You take good care of Rain?"

With all six inches. "Yes."

"You hungry?'

"Yeah."

"Come." We follow Mama forward to a plastic table placed on a spotless dirt floor, a chair on each of the three sides not up against the wall. On the other end of the rectangular room, a frayed sofa faces a flat screen TV. As I wonder whether this babble box was bought with my darling's gash or her daddy's cash, Mama scrapes room temperature rice from the bottom of a pot, a clump plummeting to the cluttered counter as the rest of my ration lands in my bowl. Chucking some chicken on top of my tuck, she serves me as a rat rushes from the wall to run away with the spilled rice. Mama serves Rain.

No utensils. No napkins. Just two ladies looking on like food challenge finalists awaiting my word. In an epicuriocultural panic, I measure the merits of sticking my face in my food or fashioning a fork from the thighbones. Fathoming my fluster, Rain clutches rice between four fingers and a thumb, looking like one of those coin-operated arcade claws trapping a trinket. When I attempt her trick, steeling myself for the suffering of being tethered to the toilet erupting from both ends, half the clump slumps back to the bowl.

I wolf it away, praying my pace will prevent any organisms from organizing against my innards. The rat runs for another nibble, returning to its roost. Giggling boys and girls come up to the open door to gawk at the grandeur of my kingly white complexion, tittering and tearing away when I return their attention.

"You like the food?" Mama asks.

"Yeah, it's good." It's a tepid intestinal time bomb, but you don't disparage someone's dish when you're diddling their daughter.

The women wallop one another with volleys of Visaya, the local language. My destiny decided, my peach plies me with peepers puddly with the passion a lassie saves for her savior, a piety unparalleled in the western world, where the dependence a damsel aches to savor in surrender is stolen by the state, leaving nothing left for a lad but to scratch the animalistic itches of her ephemeral flesh. "Baby ko, we go hotel now. Just one minute, *okay?*"

I nod, agreeing it wise to give her the goods before the bugs in my belly brew my bowels to bursting. Heady with the highs of good fortune flaunted to envious eyes, my scrumpet scampers up the stairs to the bedroom where she'd bunked with several siblings, swapping some belongings in her bag. A few more volleys of Visaya and Mama's worries are in our wake.

We turn right at the road, the shacks soon shifting to churches and markets, the air a muggy melange of durian and destitution. A few more minutes and the markets are replaced with low rises, city garishly glittering with Christmas glitz. Amidst the masses we come to a hotel, a projecting sign promising repose for 250 pesos.

"Is this okay for you baby ko?"

"Yeah, it's fine."

250 is for 12 hours. A decent deal if you're porking a prostitute, but since I'm no longer paying my peach per poke, having leased her love for the low fee of my freedom, I pay the full 500. Impatient for privacy, we tear through two flights of stairs and a fluorescent hallway to number 307, an all white womb with a washroom but no windows. Its sterile style stemming, I suppose, from the third world fantasy of the first as a place without impurities, a pestilence free paradise.

Not being one to brag, I will leave you alone to imagine the mania kindled by the covetous poonanis of her neighbors, the fantastic fervor fired by the envious eyes of female friends and family who will live their lives on the edge of enough, knowing naught but the tight wallets and tiny wieners of their malnourished men.

5:05 p.m.

I awake not to the tummy torques of bursting bowels, but with my mighty member pressed to her promised land.

An idea dawns as I swab my seed off my sweet: take a picture of my pole milk on the backdrop of her belly and see which of the world's islands it looks most like, then dash off with my darling on a romantic retreat. It could become the new honeymoon mania, or a spritz of spice for moribund marriages. Maybe I might become a consultant. Show me a shot of your load on your love and I'll wise you where to whisk her away. At last a calling curious enough for my parents' approval.

Unmolested by a man's imagination, my peach is posting tired tropes to her timeline, seeking her peers' approval of her derivative individuality. "Baby ko! We sleep so long! We need go back for dinner with Mama and Papa! But first we shower, okay?"

"Yeah sure."

In sanitary standards I stray from my strumpet's devotion to lotions. For mere sweat drips and sploodge drops I'd rinse, dry, and be done with the deed, but before I can convey my hygienically frugal philosophy, my beauty is blathering about the dirtiness of my dingis, lathering with love territory til now only touched by toilet paper.

6:07 p.m.

"It is okay for you?" Mama asks.

I take a second to swallow and simulate sincerity. "Yeah, it's delicious." The dried fish was mummified moons ago and if you told me the fish sauce was fermented from a crumpet's clam juice I'd not question your claim, but at least the rice is fresh.

My perseverance provides me an empty plate, a seeming success until I intuit too late that my fortitude will only find more food in front of me. "Mmm baby ko! You like our food!"

"You want more?" Mama enquires on cue.

"No thanks, I'm full," I reply, silently beseeching my maiden for mercy, merely to be met with the mirth of a beauty too blinded by the light of love to see my suffering.

"Have some more baby ko."

"You are growing boy!" Mama proclaims, proceeding under the pretense that my refusal of food is purely politeness rather than a prostrated palate pleading for reprieve and piling on another portion as fishy as the first. "Please have more, there is plenty."

You must understand that this might be a test to tell if I'm a man of adequate appetites, and therefore bold enough to build a better life for my love. Failure to finish this paralyzing plate would be an unforgivable affront to my host's hospitality. Setting to it somberly, I feign gusto for my girl through the longest minutes of my life.

Impressed by my ability to withstand his wife's hospitality, Papa ponders me with high hopes tempered by deep doubts. "It cost much money come here, no? How you afford it?"

"I worked and saved."

"What you do?"

"I'm a waiter." Why do I use the present tense for a position I'd departed for the sake of my sanity? Why do I proclaim a profession too meek and menial for my majesty? Could this be a kind of Stockholm Syndrome, like the self-loathing suffered by soyseffetic male feminists?

Papa crumples his countenance into a question mark until my trollop says something in Visaya, eliciting a nod of acknowledgment. "You can travel doing that?" he asks.

"Yeah."

"Your family have money?"

"Some," I reply, refraining from relating the financial fallout of our farm's fecal fiasco.

"You take care of Rain?"

"Yes."

"So you want to marry Rain?" Mama asks, reaching the intent of my interrogation.

"Yes," I reply, wising it the answer wanted.

"It is okay with me," Papa pronounces in approval of me taking over payments on his princess.

A flurry of Visaya. Everyone is pleased. Particularly my peach, who squeezes the breath from my body to celebrate my enslavement.

"You drink?" Papa asks.

"A bit." Finally. I need something stiff to stop the parasites from propagating.

Papa excuses himself while my pookie picks up. "You get enough to eat baby ko?" she enquires, sincerely concerned that I might need more.

"Plenty, thanks."

Doing my best not to burst while the females fuss over me, five minutes of forever pass before Papa reappears, bearing a brown bottle and beaming at the boozing before us and his baby girl's new benefactor.

"We take turns," my angel explains, grabbing a glass and filling it before me. "Just one glass. You go first."

"Drink!" Papa proclaims, fathoming too fully that the manacles of marriage are not softened by sobriety. As the rum sears a trail of numb to my tum, they cheer me on with the toast "enom."

Then Papa partakes and we repeat the ritual.

Rain grabs a glass of tap water and Papa chases his shot with a shlug. Then it's my truelove's turn and I watch the water follow the firewater, its platoons of parasites marching towards yours truly. I pause in panic when my princess proffers it, but I'm too deep down this rabbit hole to return to Kansas. The glasses orbit onward til we finish round two, at which point Papa and my peach settle in to smoke.

"The rum, it is okay for you?" Papa enquires.

"Yeah, I like it." Not the flavor so much as its fortitude.

"You know..." he begins, searching his cigarette for the wisdom one might want when deeding their daughter to a man of such means. "We are not rich people. We are simple people. That is okay for your family?"

"Yes, of course."

"It okay for them that she Filipina?"

"Of course."

"Rain... she is good girl."

"Yes." Quite.

"I see in her eyes that she care for you. I see that in you too. Let us drink to that." Again the glasses go round while Mama scowls, scurries and worries over the wee ones.

"Will you stay here with Rain?" Papa enquires. "Or will you take her to America?"

"I'm not sure. America I guess."

He flicks his ash, consulting his wisdom stick once more. "Yes... more opportunity in America I think. This is good for you Rain?"

"I go where he goes."

Tuesday, December 3, 2013, 10:07 a.m.

"I love this movie!" Rain squeals, showing me a street vendor's counterfeit copy of some formulaic chick flick. "Can we buy it baby ko?" she pleads, pursing her lips and popping her peepers as she holds it to her heart.

We? You mean *me?* "How much?"

"Only 50 pesos."

"Alright."

"Mmm! Thank you baby ko."

I regret my agreement immediately. It's not the money that matters, but the overconsumption I'm encouraging by funding her frivolities. This DVD epitomizes my complicity in the Californiciferian culture of consumerism. Might its transmission be more insidious than it seems? Myself not only a seductive symbol of western wealth, but also a carrier of its contagion? How long til this cancer is all consuming, the graceful angels of the east turned fat and foul mouthed like the waddling witches of the west?

"Baby ko, everything *okay?*"

Who could behold such sweetness and remain rattled? Only a monster. "Yeah, everything's fine."

"You looked upset."

"Don't worry your pretty little head about it."

"Okay baby ko. We buy these sausages for Mama cook?"

"Sure."

"Thank you baby ko. You have 60 pesos?"

12:34 p.m.

"You get enough to eat?" Mama asks.

Am I being fattened for slaughter, or slowed for easier enslavement? Maybe it's a mental move to convince me she's curing an eating disorder I didn't know was devouring me, forever indebting me to her devices. "I'm full, thank you."

"You sure you don't want more baby ko?" Rain pouts, proving her part in my tummy's torture.

It's a trap. They're maintaining their womanly worry to persuade me I'm the one with the problem. It's gastronimental torture, it's-

Foodlighting.

"Yeah, I'm *good*."

"But you are growing boy!" Mama proclaims, heaping me another helping. "You must *eat!*"

I gape aghast at my grub, the women eyeing me expectantly as I falteringly form my fingers into a fork for a bite of rice, then sausage, then rice. The path to salvation is paved with suffering.

"Baby ko, can I have ten pesos for buy cigarettes?"

"Sure," I reply, fishing for the equivalent of a quarter that will buy my beauty two sticks of smokable vegetables. Mama scowls. Rain scampers.

"You smoke John?" Mama asks.

"No."

"Rain smoke too much, like her Papa. Why you no smoke?"

To save my bucks for beer, my lungs for the green leaf and my voice to voodoo the vixens. "I guess I just never started."

"Maybe you help Rain quit?"

"Um," I mumble. "Maybe."

After a course of questions my ruby returns, peepers popping with plans to make me feel more fully the weight of her worship. "Baby ko, someone sell banana cue, you want try it?"

"Maybe another time."

"I think you like it."

"What is it?"

"Banana cooked with sugar, um, how you say?"

"Caramelized?"

"Yes baby ko, caramelized. You want try it?"

"I'm really full."

"I think you like it if you try it baby ko," she whines, putting on a puppy-eyed pout so I'll endure the doting identity she's donned in overcompensation for her sins. "I think you don't eat enough. I worry for you."

Can't she see I'm as stuffed as a midget nine months pregnant with Andre the Giant's love child? "Alright," I grumble, giving up on my girly figure.

"Can I have twenty pesos?"

"Yeah."

"Thank you baby ko."

"Uh huh."

"Be right back."

"Kay."

She whips away, returning with four warm treats, splitting two between four bambinos and forcing a whole one on me. Demonstrating the dessert's deliciousness, she nibbles her banana with an elegant eroticism whilst I masticate mine with the solemn resolve a fox somehow finds to tear itself from a trap at the loss of a limb.

"You like baby ko?"

Entrapment! My nymph should know I've no more gusto to give. "Uh huh."

It being all I can bear to bring my belly to the bottom of the banana, I listen listlessly to the volleys of Visaya Rain and Mama return, doubtlessly disagreeing over whether I need another nibble to nosh on, being unfamiliar with the feeding of a man so majestic as myself. During the display, a bimbo between my minx and Mama's age shows up at the shack's entrance. The volleys of Visaya increase in intensity.

"Auntie, this is John," my nymph announces, fire ceased for my sake. "John, this my Auntie."

"Nice to meet you John."

"Nice to meet you."

"You are Rain's boyfriend?" Auntie asks, assuming the seat across from mine.

"My fiancé!" my princess proclaims.

"Wow, fiancé! You must really love her!"

"Yes, very much." At least I did, before the force-feedings.

Another bout of blather between my beauty and Auntie.

"Baby ko? Can we buy beer?"

"Sure."

"You have sixty pesos? I go get it."

"Yeah, here." I pull out a hundred peso note, hoping I can handle its sudsy understanding.

"Baby ko, can I get cigarettes too, for later?"

"Sure."

"Mmmm! Thank you baby ko," she coos, pecking my cheek and whipping away.

"How you meet Rain?" Auntie asks, wasting no time in her interrogations.

"In El Nido."

"You stay with her in Davao?"

"Davao's nice."

"Maybe you take Rain to America?"

"I'd like to."

A frenzied flurry of womanly worry, Mama's brain about to burst.

"She mad cause we drink. She think I bad influence on Rain. You like drink?"

"During waking hours."

After a tummy-tortured eternity of small talk my princess reappears with a liter of lager and a smitten smile, putting the change in my pocket and grabbing three glasses.

"John say he meet you in El Nido."

"Yes, he…" She switches to Visaya, and I suspect another conspiracy.

"Rain say you sing."

"Sometimes."

"You will sing for us tonight?"

"Tonight?"

"Yes baby ko."

"Um… alright."

"Rain say when you sing it cast a spell on her. She cannot look away."

I lavish the ladies with but a smidge of my smirk, still my strumpet blushes blindingly at the memory of our meeting, that longing eye lock that led us from the darkness of depravity to the light of true love. "It is okay for you baby ko? Because you know, we are poor people. If we go you will have to pay. That is okay for you?"

"Yeah, it's fine."

"Thank you baby ko."

9

The Club

"It okay with you baby ko?" my crumpet enquires, perching her paw on my pants to reroute my rationalizing through my auxiliary head, puddly peepers weaponizing her womanhood to keep my mind off the money being quaffed by her crew.

"Huh?"

"The bar, it is o*kay* for you?"

"Yeah, of course." I suppose I expected a karaoke bar, like where I met my minx but without the matchmaking, but what I get is a three walled, open air lounge with a cover band, its plastic seating all stamped with the country's biggest brands of beer and booze, its name in neon simply 'The Club.'

"Will you sing for us baby ko?"

"*Here?*" I ask, bunching my brows in bewilderment. "Is there karaoke after the band?"

"No baby ko! You sing on stage *with* the band!"

"*With* the band?" I gulp.

"Yes baby ko."

"Oh." The fact is I'm a fraud, but a karaoke Casanova. Singing without song

85

lyrics scrolling by on a screen makes me want to crawl under the covers.

"Baby ko? I tell them you sing tonight."

"Um."

"What you sing?" Auntie asks.

"Uh."

"Rain say you good singer," says Rain's friend Jenna.

All eyes are on me like that adolescent dream where you go to school in your skivvies, realizing your lapse as you recite a report to cackling classmates. "She is too kind."

"*No* baby ko! You are kind to *me!* Because you treat me so *well!*"

"Of course I do baby ko, because you're so sweet."

"It okay if you don't want to sing," Rain snivels. "I understand." Rudolph, luminescent nose confused for a cruise missile, was shot down over the north Atlantic. Christmas is canceled.

Looking out as always for our mutual best interests, His Girthiness suggests I sing. I solemnly accept his worldly wisdom. "I'll sing."

Christmas is back on, a pony stuffing every stocking, mistletoe haloing my head, which receives a rapid-fire round of pecks from my peach. "You will? *Mmmmmmm!* You make me so *happy* baby ko!"

When the band breaks my crumpet confers with the strumpet on stage, who with a smitten smile hands me the band's song list to search. I settle on 'Santeria' by Sublime, slipping back to my beer for bravery.

A few minutes pass, along with my lager.

"And now," the nymph announces. "A guest singer! Would you please come to the stage?"

All eyes are on me. I have no choice. Whatever worries are tumbling around one's tummy, show time is go time.

"Welcome to the stage!" the temptress trills, as I accept the male singer's microphone. (As is common here with cover bands, they have singers of both sexes to maxify audience mania.) "Can you tell us your name?"

"John."

"Where are you from John?"

"The United States," I reply, hooking the interest of every beauty in the bar, marking myself as more than merely a member of the master race, but also as hailing from the holy land, and therefore capable of being the conduit for cockular communion with their consumer messiah.

"Wow, you are long way from home. Everybody welcome John!" Polite applause.

Though there are only about 50 Filipinos in the audience, amounting in mass to about half as many Americans, my performance foments a euphoria ten magnitudes more than the titties in attendance. Recognizing Rain's squeal piercing through the applause, I deliver a double dose of my signature smirk and return to our table.

"You were *amazing* baby ko!" my scrumpet exclaims, bear-hugging me breathless to showcase her claims.

"Thanks," I reply, pulling loose from my lollipop to grin at the group.

"You sing in band?" Jenna asks, gulping down giddy so my sweetie doesn't see it.

"No."

"Why not?"

"Never got around to it."

"Baby ko, maybe you stay here become big star in Philippines!"

"Could happen."

"And I will be your *princess!* And you will be my *king!*"

"Wouldn't that make you my queen?"

"What you mean?"

"Queen, not princess."

"No," she whines, feigning offense. "I will be princess. I too young and pretty to be queen."

"Is there a rule about that?"

"Yes."

"Huh."

"Thank you for singing baby ko. You make me happy."

"You... uh... you have..." Rain's little brother Alex stammers. "Uh! Nosebleed!"

"*Nosebleed?*" I question, wondering where the blood could be.

"Nosebleed mean he shy about speak English," Rain clarifies. "We say that when we don't know how to say what we want to say."

The siblings confer.

"He want to know why you not in famous band."

"Dunno," I shrug. Sloth I suppose. But then, is fame not the finest lift a loafer could hope for, not only bringing in bucks far beyond the worth of his work, but also simplifying seduction, an endless effort with only trifling returns for the average American male?

"What you think about baby ko?"

"I think we need another bucket."

11:17 p.m.

The flip side of cupid's coin is the moral confusion it fosters in the fellows it favors. The leers of lovestruck ladies muddle the rock star's mind, for like your typical fella he fathoms too fully that an unfulfilled fantasy hangs heavy on the heart. Rattled by the realization that gobbling his goods will be the highlight of a hussy's cock carousel cruise, a railing to reminisce on when the wall wilts her womb and other boners are a bitter blur, he hurls headlong into his compassionate crusade, diddling a different doll daily. He is a sexual Sisyphus. Sexyphus. Endless are his efforts.

How many Hollywood harlots would go so far for their fans? None that I can name. I therefore submit Sexyphus as exhibit A for the male's superior capacity for morally managing celebrity.

"Ikaw lang sapat na," Rain coos, grasping me greedily in the giddy afterglow of making love to a legend. "Mahal kita lagi."

"What's lagi mean baby ko?"

"Always."

"Yes, always. Mahal kita lagi."

"Promise?"

"Promise."

"Baby ko… when you famous you stay with me? Because, you *know!* When you sing I see other girls watching you… because… because you so *sexy* up there!"

"I'll stay baby ko," I reply without pause. But will I? How many longing looks can my boner bear before giving these girls the goods they're gagging to gobble? Is it more moral to marry one lucky lass or to spread one's sploodge over flocks of floozies? Logically it's the latter, for how could one heart's heaving match the summed mirth of a gaggle of beguiled groupies?

Intuiting my turmoil, she heaves her head to hear my heartbeat. "Thank you baby ko," she coos, twiddling my tummy hair with a soft little sigh.

"You're welcome."

"How come you no have American girl?"

This again? I suppose somewhere in the collective unconscious the Hollywood harlot has supplanted the princess as the model for maidenhood, elevating through association the American minge in the minds of third world wenches, making any criticism of our cunts an attack on their fairy tales and not to be believed.

But if my angel can't fathom what I've fled, then how will she know what I need?

I will always be haunted, like a Holocaust survivor.

"Because I'm not a masochist."

"What you mean?"

"I like my sanity."

"But why you no like American girls?"

I let slip a long sigh, annoyed to be enumerating my grievances again. "They have a bullet point checklist that could make it to the moon and back, but make no effort to fulfill men's simplest desires, like femininity and respect."

"What you mean?"

I imagine the American love market, like the weariness of war, cannot be understood by eyes that have not endured its despair. "I mean they take without giving. Demand respect without offering it. Give blame but never bear it."

"Why they like this baby ko?"

"I don't know," I sigh, exhaling a weight from deep within. "And I don't care anymore."

"But on TV they are so pretty."

"But that's just TV."

"What you mean?"

"The Filipinas on TV, are *they* pretty?"

"Yes."

"Prettier than the *average* Filipina?"

"Yes."

"You see?"

An ounce of understanding finally hits her hamster. "Ah… okay… you mean most American girls not pretty like girls on TV?"

"Exactly."

"And they not nice?"

"Not usually."

"And men still marry them?"

"Sometimes, but it usually ends in divorce."

"Di*vorce?* What is di*vorce?*"

"They end the marriage."

Giving out a gasp, she clutches me closer to keep herself safe from this demonic idea. "But how can they *do* that baby ko! A marriage is for*ever!*"

"Not in America."

"Why *not* baby ko?"

"I don't know. Americans have too many choices to be satisfied. They're always looking for something better."

"And *you* baby ko?"

"I couldn't find what I was looking for, so I left. Now I've found you."

"You won't leave me?"

"Never."

"Promise?"

"Promise."

"Thank you baby ko… *baby* ko?"

"Yes?"

"Can we go see my brother Marco tomorrow?"

"Marco?" Must I meet all of them? I mean, after three or four, aren't more siblings superfluous?

"Yes, my oldest brother. He live on side of mount Apo, near Kidapawan City."

"Oh, alright." I've no idea where that is, but the mountain bit sounds exciting.

"Mmm! *Thank* you baby ko! And we see my friend Jaijai *too!* I'm so ex*cited!*"

10

Maidens on the Mount

Wednesday, December 4, 2013, 11:33 a.m.

Unimpressed with the pox we've left upon the land, Mount Apo stands unstirred by humanity's hubris, knowing our time is a cosmic tick and a belch would make us barbecue.

"Baby ko?"

"Yes?"

"You close to your brother and sister?"

"Not really."

"Why not?" she whines, pouting her disapproval.

I shrug at the futility of intercultural communication, the gaps we grasp at but never truly traverse. "We just aren't. We grew apart."

"What they do?"

"Well… my brother's a real estate agent."

"What you mean?"

"He sells houses."

"Is good job?"

"Well, the pay exceeds the effort, so I suppose so."

"And what your sister do?"

"She's… she's an entertainer."

"What you mean? Singer like you?"

"More of a… uh… a dancer." Stripper.

"And she get *paid?*" she asks, bunching her brows in disbelief. "What kind of dance she *do?*"

"Uh… interpretive."

"What you mean?" she enquires, curling up to be cradled.

"Well… she works with her wardrobe in a way that excites the audience." I may have only completed two quarters of community college, but at least I learned the most essential skill higher education can confer: how to say half as little with twice as many words.

She doesn't understand, but that matters not a mite, for with her head to my heart she can feel my compassion broadcast by its beat. "Is good job?"

"Well, the pay is more than the effort, so I guess so."

"Mmmmm…" she murmurs. "Maybe when I come to America you get me good job like this baby ko?"

"Maybe."

Lulled to languor by the rhythm of the road, my princess shuts her eyes, drifting to dreamland as we pass palm plantations and provincial outposts populated with rollicking rascals and mangy mutts. Presiding upon these principalities so fetid with filth yet festooned with festivity, mount Apo's misty flanks portend our impermanence.

We are all just ants crawling upon a claymation set, and God but a capricious toddler with clumsy fists and a penchant for pulling his pee pee.

3:08 p.m.

"I just knock baby ko, see if she here."

My darling drums a tinny tap tap tap. Receiving no reply, she hobs her head back to holler at the second story, a slipshod spire pointing skyward like a shantytown princess tower. "Jaijai!"

After knocking another ratatatap, Rain pries open a loose strip of tin siding, revealing a dirt floor, plastic tables and chairs, a pair of pool tables and a bare-bones bar. "We go in," she says.

She sees my mortified mug, the question of whether Filipino prison food is palatable, or anywhere near the nutritional needs of my superlative self. "It's okay baby ko. I work for owner sometimes when Mama and I fighting. This secret way in."

Secret way in? Or proof of impending collapse? "It's okay?"

"Yes baby ko."

"Alright."

I slip through behind my honey, letting her take me to a table. "Wait here baby ko," she coos, a peck on the cheek underlining that our love can by no distance be defeated. "I go up and see if she here."

Nodding at my inamorata, I sit down as directed, waiting for her weight to break the bar's back. The giggles of girlfriends washing my worries away, His Girthiness requests a report. I prescribe patience.

A descending pitter patter finds my beauty sat beside me. "She come down in a minute baby ko. I wake her up."

"Alright."

"Is just bar for simple people baby ko. Is *okay?*"

"Yeah, it's fine."

"The owner, he kind to me, give me work when mama and I fighting."

After a minute of mush Rain's amiga emerges, the transcendent sight of a mighty whitey in the wild leaving her wide-eyed and wanting for a pinch more poise.

"Baby ko," Rain coos, pulling me up for introductions. "This is Jaijai. Jaijai, this my fiancé John."

"Nice… nice to meet you John," she purrs.

"Nice to meet you Jaijai," I reply, deeding her a deniable dose of my signature smirk, watching her turn red as I reach for her held out hand. It is easily observed but seldom said aloud that lassies, because of the herd-brain's hold on their hamster, pine for the penises pre-selected by their peers. Synthesizing this surmisal with the following facts, one will see through science how I summon such lust in Jaijai's loins:

1. Meat-fed American men are gods to the girls of the emasculated east, who have been habituated by Hollywood to see our superiority as more than mortal.

2. The smirk will smite any other expression if it comes from true confidence, winning a man women and wealth beyond his dizziest dreams. (Any presidential race can be predicted by the power with which this weapon is wielded. Females, for whom the smirk is not a natural product of prestige, but a forced affectation that comes off as sour grapes for being defrauded their femininity in pursuit of a parity for which their constitutions aren't equipped, will never hold our highest office for this rudimentary reason.)

3. Chicks dig dudes with facial scars. (Have I not told you of this, dear reader? No, it is not mangling, merely a mark on my mug from falling on a rock as a rascal, but its roguery is rousing.)

I illuminate these items merely to remind that I am but the breathing embodiment of her feminine fantasies, not some hunk sent from heaven, though so it may seem to set eyes on me. Thankfully, my maiden mistakes her friend's aphrodisia for mere mirth, and the girls gabble on in Visaya. His Girthiness proposes a pillow fight.

"You want a beer baby ko?"

"Yeah."

"I tell Jaijai you good singer. She want to hear you."

Jaijai nods, wolfing down woozy so her words don't waver. "You sing for us?"

"Now?"

"Sure. I set up machine."

"Alright."

Jaijai brings beers, sets up the machine. Never have two nymphs so filled the air with pheromones. When Jaijai sings, His Girthiness offers himself as microphone. One beer and my beauty is ready to roll, melted by my melody.

"Baby ko? We go check into hotel now, *okay?* Then we come back tonight."

"Sounds good."

Agiggle over my glory, the cuties confer.

"Jaijai give me directions to hotel."

Picking up our packs and bidding goodbye, our passion propels us towards privacy through surprisingly suburban streets. And yet, even in our ardor it occurs to me our quest has yet to be addressed. Are we not here to brag to her brother of the western woozy his sister suffers?

Of course, I do not blab it so bluntly. In tact I am topless.

"We go see him tomorrow. Is on road up Mount Apo. Take maybe an hour get there. Is okay for you?"

"Sure."

"Jaijai and Alexa come too. Maybe we go hot springs? Is okay for you?"

"Yeah, it's fine."

"Because, you *know* baby ko, we are *poor girls.*"

"Don't worry about it," I reassure, knowing the economic inequality plaguing our partnership is but a product of provenance, and that our true treasures are internal.

Thursday, December 5, 2013, 9:23 a.m.

They comb the aisles like stoners stocking for a storm, snatching every snack whose glitz makes them giddy, clutching every candy whose carbs they crave. What curse have I cast upon these gullible girls, so keen to catch the cancer of consumerism?

"Baby ko, you mind pay for this?"

"It's fine," I reply, wising from where her greed is growing. Does it not make sense, in this poverty-stricken province, for a man's money to make her moist? What wiles would it take in a world of such want to win oneself wealth so mighty as mine?

We head to the highway to hire a driver. The first two fellows reprove our request to be carried to the clouds by one mere little moto. Thankfully, a third driver can see past the possibility of a fatal fall to the promise of a paltry profit.

Mounting the moto proves an act of ingenuity. Behind the driver jiggles Jaijai, then magnificent old me begging my boner not to bulge, and in the rear my ruby with our pack of provisions. Backwards on the handlebars sits luscious little Alexa, jean zipper dead center in the driver's vision, forcing the fellow's face sidewards to see.

Casting civilization aside as we close upon the clouds, our majestic mountain hovers ahead, its canyons inclined to collect our corpses like a fatty's folds accumulating crumbs.

10:32 a.m.

Bound between my blossoming beauties, I endure our ordeal as I fancy a fetus does sky diving. That is, comforting myself in a cradle of flesh.

Up where the sweltering smog gives way to a veil of fog, the ravine's primeval depths disappearing into the murky mists as if providing padding for our fall, we stop at a curve in the canyon, a thatched shack perched on the promontory side with a postage stamp for a pig sty and produce patch. Unmounting the moto, Rain bounds towards her brother, a stickpole of a stoner with dirty dreadlocks and a glued on grin.

"Baby ko, I want you meet my brother Marco," she says, having hugged him hard enough to puncture his lungs with his rawboned ribs.

Shaking my hand, Marco's grin defies gravity and grows even grander.

"Nice to meet you Marco."

"Nice to meet you, uh…"

"John."

For the sake of succinctness I will not bore you with the banalities foreigners force upon one another when incapable of communicating pithier points.

The estate toured, we find ourselves inside the shack in the loosest sense of inside, repeating the platitudes that keep a girl's beau and brother's fight for her favor seemingly civilized. Munching a meal of corporate candies and mummified fish, we wash it down with a bottle of rum and Marco's homegrown, remounting our ride with newfound fortitude.

1:46 p.m.

I cannot convey the torturous temptation as the maidens remove all but their unmentionables, all the vivacity on view not letting me linger beside the spring, lest my trouser tent attract attention. Jaijai is especially juicy, her baby fat filling out her features without furrowing into folds. A shave short of my five foot eight, she has a shape I could really shake, really rail without worry of wounding. It seems so long since I've laid with a lass like her. Before Sarah.

No, I must not look.

There is nothing wrong with Rain. Rain is 95 pounds of perfect, but sometimes I feel like I'm fiddling a fifteen year old. Not that anything is wrong with that.

Wait, don't quote me on that.

Subconsciously sensing that I'm scoping her skivvies, scarcely disguised desire drips from Jaijai's dewy lips, her hamster wheel whirring out a way to wise me her weakness for white willy without tipping her hand to my honey that she'd wolf mine without remorse. "You have brother John?" she asks at last.

The primordial cloud forest fades from focus, leaving a tunnel vision of vixens tuned on yours truly in wanton anticipation. "Brother?" I parrot, like a toddler taking his first faltering whack at the word.

"Yes."

"Yeah."

"You invite him to the wedding?"

"Uh... yeah."

"He have girlfriend?"

11

Opportunititty Knockers

Friday, December 6, 2013, 8:13 p.m.

Back at The Club with Alex and Rain. Alex likes me. Probably because I buy him beer and not because I boink his big sis, but he seldom says more than a sentence in the language of our lord, so it's hard to say, as he mostly masks his mug with a goofy grin like a Make-A-Wish sponsored mute meeting his favorite actor.

Of course we're here because my harlot is crazy for a crooner, a Romeo who rouses the room to rapture. To keep her googly gleam glinting I must endlessly enlist her fellow females to affirm her fortune. This is what women want but can't word without a critical dose of cognitive dissonance. A man might imagine a minx his angel evermore, but even if her hamster wheel head insists he's her soulmate, he is but a beau who sees through her bullet point checklist with his boner's blind eye, for he'll ruin the relationship if he becomes too comfortable, as a retired snowflake is but a drop of water.

I'm called up for an encore of 'Santeria.' The crowd has grown since Tuesday. Glowing with glory, I smitten my smirk, siphoning the salacity from my sycophants and belting it back to their bosoms.

Sitting back down beside my darling, my crumpet makes it clear to every bimbo in the bar who's gobbling my goods whilst Alex smiles on stupidly, as dolts often do when met with majesty like mine. "You are… big star," he stammers.

"Yes baby ko," my princess purrs. "Everyone here see you, and they wonder, who is *he?* And me *too!* I wonder… why you *here?* Why you pick *me?*"

"You picked me."

"You had eyes like a tiger! I was helpless. I could only say yes."

Her woozy doozy eyes devouring me, I turn putty at their piety. She's sweeter than a lollipop at a sweet sixteen, as savory as a fish taco at a quinceañera. "How about now?" I murmur. "Still yes?"

"*Al*ways yes baby ko. For*ever.*"

My fingers frisk her skirt for the silky skin beside her squiz, my mind's eye meandering from her minge's fringe to forevermore, only to refocus on a well-fed fellow of forty or so summers, awaiting my attention beside the table. With shoulder length hair, a red silk shirt tucked into pinstripe pants, and a smile that could sell dirt floors from door to door, he displays a dignity almost equal to my own, despite his dimensions.

"Pardon my interruption," he says, holding out a hand and giving me a grin as I pull my paw off my peach to share in a shake. "My name is Miguel. Welcome to my club." Besides his kingly countenance, what strikes me most about the man is that, though his skin is the olive of the orient, his pronunciation is more Russian than Pinoy.

"It's a nice spot. I'm John."

"Pleased to meet you John. You mind if I sit?"

"Please do," I reply.

"Your singing, is very good," he says, settling into the empty seat.

"Thank you."

"And not just your singing, but also your, how you say?"

"Stage presence?"

"Da, that's it. Your stage presence. Is very impressive."

"Thank you."

"You live here in Davao?"

"I do now."

"You like it here?"

"Yeah."

"You have job here?"

"No."

"I want you to sing for me."

"Another song?"

"*Many* songs! I want you to be the new singer in my band what plays here on Thursday and Saturday."

My peach's peepers are orgasmic orbs of puppy love paranoia. Alex's grin has grown even grander, becoming all but unbreakable. "Um," is all I manage.

"Think about it."

I am. Not the singing so much as the frenetic fits of possessive passion to be kindled in my crumpet by the covetous cuties in the crowd. "I'll do it."

"Great! Wonderful news. They will love you. I see your beers are empty. You want another round? On the house."

"Sure."

He barks at the bitty beauty behind the bar, who drops what she's doing to press through patrons with four bottles of beer, as if magnetized by my majesty.

"Cheers," Miguel toasts. "You like the Philippines?"

"Yeah."

"And what you like? The *girls*, no?"

"Everything."

"Ah... is *this* girl, no? I can see that you are in love."

"Yes," I reply, reading Rain's need for romantic reassurance bestirred by the bartender's envious eyes and adding, "very much."

"Her eyes say she care for you deeply. Philippine women are very devoted. They care very much for their men and children."

"Very admirable."

"Yes, I think so..." He pauses, taking a pull of Pale Pilsen as he mulls the money to be made off my velvety voice. "If you sing here you will have to sing for maybe two hours straight, is okay for you?"

"Don't see why not."

"Great! A cheers to my new singer." We clink and swig again. "You can come by tomorrow to talk?"

"Sure."

"Two in the afternoon? Is good for you?"

"Sure."

"Great! I will see you tomorrow then."

"Sounds good."

Miguel excuses himself. Rain's head, a swooning swirl of insecurities, settles on my shoulder. Lord I'd like to boink that bartender! But dammit... Rain. That mushy little minx will never leave me alone long enough to give a groupie the goods. But a peach's possessiveness is a double sided sword, for though my goods she may guard from other girls, she'll give it up more than an amnesiac nymphomaniac at a nude beach oyster roast.

"Baby ko, what you think about?"

"Hmm?"

"It feel like you somewhere else baby ko. What you think about?"

"About the future. About us. About singing here."

"You will be a big hit baby ko."

"I hope so," I say, squeezing her squiz through her skirt to hush her harried hamster.

Alex looks on at my lechery with the same silly smile. Amazing. It's too bad he was born in this catholic country of puritanical princesses and sex industry sluts, for though his nonchalant numbskullery might not fit him well for fatherhood, it would melt minges in America, where he wouldn't have to worry about wenches wanting him to wed, and any brown bastards would be bankrolled by big brother if the bimbo didn't abort.

"Can we go soon baby ko?"

"Tired?"

She nods, puddly eyes pleading for lovey dovey wuvvy forever and evers. "Yes baby ko."

"Alright. After these beers then."

"Baby ko? Can we eat Balut first? Before we go hotel?"

"Balut?"

"It is, um, how you say? It is duck egg, but with… with baby."

"Fertilized?"

"Yes baby ko."

Eleven minutes later we find ourselves facing a street vendors stock of otherwise ordinary eggs, each one a life lived and lost in that limbo between oblivion and birth, a life not unlike the over a billion unborn babies sacrificed to Satan since the abortion holocaust began.

"Just one baby ko?"

"Huh?"

"You want just one?"

"Kay."

There is an art to Balut. One doesn't simply shuck the shell and cram it in one's kisser like some Easter Sunday stoner. One teases off the shell's top, slurping the brine gathered there and sighing exaggerated satisfaction. Salting and saucing it to taste, one bites into the baby with its fledgling feathers and ambitions of bones, finding it surprisingly savory.

It's what's left of the white that torments one's taste buds. As rubbery as a bouncy ball, biting it only breaks it into puny pieces that refuse to be pulverized into a paste.

I know, you'd spit them out, right?

You aren't here, with my darling's eyes devouring you.

I bet you'd swallow too.

Saturday, December 7, 2013, 2:01 p.m.

Faced with eyes that could squeeze a million dollar home equity loan from a cardboard fort, I could only acknowledge the inevitability of my crumpet coming down with the consumerist contagion and provide her with pesos to scratch the itch while I meet with Miguel. Certainly you must see my sensitivity to her sweetness, as American men have no immunity to bona fide femininity, our soil being too acerbic for its survival. I am an Indian. Her love is a smallpox blanket.

Miguel is sliding back the metal grate that spans the missing wall overnight. "My friend," he says, greeting me with a grin and a held out hand. "Good to see you again."

"Likewise."

"Come, sit down," he says, motioning towards a table. "You want a beer?"

"Sure."

"Pale Pilsen?"

"Sounds good."

He hollers at the lollipop from last night, who turns from the task of stocking the straws to assemble our order, gliding over with glasses, ice, tongs and a liter of Pale Pilsen, gulping down giddy so her tray doesn't tremble in my princely presence.

"Don't tempt him," Miguel chides as she serves our suds. "He is already happy man."

Seamlessly slipping from passion to pique, she snaps back at her boss, turning tail with a feisty flourish to flaunt her fanny wiggling away.

"I think she likes you," he says.

"Oh?"

"Yes of course! Don't you notice? You are singer! Girls love singers, da? Maybe you don't see it because girls always this way to you? I bet you meet your girlfriend singing, no?"

"I did."

"You see what I mean? You are lucky man to have gift of voice. Some men have to try with the clothes or with the job or with the muscles, but you just open your mouth and they come to you! Of course, it is shame that you will not be able to please your, uh, how you say? Those girls what like musicians?"

"Groupies?"

"Yes, *groupies!*" he agrees. "Maybe you can still give them hope, you know? Is good for business if they think they have chance."

"I'm sure."

"You sure it will not be hard for you, with your girlfriend?"

"I'll manage."

"Yes! Of course you will. I can see your girlfriend knows that to keep hold of you takes *passion!*" He mimes *passion* with a furled fist, making me mindful of the grip a girl gets on her boyfriend's balls if he isn't careful to keep her auditioning for his devotion.

"Oh, *she knows.*"

"You hungry? I own pizza place next door. Is good business pizza. You take bread and this cheese what you make from the milk from cow tits. You not even need kill cow. Is like, how you say? Like the sun how it keeps shining?"

"Renewable resource?"

"Da! Renewable resource! Is good profit! But is baby food for grown ups, no? You American's what eat pizza all the time look like big babies with the puffy faces and the big bellies. Kind of like me but even bigger. But is tasty, no? You want me get you slice?"

"I just ate. I think she's fattening me."

"Of course she is! A woman's job is to care for her man. Why you think I so fat?"

"You have two girlfriends?"

"Haha!" he cries, slapping my shoulder. "Is dream, no? Or maybe nightmare. One woman make enough problems. Cheers! To women!" We drink.

"So... uh."

"Ah," he says, setting down his suds. "You want to talk business, no?"

"Sooner or later."

"You Americans, you are in love with money, no?"

"Um."

His mouth grows into a grin. "I joke. Me too, I love money. When I grew up, I was poor, but there was fire in me." This time the emotion he mimes makes me think of the morning after an authentic Mexican meal. "The other kids would waste time playing games, waste time going to school. But not me, no. I go to the beach and sell sun glasses to tourists. I save money, buy cooler. I fill cooler with ice and beer. Sometimes they not let me buy beer because I too young, so my uncle buy it for me. Family is very important here in Philippines, da? I sell cold beer on beach. I bribe first policeman age twelve. Is not skill you learn in school, no?"

"I suppose not."

"I wanted to be the man, you know?"

"I can understand that."

"I'm sure you understand that the Philippines is poor country. My club is modest club. Is place for the people, you know?"

"I see that."

"I cannot pay as much as I would like."

"And how much would that be?"

"You are *star* my friend! If I could, I would pluck a Porsche from the heavens for you," he declares, miming the motion of plucking a piece of fruit from a tree. "I would fish a yacht from the sea for you, mine a mansion from the ground for you. But sadly, I cannot."

"So what *will* you pay?"

"Well... I thought maybe you had an idea what *you* wanted."

"You first."

Stalling for time, he frisks my face for signs of a sucker, merely to be met with the majesty of my signature smirk. "One thousand pesos a week," he finally offers. "Is good, no?"

Negotiating wages is like a family reunion, always go high. "I want two thousand."

"Too Much. I can do one thousand two hundred."

"Eighteen hundred."

"One thousand four hundred."

"Fourteen hundred and free drinks."

"Okay, okay. You are my *star!*" he states, punctuating my importance to his plans with a paternal shoulder pat. "I take care of you! One thousand four hundred and two hundred pesos a week for drinks. I suppose you want to know when you meet the band?"

"I suppose I'll have to meet them sooner or later."

"You are free tomorrow? Band practice on Sundays."

"I could fit it in."

"Ah ha ha yes! Pull your girlfriend off you long enough to come in! I hope ten tomorrow morning is not too early for you? I know how you singers feel about mornings."

"That's fine."

"Good… good. Cheers."

As I go for a gulp with Miguel, my peach appears with a couple of counterfeit films, antsily awaiting my attention.

"Oh hello again! Please join us. We are just finishing." Miguel barks at the bartender, who begrudgingly brings an extra glass, glowering at my girl as she sets it before her and smittening me a smile as she walks away.

"She is very expressive no? Maybe sometimes too much," Miguel muses, pouring for Her Poutiness. "So John, band practice tomorrow morning before club opens. Is okay for you?"

"That's fine."

"You will be ready for Thursday with only two days practice?"

"Not really."

"Of course not! Cheers."

12

Bungling the Beat

Sunday, December 8, 2013, 8:24 a.m.

I wake to weeping.

"Baby ko?" I query, shaking her shoulder. *"Baby* ko?"

"Mmmmmmm," she murmurs, unmoving.

"You okay?"

"No baby ko!" she cries into the covers. "I *not* okay!"

"What's up?"

She heaves her head to behold me, wrenching my gut with her grief. "I dream you with other *girl! That* girl from the *bar!* She give you those big *eyes!* She want to *steal* you from me! I *feel* it!"

I let slip a slow sigh. Is this why Sexyphus suffered through a life without love? Because his majesty was too much for jealous worry not to wear down any wench he was with? Is this the price I must pay for the life of a legend? Sure, I'd bone that beauty behind the bar in a blink, but should my sheila find out of the affair, then I fear in forlornness her heart would lay forever fallow, nevermore to know love's giddy growth again. "It's just a dream," I reassure.

"It *not* just a dream! I *feel* it! I see how the girls look at you like... like they want to *take* you from me!"

From where wells their womanly worry? Is it a communal capital culled from the collective uncuntscious? Or is it furiously fabricated by some feminine faculty? "They won't baby ko," I console.

"Promise?" she implores.

"I promise," I reply, tenderly swabbing tears from my love's leaky eye.

"But they want to."

"I won't let them," I reassure, a delicate kiss confirming my passion is pure.

"Promise baby ko?"

"I promise," I repeat, paws pledging to her plums her never to mistreat.

"Okay baby ko. Ikaw lang sapat na."

"Ikaw lang sapat na."

"Mahal kita lagi."

"Mahal kita lagi."

Polly wanna cracker?

9:59 a.m.

Oh wondrous world! Have I cut my mortal coil and through clerical error come to the gates of God's kingdom? Is this not an angel before my eyes?

The cutie in question stands beside the side door, tilting her head back to contemplate the clouds, a lock of her hair falling past her bit lower lip to land on the wagging tongue of a Rolling Stones T-shirt.

"Good morning."

"Good morning. You are our new singer?" To simply say she smiles cannot convey the compassion popping from her peepers, the understanding eyes that delve into my depths without a joule of judgment.

"Apparently."

"I heard you sing the other day. You have very nice voice."

I also have a really nice... "Thank you."

"What is your name?"

"John. And yours?"

"I am Trisha," she replies, proffering her paw. Without missing a move, I lay it to my lips, bringing out the blush Tinker Bell would bestow if the sprite were to spy Peter Pan's Peter. "I play keyboard, sometimes I sing."

"Where are the others?"

"I don't know," she answers, shrugging to show her ease with uncertainty. "They come soon."

"So... uh, what happened to the last singer?"

"He no longer with us."

"Oh shit, I'm sorry."

"It's okay. I think he happier in Manila."

"Oh... I thought you meant, that, uh..."

"Yes?"

"That he was dead."

"No, he is okay I think."

A fracas inside. A foreign flurry from whose timbre I intuit to be between a floozy fishing for a fight and a man who can't be bothered to participate.

"Miguel's girl mad cause he kick her out before band practice," Trisha clarifies for me, seeing the question mark on my mug.

"He lives here?"

"In the apartment upstairs," she answers, signaling toward the second story.

The door opens and a maiden my age emerges, giving Trisha a glower that transforms into an eye fuck as she glides past my grandeur.

Miguel appears, evidently indifferent to her fading fanny. "Ah, good morning, come inside. No others?"

"Not yet," Trisha replies.

"You see? This is why you two are my favorites."

"But I just started," I say, not wanting to jinx it.

"Exactly, you haven't ruined it yet." As I muddle his meaning, Miguel's guffaw severs the silence. "I joke. Is funny, da?"

"Uh, yeah."

"You Americans are funny people, no?"

"Sometimes."

"Maybe just not in the morning?"

"Um. Maybe."

"Don't worry my friend!" he cries, slapping my shoulder sympathetically. "It will be okay! You are my *star!* You too Trisha. These other guys I not so sure of, but they are musicians, da?"

"Something like that."

"Yes. Something like that. Best musicians I can afford at slave wages. Now if you don't mind, I have some things to do upstairs."

"Are they always this late?" I ask Trisha once Miguel is gone.

Again she gives me a nonchalant shrug. "Sometimes they are late," she says, her right hand rubbing below her left breast. "But the music always starts when it is meant to. You in hurry?"

"No."

"Americans often in hurry, no?"

"Pretty much always."

"Why?"

"Distraction."

"From what?

"The lack of meaning in our lives."

A frown flits across her face and melts into amusement, as if she'd rendered my remark's negativity inert. "The lack of meaning is meaningful itself," she offers.

"I suppose so," I reply, again catching her scratching beneath her breast. "Is it a rash?" I ask, a pang of the hypochondria drilled into the American mind by our pharmaceutical slavemasters making me imagine myself melting from flesh eating fungus.

"Sorry?"

"What you're itching. Is it a rash?"

"No," she blushes. "Just an itch."

When the others at last arrive, practice goes as well as could be wished, meaning I've no idea what I'm doing and drive the band bonkers by coming in beats off cue. There are six of us if you count our drummer Manuel's hair, which whips with every whap like a weeping willow in the wind. Bong, Weezer's lost Asian member, is on bass, glasses and all. Mica is my guitar whiz, an unremarkable man until he grabs his guitar, at which moment his mug plugs into his pick. There is no strum that doesn't stretch his lips, no chord that can't titillate his tongue. It's like watching a spastic schizophrenic make out with their imaginary friend.

And Trisha? As a keyboard player she's passable, but her voice is as velvety as an angel queef.

2:15 p.m.

Practice ends when The Club opens at two. In repentance for poor rhythming, I offer the band a bucket of beers, but Miguel insists on being the big shot. Having suffered through several hours without me, my jewel joins us.

"So how you two meet?" Trisha asks.

Rain purses her lips, peepers imploring me to make our meeting sound romantic. "I was singing karaoke and she was in the audience. She kept looking at me."

"You looked at *me!*"

"You looked first."

"Because *you* looked!"

"Well, it's either the chicken or the egg, eh?"

"What you mean baby ko?" Oh right, she's Catholic. The chicken and the egg fell from an apple tree and took an ark ride.

"Don't worry your pretty little head about it."

"That's sweet," Trisha says, glowing at our good fortune. "It sounds like you are meant for each other."

"What about you?" I ask. "Do you have a boyfriend?"

She frowns, but not a frown of failure so much as a metaphorical making of lemonade from life. "I had a boyfriend but he didn't like me on stage. Said he shouldn't have to share me with the audience. He wanted me home with him every night, so he left me for another girl."

"That's shitty."

"It's okay," she shrugs. "Love will happen when it is meant to. You cannot force it."

"True."

"But sometimes I have doubts. I am already 23. Maybe that is not old in America, but here most girls start family by then. My younger sister married already with two babies. My mama tell me if I don't marry soon I grow old alone, but maybe it is better to be true to yourself than with someone for the wrong reasons?"

Monday, December 9, 2013, 11:13 p.m.

"Baby ko?"

"Yes baby ko?"

"Now you in band, we stay in Davao?"

She's groping His Girthiness. Not looking to be layed, just flipping and flopping him this way and that. A compromising position for the romantic intention interrogation her inflection implies is impending. "Yeah, we'll stay."

But maybe I don't mean it the same as my sweet. She wants the world from a beau slow boiled from birth in a cultural broth of debauchery. When finances force me back into bondage, would it not ruin my ruby to bring her back to Babylon? Sort of like saving Frosty from freezing? Americunt culture would curdle my cutie to the core.

Can our love last even as our designs diverge? Have I not been true with my touch, even as I vowed evermore too easily? Is love not more skillfully scribed with skin against skin than diamonds and I dos?

"Baby ko, if we stay in Davao, how come we stay here in hotel?" *Flip.*

"Good question." *Flop.*

"It is? What you mean?"

"I mean let's get an apartment. The two of us." *Flip.*

"You mean it baby ko?" *Flop.*

"Of course."

"You make me so happy baby ko! You and *me!* Our own a*partment!* I love you *verrrry* much." *Flip flop flip flop.*

"I love you too."

"Ikaw lang sapat na."

"Ikaw lang sapat na."

"Mahal kita lagi."

"Mahal kita lagi." Lagi – always. Is it profane to promise my darling all my days, when her always is my indefinitely?

"I so happy for us... *oh! Baby* ko! *Mmmm!*"

Always...

Indefinitely...

Are the duo so different?

Tuesday, December 10, 2013, 1:43 p.m.

My swoony sweetheart is in the communal courtyard squeezing the scuz from my skivvies, overjoyed by the opportunity to take care of yours truly. Perhaps in poverty is Lucifer's allure lessened, a lass more likely to lead the godly life of mother and wife without her hamster harrying her to role-play as a professional, vacuuming out any wee ones in the way of actualizing her life only to lament her fallow loins at the eleventh hour and lay out a fortune for fertility treatments, beseeching Science for success as she plays retard roulette with her aging eggs.

I am blessed.

Mama scrubbed my duds the other day, and I could not help being horrified that the crust created by sweetly swabbing my liquid love from my baby's belly had suffused the suds, making me gape aghast as glubs glopped down Mama's arms. When a sploodge spritzed splash sploshed the spot from which my little spoon had sprung, I spluttered a speck of spittle upon my pants.

"Rain say you get apartment," Mama states, returning me to the moment.

"Yeah."

"You find one yet?"

"We're looking."

"When you two get married?"

God, that scowl. Who could artfully articulate whilst facing such ferocity?

"Um."

Mama wants answers, not hesitation. Utmost on her mind is the remittances to be wrested from yours truly, cash she can't kosherly request til after the wedding in white, which must occur quickly if the apathy accompanying a daily drained dingis is to make me amenable to the milking. "Rain love you very much. You two get married we have big wedding."

As the rat runs to nab a nibble, Rain lobs a lance of Visaya and Mama returns fire, their squabble squeezed into earsplitting spurts, like sentences shot through machine guns.

"Rain mad cause I ask when you two get married," Mama clarifies for me, once fire is ceased.

2:17 p.m.

Into the humid streets, burning sun. Past tricycles, tin shacks, markets, old ladies hawking chicken innards on sticks, Balut, fruit. Christmas is a rash upon the city. These people sure have plenty to peddle for paupers. So many maidens mooning me. Lucky lady landed the only white willy in sight without a saggy sack.

"Baby ko, I'm sorry about Mama."

"It's okay."

"No! It *not* okay!" So sweet when she insists, like a princess protecting her kitty from castration. "Because you are my true *love!* My one and *only!*" That doesn't limit me, does it? "I know we get married, when you are ready." Don't hold your breath honey. "Mama mad cause she think to live together we should be married, but I think it not matter if we marry now or in a few months, because I know we together always baby ko, forever. I don't like her pressure you."

"Don't worry about it." *Always...*

"My family okay for you?"

"Yeah, of course." *Forever...*

"I know Mama worry. Always something worry her. Make me want to be away from her."

"I understand." *No divorce if I marry her here. Half my money or more if I marry her in America...*

"But it o*kay* baby ko! It okay because we get a*partment* baby ko! I'm so *happyyyyy!*"

"Me too." *Aaaaahhhh!*

"When we get apartment baby ko, I cook for you! Every *day* baby ko. I make you breakfast, lunch, dinner, dessert, snacks. *Mmmmmm!* And baby ko, when we get apartment, we throw big party, o*kay?*"

"Okay baby ko." Do I have to be present? I mean, emotionally?

"Baby ko? Can we visit Jenna and Marcel tonight?"

"Sure. No dinner with Mama tonight?"

"*No!* Baby ko, I'm sorry."

"It's okay."

"Jenna ask when we come visit her. Oh baby ko! You want try kwek kwek?"

4:43 p.m.

An all but broken-down boardwalk brings my beauty, myself, and a fifth of firewater to the couple's cabana, low tide leaving a badlands of bags and bottles mired in the muck below.

Lazing on plastic benches fronting the shack for the 'enom' ritual, the rum rolls round the group in a single glass refilled afresh for each imbiber, spirits suppressing the scent of sewage and dead fish, mixing with the mugginess to lull me to languor.

Marcel is saying something, but his gibber is garbled by my grogginess, as if my head were under water.

"Huh?"

"What you do in America?"

"I wait tables."

The pair appear perplexed. They know what it means to wait, and that a table is a place upon which you put your plate, but the combination is confusing. Perhaps I'd misplaced a preposition between the two? "What you mean?" Jenna asks.

Rain says something in Visaya, Jenna nods.

"Ah, you work in restaurant."

"Yeah, I serve, or I did anyway."

"Ah, okay, you serve," Jenna replies.

"What kind restaurant you work?" Marcel asks.

"Upscale west coast American. Burgers, pasta, seafood, steak. That kinda stuff."

"How much it cost eat dinner your restaurant?"

I figure the exchange. "About one thousand to fifteen hundred pesos for dinner, without a drink." Or appetizer, dessert, tax, tip or ball cupping surcharge.

A congress of confused eyes comb me for a misused zero. A thousand pesos is half a weekly salary here.

"People spend that much on dinner?" Marcel asks.

"Some of them."

"It take me three days make that much. This normal? Most restaurants in America so expensive?"

"No, not most."

"Ah, okay. Is expensive restaurant."

"Fairly."

"For rich people."

"Or those aspiring to poverty."

"Sorry?"

"People who are bad with money."

"You have big house in America?" Marcel enquires, questing for a vicarious fix of my fortune.

"No, I lived in an apartment."

"But big house is American way, no?"

I clear my throat. While a soycialist would seize the chance to charge their capitalist countrymen with criminally careless consumerism, my spartan superiority is indisputable, so I've no need to virtue signal my values. "Sure.

Big houses with a TV in each room, so no one has to sit with anyone else unless they want to."

"This true baby ko? People don't sit together in America?"

"It's not so bad. Sometimes they meet in the kitchen while microwaving their meals."

"So they *do* eat together baby ko?"

"Well, if they want to watch the same show they might eat TV dinners or take out in front of the living room TV, but with so many viewing choices they rarely agree, so they eat alone, in front of the TV in their bedroom."

"That sound lonely," Rain repines.

"A bit, yeah. It's not *my* thing, but some people view it as freedom."

"Why that freedom baby ko?"

Such a perceptive point from the pert little pouter in the front row. A gold star. "Well... I guess it comes down to the American i*dea* of freedom, a concept inseparable from conspicuous consumption. In America we buy big cars for the freedom to drive them wherever we want, but spend so much time working to afford gasoline, insurance, and car payments that we mostly just drive them to work and around town. We buy big houses for the space to indulge in hobbies and self improvement, but we're so tired from working to pay the mortgage that we usually just lounge in front of the TV, where we have the freedom to flip between three hundred channels. Even here our freedom is underused, as we mostly stick to the same three or four channels. But here, in these *unused channels*, is the quin*tessence* of our freedom, for to have freedom we must have something to say no to. We stock our kitchens with gadgets and gizmos and stuff the fridge with food from afar, but we're too tired from working to pay for it to bother cooking it, so we order takeout instead, and let the food in the fridge go bad. This fridge's existence, the idea that at anytime we can get up from the couch and get ourselves a snack, is the em*bodiment* of American freedom, as is our right to let its contents spoil, for to chain our culinary choices to the time-line of our grocery's biological decline, however artificially altered it may be, is gastronomic tyranny."

I lost them. Should I have simplified it?

"Could you say again slower please?" Marcel asks.

Again? He wants me to repeat a once in a lifetime monologue? Would you ask what's his name to paint a second Mona Lisa? "Well, what I mean is that in America freedom and excess are inseparable, two sides of the same coin."

Still their peepers imply perplexion.

"Sorry?"

"Americans mistake freedom for being corporate tool bags."

"What you mean baby ko?"

"They use freedom to justify waste."

Budding understanding. "This normal?" Jenna asks.

"Mostly."

"Why?"

"I dunno," I shrug. "Shall we buy another bottle?"

13

Stumbling Star

Thursday, December 12, 2013, 8:02 p.m.

Surveying the scene, my butterflies bumble between daring and dread. But though my guts are agambol my golden voice galvanizes every cloozy in The Club, and any terror in my tummy turns to tingling titillation, spreading from my spine to every tart in attendance, growing til my giddies go straight to the girlies' titties.

An arithmetittical miracle manifests, the swoons swelling these beauties' bosoms build above and beyond the mere number of their nipples. As Joseph Stalin so stirringly stated at a cut-rate strip club, 'quantititty has a qualititty all its own.' A pair of peaches without other plums to pump for second hand hankerings will know no more than fuzzy fancies, but get a giggle of girls gabbling and their greeds will grow to lemmingual levels. How else can we explain a decline in media quality inversely correlated to the increasing connectivity of an ever more populous planet? Incontrovertible evidence for the lemmingualitty of the titty. But the million melon question remains: from where flows women's herd-brain ambitions? Does a queen titty spray some subliminal serum? Do the titties tap into a tit-hive think-tank, powers comboouboulously intertitualizing? Is it more mysterious, a cabal of cans

120

powwowing in private like the Bilderberg group?

The Tittyberg group?

10:22 p.m.

"Baby ko! You are a*mazing!*" my scrumpet exclaims, sloppy kisses and coos demanding my distraction from the rabble of rubies rutting to ravage me. "You sang so *well* baby ko!"

"I try."

Alex's mug is unmoved by my darling's display. Stupendous state control. He'd be quite the Casanova if he got rid of the goof and added a wink more woof and a little more aloof. "You are... big star," he stammers.

"You have single uncle? Older brother?" Auntie asks.

"No."

"Too bad."

"Baby ko? We get another bucket of beer? Cele*brate* baby ko! I'm so *happyyyyyy!*"

"Yeah. Another bucket sounds good."

"The stage... it made for you," Alex stammers. "Someday you... uh... *nose*bleed!"

Alex and Rain confer.

"He say someday you famous baby ko."

"Big star," Alex says, giving us his grin.

Friday, December 13, 2013, 9:46 a.m.

Goaded by other girls' envious eyes, a damsel's dread will roil to a boil, her hamster wheel redlining under the weight of her worries.

"Baby ko, what you think about?" Why must she mine my mind? Is it not enough to clutch me close and hear my heartbeat?

"The show last night." All the minges melting at my majesty, the fillies from

121

whose fruits my cutie's clutches will keep me. That and the twins I've been twiddling.

"Mmm! Baby ko, you sing so *well* last night!"

"Thanks."

"You always playing with them baby ko. With my, uh, how you say?"

"Tits?"

"You call them tits?"

"Sure do sugartits."

"Sugartits?"

What's not to understand? She's sweeter than syrup and blessed with breasts. "That's you. It's a term of endearment."

"It *is* baby ko?"

"Sure. It's what we say in America instead of baby ko."

"Hmm. Okay baby ko. I like it. Boys are sugartits too?"

"No... uh, boys are sugarballs."

"Ahh... okay sugarballs. So why you always play with my tits?"

Because eons of evolution have favored guys who go for it. "Cause they're nice."

"But they so *small* baby ko. Not like American girls'. American girls' are so *big!*"

What is this, an itty bitty titty pity party? "American breasts are corn fed and misshapen. Yours are rice fed and perfect."

"You really think so?"

"I know so sugartits."

"Mmm sugarballs. You are sweet. You mean it?"

"With all my heart." But mostly my member.

"Thank you baby ko. Mahal kita lagi."

"Mahal kita lagi."

What's that dear reader? My narrative is as nuanced as the notes of a rapacious poet pillaging the land of lost similes? I like that.

Not a compliment? My heterocisnormapatriartypically privileged prose is more than merely offensive to the floozies so long oppressed by God's plan, but also insulting to the soydomites bravely fighting the bigotry of biology to achieve ecuckuity of outcome for their sisters in suffrage, courageously castigating mightier men for failing to follow ever expanding speech codes, bowing before their ovarian overlords to virtue signal themselves safe for the social justice Shangri-La the thought police are plotting?

3:32 p.m.

Though we must never misunderestimate mental machinery so mighty it can make a maiden forsake her femininity for a cock hopping mockery of masculinity only to demand a diamond ring when her baby clock is closing on midnight, we must remember that a woman's hamster wheel head is often overheated from kneading the narrative to fit her feels, and that during this debility any failure to follow the lassie's illogic will hurl her into histrionics.

"Baby ko?" my beauty beseeches as I return to our roost from flushing my little fellas. "How come you always come... how come you always come out*side* of me?"

"Um," I mumble. Pulling out being as habitual as breathing, I'd not thought through the act that, when employed with a fake name, provides near perfect protection from pregnancy.

She wraps herself around me, peepers imploring me to give her the gift of maternal meaning, a worth to outweigh the wilt of her womb, to not suffer the sorrow of a barren bosom never chewed on by child, a cancer consuming the witches of the west. But unlike in the land of the bold and the brave, there will be no brunches to balm the hole in her heart, no cats to collect if she can scarcely feed her own face, only the melancholy of old maidery, spinsterhood sputtering towards its Darwinian dead end. "Why we have to wait?"

"Um... wait?"

"Why we have to wait?"

"Wait for what?"

"For make *babies!* If we are forever and always, then why we *wait?*"

"Well... because."

"Because *why?*"

Because we're not forever and always, we're here and now until the newness of our fantasy fades, laying bare hearts brittle from too many mendings. "I want to wait til we get married baby ko."

"Okay baby ko," she coos, lightening at the M word like a dove flying above a DEA weed burn. "We get married soon?"

"Of course."

"When baby ko?"

"Um." Why give love a time line? "April baby ko. I want my parents to come, but they can't make it til April." What's a little white lie when love is on the line?

"Your parents come baby ko?" she asks, perking at the prospect of employing my parents as partners in my imprisonment.

"Yeah."

"Mmm! I'm so ex*cited!* You think they like me?"

"Of course."

"But baby ko, if we get married in April, how come we don't try make baby *now?* It still… baby still come after April baby ko." Dewy eyes demolishing my defenses, I find my heart melting to the prospect of parenthood.

No! I must fight for my freedom. "That's not really traditional in America. My parents would be shocked if it didn't take at least nine months after we marry." Actually, my mom imagines it would take a tike to make me marry, and even so she'd assume I'd fake my own death and don a new identity before doing the deed.

"They *would* baby ko?"

"Yeah. Wouldn't your parents?"

"No. I don't tell Mama and Papa what we do but I think they know."

"They do?"

"Of *course* baby ko! Because I stay with you every *night!* What else people do when they spend night together?"

"Play cribbage?"

"What that baby ko?"

"Don't worry your pretty little head about it princess," I reply, running my hand through her hair so her hamster doesn't overheat. "But isn't it traditional to wait?"

"Sometimes," she shrugs. "Sometimes girl already making baby when marry."

"That happens a lot?" I ask, simulating surprise.

"Yes, of *course* baby ko!"

"Oh."

"So we try make baby?"

"Um."

"Baby ko!"

"Hmm?"

"You make me sad. I think you don't want make baby with me."

"Of course I do baby ko."

"No you *don't*," she whines, turning away with the blanket bunched to her bosom, leaving my body bare. "Maybe you have other *girl.* I dream a*gain* baby ko! I dream you with that girl from the *bar.* I dream you leave me for her and I grow old a*lone.* And she have your *babies.*"

Wishing I had words to pacify my peach, I go with titty twiddles and neck nibbles, cradling her close to wash her worries away.

"*Baby* ko? How come you not *say* anything?"

"It's just a dream."

"No it *not.* It feel *real,*" she sniffles.

"Don't worry about it baby ko."

"I can't *help* it."

Is it not natural for a crumpet to crave her lover's load? Maybe creaming her quim will wash her worries away. Her sea should be safe for my little navy by now, having not carried the crimson tide to my Sheila's shores since before our first boff, but I'll have to fake it when she's ovulating. Alas, the coos and quivers of climax are so much simpler to simulate than semen. A loogie while I'm licking her lollipop perhaps? I could hock it in the bathroom beforehand and hide it in my cheeks, but then there's the problem of putting it in her pooter. If I tucked it in with my tongue, would it even look like a load?

Honestly, the lengths I'll go for love are worthy of award.

"*Baby* ko?" I murmur.

"*Yes* baby ko?" she coos, torment tranquilized by my tenderness.

"Nothing. I was just thinking."

"About *what* baby ko?"

"About *you* baby ko. About *us*. About making *sweet sweet love. Babies.*" I look lovingly into her eyes, fingers threading through her thighs to their superlative prize.

"Mmmmmmmmmm *baby* ko."

"I want you," I whisper, voice as silky sweet as cotton candy. "*All* of you. *Al*ways."

"Mmm. I'm *sorry* baby ko."

"Why?"

"Because I am so *sad*. Guess I just nervous, because, you *know!* Because you so popular at The *Club* baby ko!"

"Don't worry about it baby ko."

Accenting my saccharine syllables with a delicate kiss and a tenderly cupped titty, I transform her fears into a frenzy of flesh aching for evermore, my darling desperate to milk my mojo, lest another tart take a taste. Without the leash of logic a maiden's emotions must be as heavenly at their heights as they are despairing at their depths.

Though compared to her crazy my emotions may be muted, just to drink of her delirium is divine.

Saturday, December 14, 2013, 11:02 a.m.

In this wild new interwebual world, one's online presence is presumed. Taking time to return your mother's messages whilst away will drive her to develop dire ideas of your demise. Following are a few that might harry her hamster:

A: You took a self-guided tour of a coca plantation and found yourself turned to fertilizer.

B: You brought bud into Bali up your bumhole and wound up in deep shit.

C: You're learning about sex trafficking the hard way.

D: You learned a gut-wrenching lesson about the international organ trade.

E: You went on an absinthe bender and, following a failed attempt to mail an ear to an ex, woke up in the French foreign legion, having apparently sold yourself into the service for an emergency blood transfusion.

Mom: **Who is this girl posting pictures of you? Is her name really Rain or is that a nickname? I hope you aren't making hasty decisions. Be careful which head you think with. Hope you are well.**

Mom again: **I know you're alive because this girl has been posting pictures of you constantly. I will concede that she is prettier than Sarah, or Amy, or Heather, or any of the other poor girls you dated back home, but I'm worried about her motives. Do you get hints that she's using you to get to America? Do you find her quoting Hollywood films or listening to American pop songs? Did I see a picture of you singing with a band? Do you take any nights off from drinking? I hope you have time to take it easy, to connect with nature. I was really hoping this trip would give you a chance to do that. I think that was what was wrong with your job. Eating at restaurants is so disconnected from the source. When we eat food we grow ourselves it connects us back to Mother Earth. We see it from growth through preparation and consumption. People lose that eating out. Their belly gets fed but their soul starves, so they eat until they're fat. You needed to get away from that scene. You can't serve the spiritually malnourished without them sucking up your soul like spiritual tapeworms. Speaking of tapeworms and other parasites, be careful over there. Can you find oil of oregano or goldenseal? I'm guessing your liver could use some milk thistle. Do you need me to ship you some? Hope you are well.**

Me: **Don't worry mother I am happy and well hydrated. I went and saw a volcano. Its menacing ambivalence made me feel spiritually connected.**

Annetta: **Having fun over there drunky pants? It looks like my bunny fish didn't waste much time. I hope you're being safe. Hate to lose**

127

my Johnny to super syphilis. When's the marriage? You better let her know I still get conjugal rights LOL.

Me: We're waiting for you to get here. It's gonna be a trifecta. A Johnny sandwich. Don't worry you're not a lesbian if I'm in the middle.

Jay: Hey bud you in a band now or something? Finally graduate from karaoke? You always had pipes. Looks like the anatomical studies are going well. Can't say much has changed here. Ed's over there somewhere taking care of his 'needs.' I think he said he was going to Angeles? That anywhere near where you are?

Me: Angeles? Never heard of it. Yeah, I'm in a band, I have a girl-friend and theoretically we're getting an apartment together. What the hell is wrong with me? I thought I was running away from commitments.

Lacking further business, I log off.

"Done already baby ko?"

"Yeah."

"Okay, one minute, I finish."

She finishes. We pay.

"Baby ko?" Rain coos, pulling me into her arms as we step into the streets. "We get you phone?"

"What for?"

"So I can *call* you baby ko!"

"Oh, alright."

"Baby ko," she says, getting a giddy grin. "I think I find us *apartment!*"

14

Three Sizes

Sunday, December 15, 2013, 2:07 p.m.

"Is on me," Miguel states, setting our suds atop the table. "My stars have nowhere to be?"

"Nowhere I'd rather be," I shrug. That's a lie. I'd rather be marooned on Maui with a minx who makes a mean mojito, communicates mouth to member, and wears not a whit but the gifts God gave her, but I'll manage in the meantime.

"Ah, okay. Your girlfriend wait patiently?"

"Impatiently probably."

"Ah, she good girl, cheers," he says, wandering off to his upstairs apartment.

"Enom," I say, raising my bottle to bonk Trisha's, showcasing myself considerate of her budget culture's customs.

"Cheers," Trisha replies. "So where *is* your girlfriend today?"

"At her parents'."

"Ah... I *see.*"

"Why do we practice Sunday mornings? No one in the band goes to church?"

"No."

"None of you?"

"None."

"I thought most Filipinos went to church?"

"Most of us, yes."

"But not the four of you."

"Why? You want to go to church?"

"*God* no!" I snort. "I'm glad for the excuse *not* to go. I just wondered why none of you went."

"I can't speak for the others," she shrugs. "I think I feel that, as a musician, I carry church with me."

"How so?"

"I just mean…" she begins, taking a tick to word her wisdom. "I think people go to church looking for something bigger than themselves, but I feel that playing music, you know?"

"I can dig it."

"How come *you* don't go to church John?"

"I guess it's… it's like you. I'd rather worship with my senses than worship nonsense."

"It is not nonsense," she reproves. "Some people just need symbols for it. Some don't." A pregnant pause italicizes the tacit attraction between us. "Rain know you here with me?" she asks, putting her paw on my pants only to sheepishly shed it, doe eyes darting for witnesses to her warmth.

"She knows I went to band practice."

"I think it dangerous," she whispers. "For us to drink here together."

"You think so?"

"Come now John, we are similar, *no?*" Her peepers perk as they meet mine, inviting me into that little cosmos lovers create whilst the world falls away. "But you are with Rain… and she loves you very much. She makes you feel special, but she doesn't understand you, no?"

"No… she doesn't."

"So, it is up to you."

"Up to *me?*" I say with a swallow.

A pointed pause precedes her reply. "Yes, it is up to you."

"You think it's safe?'

"Safe? If you mean, will it stay between us, then yes, no one else should know."

My poor heart palpitates. What a cumundrum, where to sow one's seed. "I want to," I whisper, wishing it weren't so morally muddy. It would be clear cut if only my crumpet and I had quarreled and for the evening estranged, lending me license to get lit and boff some bimbo to console myself. That was the way I worked it with the witch.

"I don't mean leave Rain. She love you very much, but I think you not so sure about the future as she, *no?*"

I imagine that maidens, lacking the logic that leashes us lads to the reality around us, are better equipped for catching subconscious cues, but even so a siren has never read me so readily. "You're right. I'm not."

"So maybe we can help each other. Give each other understanding, you know?"

"Understanding?"

"Yes, understanding. When you have to meet Rain?"

"Rain?" I reply, taking a tick to remember my ruby's plans for after practice.

"She is anxious girl, no? Always worry in her eyes."

"Her well is deep."

"You have a couple hours?"

"I have as many as I *want*," I snip, insulted by the insinuation that my wench's wishes might matter as much as mine.

"We go hotel?"

The beauties battle in my brain like metaphors fighting for a place in a poem. Wiser than my head, my heart adds another line to make room for them both, growing three sizes as it does so.

3:23 p.m.

Alas I have but language to tell my tale. Though the molding of our minds to the tongue of our tribe makes our musings superficially transferable, I dare say words deliver but a fraction of the feeling that touch may transmit. I pine

131

to put you in my place, but sadly I can summon but a figment of our euphoria.

Trailing fingers tenderly from her tits to her treasure, they pause as a shiver shakes her, and I look to see I'd landed on a mole below her mammary.

"Is third nipple," she remarks, severing the silence.

"It's cute."

"You think so? It make me self conscious."

"You get self conscious?"

"Everyone is about something John. Sometimes I think… I think it try to tell me something."

"Tell you something?"

"Sometimes I get a feeling, and it itches."

"When we met… in front of The Club."

"Yes?"

"You were scratching yourself."

"Yes… I had a feeling about you. You don't think I'm crazy?" she asks, her almond eyes opening with an ache for understanding, melting as mine answer with empathy.

"Crazy?"

"Because I think my nipple is… uh…"

"Psychic?"

"Yes."

"You're not crazy," I reply, a quiver coursing through her as I lick it for luck.

If you found a genie in a bottle, you wouldn't *just* rub it with your hands would you?

15

A Lease and a Leash

Monday, December 16, 2013, 3:17 p.m.

"Mmm baby *ko!*" Rain squeals, setting her effects on the floor and pulling me into her arms to caption my captivity with a breath squeezing embrace. "Our own a*partment!* I'm so *happyyyyy!*"

"Me too," I mumble, contemplating the counters to be cluttered with kitsch, the floor to be furnished with representations of my interment. For though fellows may fathom that chattels are shackles, only women have the wiles to pamper their paramours into self-imprisonment.

"Baby ko. I know it empty, but, we buy *furniture!* We *decorate!*"

"Great." You decorate. I'll inebriate. We'll call the effort equal.

"Aren't you excited baby ko?

"Yeah."

"You don't sound excited."

Why must women look into little white lies and tear out the truth? "Of course I am," I reply, faking offense as a damsel would do when denying her duplicity. But my walls are weak, as girls are great at sussing insincerity thanks to their custom of communicating between lines of illogic. Seeking something that excites my little Sargent so she doesn't think me unenthused, I

133

smitten her a smile, pulling her into my arms to consummate our cohabitation. "Let's break it in."

"What you mean?"

"Take these clothes off," I murmur, nibbling her neck. "Roll around the floor," I suggest, shedding her shirt. "Give these walls a show," I add, unbinding her bra.

"But baby ko, I *bleed*," she bemoans.

"So?"

"It *messy* baby ko."

"So?"

Picking up my peach, her legs entwine me as I twirl her, swirling her swoons into a frenzy as we French, falling to the floor as flesh fumbles for flesh.

"It *okay* with you?" Those woozy, woe is me eyes want it to be, but she needs sweet nothings this tender time of the month.

"Of course baby ko," I murmur, fingers migrating to her minge.

"Okay baby ko. I go take it out."

"No need," I tell her, tugging on the cord and tossing the tampon aside.

"Baby *ko!*"

16

Christmas Comes

Wednesday, December 18, 2013, 9:40 a.m.

"Baby ko, it Christmas soon."

"Oh... yeah." Shit! I can no longer ignore the creeping crescendo of chintzy cheer coming for my cash.

"Don't you like *Christmas* baby ko?"

"It's okay," I reply, praying she won't press the point.

"I don't think you like it baby ko," she whines, weaponizing her woe with a puppy-eyed pout. It's not like I fed her Donner kebab, Blitzen bangers or Vixen venison. I should be offered amnesty and supplied a safe space to forgo the festivities in inebriated neutrality. "Why you not like Christmas?"

"You really want to know?"

"Yes baby ko."

Cause corporations cash in on it by co-opting the fuzzy feelings we get from feasting with friends and family to sell us sundries bound to be broken or boxed before Christmas rolls around again, inciting an arms race of monetized amour in which we one up our neighbors in how much we care for our kin, initiating our nippers into an enslaving cycle of consumption. "Cause it's too commercial."

Sniffle snuffles, snouty pouties. "So you don't like Christmas?"

"No."

She turns her pout up further. A look like hers declares undying devotion whilst simultaneously threatening something just as worse. "Can I have money for buy presents?"

"Fine." I usually give her a couple hundred pesos before practice, so I hand her five hundred, about eleven bucks.

"I was hoping buy *many* presents baby ko," she whines, unmoved by my magnanimity. "Maybe I have some *more?*"

"No," I say severely, not caring to encourage the cancer of consumerism infecting modern femininity, the mall culture metastasizing from America as the third world westernizes.

"Why not baby ko?"

"I said no." My words are Prancer lancers, Dasher mashers. My words would roofy Rudolph on Christmas Eve only to sell him to the highest bidding zoophiliac on Boxing Day. I slip on my shoes, shielding my eyes from my amour, lest her suffering slice a hole from my heart all the way to my wallet. "I'm not Santa Claus," I castigate, leaving my love to mull her misdeeds.

Have I been too harsh on my honey? Are the desires that drove her to sell herself not still bubbling in her bosom? I must face the fact that living muff to mouth has not given my girl the brains for budgeting. I must admit that our fiscal philosophies are essentially irreconcilable.

Rain deifies the dollar, but money merely milks her amour. On Friday night money takes her clubbing, whisking her away for a water closet quicky. On Saturday she calls, still bashfully beaming from the blustery bathroom blitz-boinking, but money is burping bubbly in some bougie bar. She calls again Sunday, but money is yachting. She finally gets ahold of money on Monday. Money drives her down a side road and demands his dick sucked.

Following a fleeting but fiery affair, money and I have been but friends with benefits. This isn't to say I never sell myself for the sake of simoleons, repeating pleasantries to pissants, but that I do so for survival, not some kick for hard cash. In fact, money has many times left me feeling defiled for the deeds I've done for it, and in return I've taken it out on the town only to head home alone, but we've always made up in the end.

2:47 p.m.

"What you do here John?"

"In this hotel room with you?"

"No! I know what we do here. We are giving just each other understanding, *no?* I mean, what you do in my country?"

"Just traveling. Looking for adventure."

"I think you run away."

Why do I tinker with the truth, when no fudging of it will fool Trisha's supernatural nipple? "Run away?"

"Yes."

"Why do you say that?"

"I am wrong?"

"No... I guess I did."

"Your eyes are not a traveler's John. They are... a refugee's."

Never has a nymph so nuanced my needs. Beswoondled by the bond blossoming betwixt us, I drink from the depths of her almond eyes, quenching a thirst I'd long thought to be but a burden I must bear. "I guess that fits," I murmur.

"What you hide from?"

"Everything," I sigh.

"A girl, no?"

"Yes."

"A job too?"

"Yeah. That extra titty of yours read minds or something?"

"No, it only gives me feelings. It is written on your face. I have met other western men that come to my country. They run away from their women, from their jobs... from all of it. Most of them not so young like you. Most of them old, with full wallets and empty hearts. They come here thinking they can make up with money for the ways they are spent, but they are wrong.

You can sell your soul for money, but money cannot buy it back."

Deliberating that doozy, I consider Sarah, and how close I'd come to living a life of self-loathing servitude, suffering the slow death by disenchantment that comes when one cashes in the gamble of greatness for the certainty of insignificance. "I know what you mean," I bemoan.

5:46 p.m.

"Mmm," Trisha purrs, her lips smittening me a smile even as her eyes deny reality's rays. "Good morning."

"Good evening."

"Mmm... what time is it?"

"Almost six."

Her almond eyes open with a plaintive plea, countenance crinkling into a pinch of a pout. There is no peril in her peepers, like Rain's cold war of the heart pout, merely the admission that my sheila would be shattered if she found out of the affair. "You need to go, don't you?"

"I probably should."

"You think she is mad?"

"Sad anyways. We fought this morning."

"She is an emotional girl, no? Very Jealous."

"Pathologically," I reply, getting up to go. "She thinks all the girls want me." I put on my pants while my siren sits up, sweater puppies and peepers boring into my being, imploring me to promise them goodbye will not break us.

"I don't think that make her crazy John," Trisha declares between tender kisses and titty cups. "Many girls want you. You only American boy in Davao who sing like rock star. Girls like singers."

"That why you like me?"

"No John, it is because you are like me. You know the spiritual power of passion. You think she suspect us?"

"I don't think so. She suspects the bartender though."

"Yes, because the bartender is hungry for you. Rain think she wants you to herself, but you have too much passion for one girl."

She is too kind. I don't think an overpouring appetite is foiling my fidelity so much as a failure to focus my affections on one woman, a dongular ADD.

My phone is overflowing with my wench's worries. Am I mad about money? Will I please hurry home and let her burst my belly and wolf my willy? Did I get more than a liquid lunch? Is our love still everlasting? Is my phone still functioning? I reluctantly let my inamorata know I'll be beside her soon. "She's been messaging all afternoon."

"I hope this not cause fight tonight?"

"Don't worry about it."

"Maybe it too predictable for us to meet after practice. I give you my number. Call or message if you want to see me, *okay?* I won't call or message first, cause I know you don't want Rain see it."

"Alright," I say, handing her my phone. You must provide a peach ample opportunity to assist you, for her hamster wheel head interprets her every toil as another stake in your stiffy. In turn your time must be spent on her sparingly, lest your pampering prompt her to overvalue her vaj, bringing her to believe she could find a better fella for more than a fling, precipitating an empowering parade of penises that, though it commences as a quest for the best lad she can land, habituates her to the highs of new throbbers in her thighs, making it impossible for her to pair bond and perverting her maternal instinct into lavishing what's left of her love upon a clowder of cats. (Unfortunately for fellows swiping for sweethearts or navigating the night life meat market of America, the continuous attention finds strumpets' stocks in the stratosphere, making a barrage of bids necessary to nab a single night of nookie and a melancholy morning of wiener infection worry.)

"This number safe for you to call or message," she informs with my phone's return.

"Safe?" I reply, cocking an eyebrow into a question mark. Struck in the stomach by her profession's implications, I've an urge to bleach my boner before any parasites pierce through my willy's fleshy walls. "Why *wouldn't* it be safe?"

"Don't worry about it," she snaps, realizing what she'd revealed.

"How can I *not?*"

"It better if you don't."

"That's kinda cryptic."

"Don't worry John."

"Sure. Whatever. I'll see you tomorrow."

"Goodnight John."

"Good*night.*"

Any designs I'd drawn up of decamping without a kiss are thwarted by the threat of a tear in Trisha's eye. Wallowing in the wistfulness of our affair's uncertain future, our lips linger longingly.

8:13 p.m.

My pouty little peach dwelt all day on our Christmas clash, her worries weighing woozier as the hours elapsed. If she deduced my adultery, then she simply showed me to the shower to wash the other woman away. I needed no excuse, for she bore the blame that was hers to hold.

We're moored to our mattress quaffing cans of Pale Pilsen. She's wearing naught a whit but pink little panties, a white titty-telegramming T-shirt, and ebullient eyes emblazoned from cornea to kumbaya with cupidity. She could give western girls such a wealth of wisdom on the fulfillment of femininity, if the message could merely be laid out in their language. Through emojis maybe.

"Baby ko?" she coos.

"Hmm?"

"I want do something special for you."

I smitten her a smile, as nothing melts a heart more than a peach who pleasures in her place. Before I came to this country I'd no idea how darling a beauty could be without the quest for equality harrying her hamster.

I am blessed.

"What is it?" I ask.

Licking her lips, she cranes forward to kiss me. "A surprise baby ko! Because you are so good to me. Lay back."

I settle back in bed as she pulls my underpants away, a worry washing over me that I might not manage to give her the go she so desperately deserves.

Sloppily she slurps me. Loyally she licks me. Only slightly inspired is he.

"Baby ko," she complains, removing her mouth from my manhood. "I don't think he like me." His fatigue is hardly her fault, for any failure of expertise is earnestly erased by her enthusiasm.

"I'm just tired baby ko."

"But baby ko, you always…" she sniffles. "You always have energy baby ko."

Sympathetic to the suffering a failure to firm my willy would weave, I imagine munching Trisha's treasure, rising my rod to three fourths full measure.

"Baby ko! He get ex*cited!*"

"Let's sixty nine."

"What you mean?"

"I mean I kiss you *there*," I reply, rubbing my ruby's clit to clarify. "And you kiss me *there*."

"But baby ko! I *bleed!*"

"So?"

"Cause I want you *like* it baby ko!"

"I will. I want to taste you."

"You want taste *that?*" she asks, bunching her brows in disbelief.

"Yeah, I need the iron."

"Okay baby ko, if that what you want."

No sooner does she sit her fanny on my face than her worries wash away, for I have a way of warming a wench from her mink to her marrow with but the tip of my tongue. The trick you pray tell? I regret to relate that no magic move will melt every minge, for every nymph is unique.

The trick is passion, perseverance, and poetry.

Poetry you ponder? How can I prattle off poetry with a mouth full of muff? Easily enough, for poetry is purely the language of love, my mouthings merely the medium of my message.

Thursday, December 19, 2013, 8:12 p.m.

I am Sexyphus, king of The Club.

But my quivering queen, and not my lascivious subjects, sits foremost on my mind. Taking off from tapping toes, lifting lust from longing loins, and hurling through a heart filled with fealty before finally conferring with her hamster wheel head for a wallop of womanly worry, Rain's passion pops from peepers wide with worship.

But hers are not the only eyes on my prize.

Ever alert for territorial trespassers, my darling detects a twinkle of tenderness flashing from Trisha towards yours truly, and dons green shades for the show's remainder.

11:49 p.m.

"Why Trisha look at you like that baby ko?"

I've thought thoroughly through that cursed question, concluding that the prudent position is to act as if I hadn't. "Like what?"

"Like she *want* you!"

"She *did?*"

"*Yes* baby ko! She look at you like she want to... make *love* to you baby ko!"

"At the show?"

"*Yes* baby ko! When you sing that *song* together!"

"Which song?"

"I think it called 'Love Shack.'"

"*That?*" I dismiss. "That's just an act to go with the song."

"It seem real," she whines.

"Trisha's a good performer."

"So it nothing baby ko?"

"Nothing." If such a reasoned rebuttal fails to snip the suspicions from your lover's lips, then they have trouble trusting and you should reconsider the relationship.

"Promise?"

"Promise."

"Okay baby ko, sorry I am so suspicious," she coos, craning forward to request a conciliatory kiss. "Because *you know!* Because you are *singer!* I cannot blame other girls for want you! I could forgive you if something happen with another girl baby ko, but if you leave me my heart break forever."

A girl who gives you the go ahead to give other girls the goods without unfurling her flower for other fellows is not a nymph to let go lightly. Warmed by her wisdom, my rod rallies to reassure her.

To plant a posy, you must sow a seed.

To sow a seed, you must soften the soil.

My penis is the plow, her gash the garden.

Our rapture is roses.

17

Party People

Friday, December 20, 2013, 8:23 p.m.

"Now you live together," Auntie slurs, cutting through the cacophony of forshnickered Filipinos. "When you get married?"

Silence.

"April!" my princess pronounces, squeezing the breath from my body while I wrench my grimace into a grin, all eyes in the apartment upon us.

"Why you wait so long?"

"His parents come in April!" Rain squeals. "They come for *wedding!*"

"You pick day yet?"

"Not yet," Rain replies, putting on her pout. "Baby ko? How come we not pick day yet?"

"Not sure." The standard fears one feels before signing themselves into servitude.

"Baby ko, if we pick day we can send invitations."

"Oh… right."

"What day you pick?" Auntie asks.

"You want me to pick now?"

"Yes! Then we can start *planning!* A wedding day is very important to a girl.

There are many things to do," Auntie declares, poising her paws to tick off the tabs to be paid for my imprisonment. *"Location, flowers, food, drinks, dress."* My heart hanging heavier with every item enumerated, my woozy wallet is soon considering suicide. Isn't this the third world? Shouldn't a patch of pavement, a rack of rum and a flea bag on the barbie be enough festivity for her family? They wouldn't gussy it up for this guy would they?

"Um," I begin, all peepers upon me, my girl's beyond googlious. "April thirty first."

"Mmm baby *ko!*" Rain cries, clutching me close to gloat her good fortune to the other titties in attendance. "I so *happy!* We invite *every*one!"

Alex gives us his grin, probably picturing the free food and bottomless beers. "Is good day for party."

Sunday, December 22, 2013, 3:07 p.m.

"Baby ko? Where you go?"

I rise from tying my shoes to kiss my beauty goodbye. I really do want dreams to blossom in our embrace, but though our bodies may bridge the canyon between our cultures, our sweet nothings will never share a native tongue's nuance, "The internet cafe."

"You come back soon baby ko? I want see Mama and Papa."

"Yeah. I'm just checking my messages."

"Okay baby ko. *Baby* ko?"

"Yes?"

"I tell Mama and Papa about the wedding day. They ex*cited!*"

"Me too." I've never before needed to fake my own death, but I've been told many times that learning is lifelong.

"Baby ko? Maybe today we go Christmas shopping?"

"Yeah, sure." My sadistic side wants to watch her hamster overheat, but my darling's dreamy eyes find my heart melting to make her Christmas complete.

"Thank you baby ko."

I kiss her again. Such a sweetly insecure creature.

My cleansing of Christmas from this sordid saga is not a failure of the festivities to cloak this Catholic country in chintzy cheer. Rather, this glaring gap flows from my personal problems with this insufferable season, an immunity to the madness manifested in a subconscious scrubbing of celebration from the scene.

My nausea for Noel was born of that boyhood cock swinging contest that occurs after Christmas. Watching fiendish friends flaunt their fripperies to prove their parents valuable members of the machine, I savvied that Satan himself had co-opted Christmas to ravage Earth's resources, turning poor Terra into a plastic purgatory. Though I made it clear I did not care for their cult of consumption, my foolish friends still grilled me about my goodies, goading me into showing them hemp socks sewn by my mother and wood blocks fashioned by my father, tittering at the tangerines stuffed in my stocking. The tangerines being yuletide's tastiest treat, my siblings and I seldom afforded fruit from afar, it miffed me to see my mates' faces painted with pity. Surmising these supposed amigos of mine to be but sleepwalking consumers on a hedonic treadmill of trinkets, I cut ties with the troop before I caught their contagion.

Alas my love is liable to be lured by the siren song of consumerism, and just as a serpent seduced Eve to lose Eden to an apple, her hamster will hound her to feast on the fruits of the fallen.

3:21 p.m.

I settle into a corner computer with the funny feeling Rain may have informed all of Facebook of her wedding in white.

Mom: **What the hell has gotten into you? Were you planning on letting your mother know about your engagement? April 31st? You do know there are only 30 days in April, right? I'm starting to think tropical parasites might be eating holes in what alcohol has left of your brain. I assume that if you manage to maintain interest in this poor girl despite your newfound fans, that you will be inviting your father** and I to the wedding?

P.S. I know you hate the holidays and have been ruining them since you were three, but merry Christmas.

Me: I was hoping you could make it. Maybe wait until we get the date straightened out before you buy tickets though. Should we expect you? Her mother will need a rough count of attendees to know how many dogs to roast. Of course a last minute mongrel can always be found feeding from an alley trash pile should we need one, but it is nice to fatten them first.

To my surprise, a message from dad: **John my boy! Looks like I've gotta join this facepamphlet thing to get ahold of you. Technology sure moves fast these days, doesn't it? I think it's mighty fine you went on this journey, mighty fine. I'm tickled pink that you didn't even have to think about it, just took the plunge. Too many people spend their lives regretting things they never did. Now, I'm sure you're aware that I've done a fair amount of mind expanding substances in my day. Well, dropping acid is similar to this trans Pacific interculturally mind expanding journey you're on in that you can't overthink it, you just have to go with it. Your mom says you're getting hitched? I saw those pictures of that sweet thing you're with. Woo doggy! Son, that's the kind of girl you don't kick out of bed for eating crackers. If you say you're gonna tie the knot then I'm all for it. I don't blame you for picking an Oriental. Your generation of American girls can't tell a stove top from an ironing board. Don't fret about your mother, she's always been a worrier, but that's just her way of saying she loves you. I'll get her to come around before the wedding. In the meantime, don't be a stranger.**

Me: Thanks for the support pops. It will be nice to have you two here for the wedding. Do me a favor though, don't rush out and buy tickets just yet. The date isn't really firmly in place. I'll let you know when we get it sorted out. Hope things are well on Orcas.

Jay: **I'll tell you what's wrong with you bud, you've found a girl who doesn't bust your balls for sport and a job that fits your lifestyle, even**

if it does pay you in a currency on par with toilet paper. You've found azure seas teeming with tropical maidens. You've found beer cheaper (and safer) than water. The only rub is that you gotta share this land of bounty with guys like Ed. I'm not sure I could get over that, picturing every sweetie I see getting railed by Ed. But hey, at least they look like women. Even the ones who aren't...

Me: **I dunno, I guess I just feel like my potential for groupie gropes is being wasted. How's life in Olympia? You still with that same girl, or did you get her daddy issues straightened out and move on to the next one?**

That's it. No news from Annetta. Rain has Facebook officialized my impending imprisonment. For cockular convenience, I confirm my captivity.

3:49 p.m.

"You are back baby *ko!*" Rain squeals, squeezing the breath from my body.

"I wasn't gone long."

"Mmm baby *ko!* We are en*gaged!*"

"Yes baby ko. Still engaged."

"But now it on *Face*book baby ko! The whole world knows we are in *love!* That I am *yours* and you are *mine* forever and *always* baby ko!"

Alarm bells should be booming, but His Girthiness, that plucky pookie poker, has rerouted all reasoning to my auxiliary head. "Sure do," I declare, bearing my beaming beauty bedward.

"Baby ko?" she coos, arms a loose noose around the nape of my neck. "Where you take me?"

"To celebrate."

"Mmm! Baby *ko!* We celebrate *every* day? For*ever?*"

II

The Fall

18

King of the Club

Wednesday, February 5, 2014, 9:55 a.m.

"Good morning John! My *star!*" Slapping my shoulder, Miguel's grin is more giddy than most other mornings, almond eyes aglow with greed.

"Good morning Miguel."

"Come, sit down," he commands, motioning to meet him in the plotting of profits. "I trust you are well?"

"More or less," I reply, assuming the seat across from the capitalist.

"And the girlfriend?"

"Also well."

"Ah… good. And you are happy here?"

"Yeah."

"You like playing the shows?"

"Of course," I reply, wondering what plans his pleasantries are preceding.

"Ah, good. How you feel about more shows?"

"More shows?"

"Yes, my band what play on Tuesday and Friday, they no longer with us."

"Oh no. All of them? That's terrible. What happened?"

"They move to Cebu city."

"Oh."

"Yes. One of them have uncle with club there. Is hard find new band replace them. So I think, who bring in most people? So of course I think of you. What you say?"

"Um."

"Of course I pay you double. Two thousand eight hundred pesos a week and you still only practice twice, so is not twice as much work."

"Four thousand, and my liquor allowance increases to five hundred a week"

"Three thousand."

"Thirty nine hundred."

"Three thousand and fifty."

"Thirty eight fifty."

"John, we not get very far like this. Three thousand four hundred, is okay?"

"Thirty six hundred."

"Three thousand four hundred fifty. I cannot afford it, but to keep you, I cut out caviar. Make big sacrifice for my star."

"Thirty five fifty."

"Okay, *okay!* You are my *star* John! Three thousand five hundred. We start new schedule this week. Is okay for you?"

"Sure, but I want six hundred a week in free drinks."

"Fine fine," he replies, waving a paw to imply that my pints are a pittance. "Is good having you drink here anyway. Good selling point to bring girls in, make them think they have chance to love you. I like you John. You are greedy like me. Never trust a man who pretends he is not."

3:24 p.m.

"How come it so long since we do this?" Trisha entreats.

"There were reasons," I lament. "Stupid reasons."

"I think you feel guilty."

Why lie to a lass with a supernatural nipple? "Yeah... though she pretty much gave me permission to cheat, as long as I don't leave her."

"Smart girl."

"Yeah?"

"Yes. She knows you are a man of passion. She know that your penis does not have to be true for your heart to be."

"But *is* my heart true?"

"I don't know John, *is* it?"

I sigh. Why can't my conscience be clearer? Would it not be selfish to save all my glory for one girl when so many minges are melting for me? "I don't know. This doesn't feel like it."

"Maybe you cannot love her with *all* your heart, but what matters is that the part you give her is true."

Solid logic. Why can't its practice be painless, but a flip of a heart switch? "Maybe. What do you think of more shows?"

"It's okay I guess."

"You don't sound excited."

"I don't want to spend so many nights at The Club."

"It's more money at least."

"So? It's still not enough for the way you live."

"You're right," I sigh, shuddering at the shames I've endured for a dollar and will grind through again when my savings are sapped. "It's not."

"How you live like you do? You have rich family in America?"

"No. I worked at a restaurant and saved my money."

"Hard work?"

"Only on my dignity. Don't *you* need the extra money?"

"No John, I probably need it less than you."

I feel foolish for asking, since she paid for our fuck pad. But then, how the hell did she get *her* money? "You're hiding things," I state, bringing out into the open what til today had been tacit.

"Is true for you too, no?"

"For everyone I guess."

"Understanding comes not with true words John, but with a true touch, with true feeling."

It sounds like one of those syrupy spiels spoken to inspire demonstrations of desire, so I slip onto my side to give her the goods, merely to be met with melancholy.

"John, come next week I cannot see you outside of the band for some time. I hope you understand."

Sure I understand. When a lass lands a lad with more money than mojo, she recruits a cad to bring her life balance. "Sure, whatever," I reply, rolling over away from her, wondering why I mind so much being second cock to her cuck when she herself is my secret.

"Please understand John," she pleads, putting a hand on my hip to beg my body back to hers.

"Well," I grumble, flinching my ass away from her, rising to rub the frustrations from my forehead. "It'd be pretty hypocritical for me to get jealous."

"Just pretend there is nothing between us when he is here, okay? Everything will be back to normal when he leaves."

"Oh?" I ask, pacing the floor in front of her. "Will it really?"

"I hope so," she whispers, sitting up so I can see her eyes well with woe, attempting to trigger my damsel in distress script. "I don't want to hurt him."

"I don't want him to hurt me," I tell her, talking as loudly with my arm movements as my mouth.

"He is not like that. Don't worry."

"You think I can help it?"

"I know John. I am sorry I don't tell you earlier, but you stopped calling to see me, so I don't tell you. How come you never call?"

"I wanted to. I just… I dunno. Shit was weird. Rain's been so needy. I felt guilty."

"Sometimes shit gets weird. That is life, no? He flies in Monday, so from then until he leaves there is nothing between us, okay?"

"He how you pay for this?"

"John please."

"Your sugar daddy payed for this room so we could fuck?"

"He give me money to make me happy. Being with you makes me happy."

"I doubt he had this in mind."

154

"Does it matter?"

"Does it *matter!*?" I thunder, getting into her aura to make it more dramatic, beaming ire through my eyes. "Does it *matter*? I suppose when we're all dust, then *no*, it *won't*. But *now*? Of *course it matters!* I'd sure mind if *I* were him."

"John *please!*" she implores, and as if pause were pressed upon our passions, we're both suddenly silent, both sorry. "I just... I'm sorry."

"Me too."

"I hope nothing is changed between us?"

Who am I fooling? We'll be back in bed as soon as she showers the whiff of him away. "I guess not," I sigh, lying back down beside her.

"I don't want us to lose *this*," she cries, nuzzling herself into my side.

"Me too," I soothe, swabbing a tear from her cheek. "It's just a lot to digest."

"I'm sorry."

"It's okay. I guess I'll be seeing him at the shows?"

"Yes," she replies, a plea for pardon in her eyes. "He love to watch me on stage. I meet him just after my boyfriend dump me, and you know my boyfriend dump me cause he not like me on stage. He come to see my show on a Thursday. Saturday he come back and wait around until the show is over. He tell me he like to watch me. He ask to take me out. I say yes, because I am lonely. He buy me things. We travel around country, stay in nice hotels. He give me so much, but only things money can buy, things a poor girl like me has never had. After two weeks he leave. He tell me he come back for me. He give me more money than I have ever had. He only ask that I be true to him. For two years, even though he gone for months between visit me, even though I am with him for wrong reasons, I am true to him. But I think he not true to me. How can he be true if his first love is money? But I am true to him, until I meet you."

I chew that over. Wanting the wisdom to defend our deceit, I kiss her extra titty in consultation. "Why me?"

"Because John, we can have *this*," she whispers, trailing fingers tenderly from the nape of my neck to the neck of my knob to mark her meaning. "And you don't ask for anything more."

4:44 p.m.

A draft of durian meets me with a musk remindful of a bag lady's fruit bowl. The remainder of the monstrosity sits atop the table between my beauty and her brother, its prickly peel pulled apart to uncover its creamy core.

Rain has tirelessly transformed our apartment into a kitschy chintzy coochy smoochy cuddle camp, a sickly sweet retreat amidst the metropolitan madness. The durian sorta seems a metaphor for that.

"Baby ko? What take you so long?"

"I had a beer with the band after practice." A tale of truth, as Trisha and yours truly did sip on said suds between band practice and the bedroom.

"Okay baby ko," she coos, swallowing my bullshit faster than a nutritionally deficient cattle dog. "We save you some durian. You want?"

"Sure," I answer, durian, like cigarettes, being slightly less offensive firsthand. "What's for dinner?"

"I make adobo baby ko. Baby ko, I invite Jenna and Marcel for dinner, *okay?*"

"Yeah, sure," I grumble, knowing I'll be an accessory to the evening, deaf to the topics at the table until they touch upon the majesty of America and my tablemates turn to English, at which moment I must regale them with the glories of my Hollywood homeland.

"What the matter baby ko? You look upset."

Fucking Christ! Can I not furrow my face without my floozy fussing over me? "Nothing. I just need a drink."

"You want send Alex to store?"

"They won't card him?"

"What you mean?"

"Ask for ID?"

"No. They not care baby ko."

"Good," I reply, handing him 200 pesos. "Better get a couple liters of Red Horse," I say, watching him stare bug-eyed at the bills til Rain repeats the request in Visaya.

Alex pops up and pockets the pesos. "I get beer," he declares, dashing for the door.

Sitting down beside my darling, she puts her paw on my pants but a mite from my member, puddly peepers subconsciously searching my soul for reassurance, affirmation my musk is merely another maiden's reminder of how lucky a lass she is to be the one to have landed me, not a whiff of the woman next in line for my love.

"I love you baby ko."

"I love you too."

"Mahal kita lagi."

"Mahal kita lagi."

"Ikaw…"

I could go on with my nymph's inane sweet nothings, but I presume the point is punctuated.

"Miguel wants us to play more shows," I announce, my amour's anxiety at last alleviated for at least a little while.

"More shows? So more time you are at the bar?"

"Two more days," I reply, pulling off a piece of the fruit's fetid flesh. "Tuesdays and Fridays."

"Is so *much* baby ko!" she complains, wiping the sweat from my neck as she'd done that first night in El Nido, demonstrating my need for her nurturing, my inability to manage myself. "I like you *sing* baby ko, but I like it more when you *here* with *me*."

"We can use the money."

"Why it have to be about *money?*" she appeals, her pout impervious to the influence of facts.

Superficially her fussing may come off as codependent, but at its pith it's a plea not to nuke the hope in her heart. To admit my funds to be finite is to demote myself from her savior to a mere mortal man, relinquishing the role of all powerful provider she's pedestalized since puberty, that pillar of patriarchy so essential to a civilization's ascent, yet so maligned by America's self loathing soy loafs, corporate cunts, and Luciferian elite whose power depends upon breaking the bonds of kith and kin through the counterfeit compassion of political correctness, a socially pressured self-policing designed to silence dissent as it coerces consent to cultural suicide, inverting traditional values and rarefying meaningful relationships whilst encouraging us to cram the holes in our hearts with defilements of the flesh. *"Really* sugartits? What do you think paid for all *this?"* With a side to side sweep, my hand bids her to behold the bits and baubles, the pillows and Pinoy pop star posters purchased for her pleasure. "What do you think is paying for the *beer* Alex is getting?"

"Money," she mumbles, looking down in defeat.

"Exactly. And *whose* money?"

"Yours baby ko."

"Don't forget it," I shout, my voice all vitriol. "Tell me a*nother* thing, baby ko. Why were you in El Nido? I guess not for *money*, since it doesn't matter to you. So what *was* it?"

Her hapless little hamster is all but whizzing off its wheel, her kisser quivering off the cusp of control. My sadistic side wants to watch the fucker fly free. *"Well?"*

"Money," she mouths, barely whispering the word.

"Ex*actly.*" A crisper castigation was never enunciated. Sometimes nuclear is necessary to end an argument before further damage is done. Hiroshima. Nagasaki. Just a couple cracked eggs to make a peace omelet. I let her take a tick to internalize the lesson.

"Baby ko. Why you *like* this? Why you *mad?"*

"Because! I'm the only one who makes any Goddamned money around here and you're mad cause I'm gonna make more of it!"

"No baby ko," she cries. "I just sad cause you spend less nights with me."

"You're in the audience."

"Yes, with everyone *else*, with all the girls staring at *you*, while you on stage with that girl Trisha. Why you have to play at night?"

"What, we're going to play during the *day?"*

"Yes. Why not?"

"Forget it," I sigh, getting up to go.

"Where you go baby ko?"

"I'm gonna go search for the bottom of a rum bottle."

"You always drink so much!"

"Yeah, well, it's cheaper than therapy."

"But Alex buy beer baby ko."

"Good. You can drown your sorrows."

"You come back for dinner?"

"Maybe," I shrug, shutting the door on her dejection.

4:59 p.m.

The humidity hangs heavy, the stewing stench of struggle filling my olfactories with guilt for the good fortune God favored the land of the free. These wide-eyed whitey worshipers will never truly know the man that is me. They see me as a unicorn, but I am merely a horse with a strap on party horn living in their zebra herd. I shouldn't have brought up El Nido.

I consider calling Trisha for an encore canoodling. I consider rambling around until a groupie grabs me. I can't commit to either option, finding myself melancholically magnetized towards that sanctum for souls malaised by modernity.

A bar.

Specifically, The Club.

The bar wench's eyes bugging as they set upon my sight, her mouth opens mute, wanting for words worthy of my whiteness.

"Hiiiiii."

"Hey there," I reply, staking out a stool.

"Pale Pilsen?" she purrs.

"Nah, Jim beam."

"You are homesick?"

"No, I just miss whiskey. Everything else I could take or leave."

She leans in until her titties touch the bar top, or would if they were corn-fed American cans. "Where your girlfriend tonight?"

"At home cooking dinner. Where's your boyfriend?"

"I not have boyfriend," she replies, licking her lips as she pokes out her peaches even further than before.

I smitten her my smirk, hoping to mend my mood manually. "Why not? Should be easy for a girl like you."

"Maybe, but it hard to find one I want."

"And who would that be? Prince Charming?" What do you know, it's working. "Maybe you should kiss more frogs."

She leans in even further, as if to say a secret. "I wait for nice foreign man. Not many here in Davao."

"So why don't you move somewhere touristy?" Though I know she's dizzy for a dicking, I imitate ignorance. After years of feminists yammering that a fish scented fissure that bleeds madness once monthly makes females infallible, American men no longer question women's claims, and so their minges melt the more for the devil who dare do so.

I assume Filipinas have similar emotional needs.

"It hard because I don't want leave my family. I work so much here to help them."

"So what's wrong with the local guys?"

"Nothing."

"But you want a western guy."

"Yes."

"Why?"

"Is something wrong with that?" she asks, the answer being obvious that her countrywomen's worship of western wealth and wiener is a symptom of the Satanic malignancy metastasizing from the twin towers of Manhattan and Hollywood, consuming every culture its tentacles touch. "They are kind and understanding, they have money," she coos.

"Money huh?" I chide. "Is that what it is?"

"It not just money," she backpedals. "They are *fun*. They are ad*venturous*."

"Sure, the ones you meet."

"What you mean?"

"I mean of course you think they're adventurous. Only the adventurous ones come to Davao."

"So?"

"So it's not really the full spectrum of western men."

"Spectrum?"

"Variety."

"Of course, guys like you not *normal.*"

I smirk. I oughta have the expression permanently attached. Where to go for that? Bangkok? "Guys like me?"

"I mean, *you know!*" she flusters. "Western men that come here."

"Like me."

"You are mean," she pronounces, putting on a pout.

"At least I'm not the mode," I repartee.

"What you mean?"

"Don't worry about it doll."

"I think you get in fight with your girlfriend. That why you come here to drink."

I cock an eyebrow. His Girthiness and I should study how strumpets analyze others so easily. It would save tons of time if I could swiftly suss the smitten from the smiley. "You can tell?"

"Yes. It written on your face."

I feel my face, as if it were egg yolk glazing its glory. "You never really answered me."

"Answer you what?"

"Why you don't like local guys."

"They not understanding."

"Of what?"

"You really want to know?" she perks, peepers pleading for empathy, pining for me to make it palpable with my penis.

"Yeah, I do."

"They all want something from a girl, but it is something she can only give once, you *know?*"

"Yeah."

"So what if she give it to wrong guy?"

Now that hangs heavier than fettuccine Alfredo in a bulimic's belly. I wash down some whiskey, wishing for the wisdom to reply to this peach who is baring herself as bravely as an open faced sandwich at fat camp. "You gave it to the wrong guy?"

Her nod is slight, yet so yeasty with yearning that my yen to yang her yin brings a bulge to my briefs.

"I'm sorry."

"It not your fault. I was only sixteen. He promise to marry me, then he leave me for other girl."

"He was a fool."

"No, I was a fool to trust him. But western men do not care about my past. I think western girls have worse pasts, no?"

"*Much* worse. *Much much* worse."

"American women not know how lucky they are. To be able to make mistakes… maybe just have fun."

"They've no notion how good they've got it," I agree.

"You don't like them," she observes.

I've grown lazy without western women's wordfare to whet my wit with. Were I this agreeable in America I would more than merely make the minx's minge cringe, she'd accuse me of a crime for failing to flirt with adequate assholery. "No, I don't."

"What is wrong with them?"

"Well…" I begin, washing down some whiskey for wisdom. "I'm not sure where to begin."

"But what they *do*."

"It's more what they *don't* do."

"So what they don't do?"

"Well… there are a plethora of pleasantries that come as natural as breathing to a beauty like yourself yet are scorned by western women, but it's easily summed up: they don't *love*."

"They don't *love!?*" she gasps.

"Well, they *do* love them*selves,* but you'd never know it if you peeked in their pantry."

"But a girl should live for her *family!*"

"Try preaching that in America."

She slips me the conspiratorial smile jelly beams peanut butter when they find themselves set beside two slices of bread. "Sounds like we both have good reason to like foreigners."

"It does, doesn't it?" I reply, hand sliding across the counter to settle on hers.

She breaks out in a blush, her hamster wheel hurrying to reconcile her lascivity with her Catholic conservatism. I'd forgotten how much more such a move means here than in America, where a female's faith has fallen to the false idol of feminism, the flower once defended til the night of her nuptials to compensate his enslavement now desperately despoiled in her quest for equality. As emotionally muddled as a lactose intolerant mouse at a cheese shop dumpster, I pull away my paw, washing down some whiskey for wisdom.

"Maybe you should go back to your girlfriend. Maybe she done cook dinner for you. I think you hungry."

"I probably should," I grumble, downing my drink to give myself gumption. "Better give me another one of these for the road."

"You want plastic cup?"

"No. Same glass. I'm gonna slam it."

"Thank you for listen to me," she purrs as she pours. "Your girlfriend very lucky girl."

Aww, so winsome is her woozy for western wiener that one and a half of my heads want to give her the goods to keep the want from weighing so heavy on her heart. "Can you tell her that for me?" I ask, giving her a grin as I huck it down the hatch. "Guess I'll head home then."

I try to take care of the tab, but with a wink she says don't worry.

"Goodnight John."

I don't recall exchanging names. Oh, right, I'm pretty important around these parts. "Goodnight… um… remind me your name?"

"Anna."

"Goodnight Anna."

What was I doing again?

19

God's Gift

Friday, February 7, 2014, 11:57 a.m.

Dad took over messaging from mom, who never let me know if they'd be popping over the Pacific to munch on mutt steak: **Well son, I just want you to know I'm rooting for ya. I'm in your corner. Your mother and I have a wager. She thinks you're gonna pull out of the wedding, but I say you're going for it. Your mamma sure is a bundle of worries about you. She thinks you soaked up a terminal level of bad vibes whilst faking pleasantries for unpleasant patrons and had to cross the ocean to outrun your demons. She figures that due to the nonphysical nature of these malevolent monsters you couldn't get loose from their grip, and now you're drowning them in drink. Me, I see it differently. I think what you're doing over there is more like purification, or gold panning. But instead of sloshing water around a pan with some sand in search of a few gold flakes, you're sloshing beer around your brain in search of life's lost mysteries, a far greater treasure. But you're not just sloshing beer around your mental gold pan, you've added adventure and maidens to the mix. That's a full on mental reboot, retune and realignment. I think that's just swell.**

Me: **Thanks for the understanding pops. If the band's popularity keeps growing, then I'll be to the Philippine's what David Hasselhoff is to Germany. One of the other bands moved to Cebu and we took their days. Four nights a week at The Club now. I wish I could tell you the wedding date was straightened out, but she's got family coming from all over the country and we're trying to come up with a date that works for as many of them as possible. Hope all is well on Orcas.**

I wonder what Trisha is up to?

2:26 p.m.

"I wish we could stay here all day," Trisha purrs.

"Then let's, til the show."

"I think your phone rings."

"So?"

"It's probably Rain."

"So?"

"She probably *worry* about you," she says, heaving her head to behold my baby blues, bunching her brows in concern for my soul. "You don't want her *worry* do you?"

"I guess not."

"We are selfish, aren't we?"

"You feel guilty?"

"No... maybe. Sometimes I feel selfish for feeling happy, because so many people not know how to be. I think Rain ties her happiness to you, and that pushes you away. Maybe I feel guilty because when she pushes you away you come to me."

"I suppose I do," I sigh.

"Call Rain back," she pleads. "For *me*."

"Why?"

"Because she *worry* about you!"

"Alright," I relent. "I suppose I should."

"You don't need to go *home*," she hints, impish eyes implying impure plans for me. "But you should ease her fear. She nice girl."

"She is. Needy as hell, but an angel nonetheless."

"So call her, tell her everything is okay."

"Alright," I grumble. "I'll call her."

When my princess replies with her woe is me worry, I say there's an emergency band meeting, meet me at the show. She responds with a sputtering of suspicions, the sweetest volley of invectives ever hurled by a harlot's overheated hamster.

Meet me at the show, I patiently repeat, hanging up on her heartache.

Telling the truth is a point of pride for me. Although there being only the both of us a band meeting it barely is, the urgency of our ardor makes it the utmost of emergencies. If Trisha's lust is not unleashed it might streak across the stage, and though that might find envy exciting every tart in attendance, it would be cruel to concern little Rain with our romance.

"You feel better?"

"A bit."

"You see? Communication is important."

7:48 p.m.

We arrive without a wink to waste, separating blocks before The Club lest our simultaneous arrival arouse my sweet's suspicions.

Rain isn't there. But where is she?

Two songs into the set Rain and Auntie arrive, bumbling about like AWOL bachelorettes freed from their frenemy's final fling. Buying a bucket of beers, their imbibing is beyond ambitious, pound for pound peerless. I gape aghast as they guzzle.

166

8:36 p.m.

A tiff touches off between my beauty and the bartender. Ostensibly originating over opposing opinions of my inamorata's need for another inebriant, the fracas fulminates in an eruption of expletives on the part of my peach, compelling Miguel to respectfully request Rain's removal for the evening's remainder.

Incapable of conceiving separation from my side, Rain rushes to declare her rights to my rod, silence erupting in the room as she storms the stage.

"Let's *go* baby ko!" she shouts, tugging on my T-shirt.

"I've gotta finish the show," I sputter, all but speechless from her spectacle. "I'll come home afterwards."

"Come home with *me* baby ko!" she cries. "I don't want leave you here with... with these *girls!*"

"I've gotta finish the set."

It takes several minutes to pacify my peach and talk her and Auntie into a tricycle home. Say what you will about my cutie's conniption, but you can't say it didn't come from a place of passion. On the crumpets in The Club its effect is fantastic, making them more than a mite orgiastic.

Oh to be me. It is grand.

I am blessed.

20

Begending Again

My babe has bundled herself in blankets, boxed her body between piles of pillows, only forsaking her fort to bumble towards the bathroom. I'm not sure if it's a call for help or a crack at conjuring some chimera of childhood.

"Baby ko, you ready to go to The Club?" I enquire, reaching under the covers to comfort my tart with a titty cup.

"*No* baby ko," she moans. "I not feel well."

"Still hung over?"

"Mmmm hmm."

"Your stomach or your head?"

"*Every*thing baby ko. Stay home tonight."

"I can't let the band down."

"Why it always about the *band* baby ko? I want spend *time* with you."

"I have to go. Just rest. I'll see you when I get home."

"Mmmmmmmm."

11:53 p.m.

"Pale Pilsen?" Anna purrs.

"Yeah."

"Where your girlfriend tonight?" A pantywaist might presume this a platonic pleasantry, but it's actually a quest to quell any qualms about stealing my stiffy from another strumpet, reassurance that success is divinely ordained.

"Home."

"She not come see your show?"

"She didn't feel good."

"She drink too much last night. Make big scene."

"Sure did."

"If I was your girlfriend, I would see every show."

"Is that so?" I snicker, smittening her my smirk.

"I just mean she should feel lucky," she stammers, reddening as she realizes how much she'd admitted.

"Because if *you* were mine, you'd treat *me* better?"

"I not say that!"

"Not in *those* words."

Sunday, February 9, 2014, 12:57 a.m.

"I think you don't want go home?"

"Oh? *Do you?*"

"You one of last people here," Anna observes, impish simper implying an impulse to play part in any impending impropriety. "I think you like my company?"

"Sounds like projection," I reply, slipping her a sly smidge of my smirk.

"What you mean?" she asks, overplaying a pout.

"I mean *you're* glad *I'm* still here so you accuse the emotion of belonging to me."

"Maybe I am," she concedes.

I take a tick to sip my suds and powwow tactical plans with my auxiliary head. "What will you do after work, go home?"

"Why, you want to come meet my parents?" she repartees, bending over the bar with a lusty lip bite, a flood of pheromones bringing my tool to attention. "Or maybe you have a better idea?"

"Sure do."

"What is your idea?"

"We grab a couple liters of Pale Pilsen and go somewhere quiet."

"This how you do it in America?"

I shrug, smirk. (I shirk? I smug?) "Sure. Our great nation was built upon beer. Well, that and smallpox."

She simulates my smirk, but it comes off more cute than conniving. "No wonder American girls way they are. I think about it."

It's a bluff. An inferior fellow would fluster, bluster, and backpedal for his boldness, freezing her butterflies like a blizzard. "Take your time," I tell her, spreading my arms across the neighboring stools. The ego, like a goldfish, needs room to reach its peak potential.

"Okay," she shrugs.

"Yeah?"

"Yes, why not? Why shouldn't I have fun? But where we go?"

"I know a place," I reply, giving her a grin.

Call me Sexyphus, for my efforts are endless.

2:12 a.m.

"You only second guy I do this with," Anna confesses.

"Oh?"

"Yes, it's been a long time."

"How long?"

"Two years."

"Oh," I reply, pulling my paw from her panties to take it more tenderly.

"I know it's a long time."

"Not so long," I reassure.

"You don't have to stop. I want it."

Flitting two fingers into her flower, her kisses quicken, back arching in orgasm as claws clutch cotton to hold her down from heaven.

Pulling my paw away once more, my lips linger over her silky skin, pausing to titillate the twins, promising her belly button a belated birthday gift, alighting at last on that long unloved lily between her legs, its landing strip luring me like a songbird to an orchid.

Is it strange for a strumpet to keep trimming her treasure without reward for her work? A refusal to admit defeat? Like the old man who mows his lawn twice weekly?

As I scarf her squiz she squeezes my skull in ascending crescendos of ecstasy, years of yearning for white wiener soaking the sheets. Only when Anna is on the edge of epilepsy do I loosen my lips from her loins.

"It's so big!" she cries, blushing at my boner.

"He won't bite," I reply, positioning myself for penetration. "But he does spit."

And yes, it may be the motion of the ocean that drives her devotion, but the more impressive your paddle the more rousing her ride.

I am blessed.

3:37 a.m.

"Why you here John?"

"Why is anyone anywhere? A serendipitous series of dubious decisions. Why are *you* here?"

"In Davao? I was born here."

"In bed with me."

"Why not?"

"Because I have a girlfriend. Because I'm a heartbreaker."

"Why should I care you have girlfriend? You wait around bar for girl to go home with. Why should I not be the one? I *know* you are heartbreaker John, So don't worry for me."

"Yeah," I sigh, regretting Rain's impending pain. At least I haven't lied about my loyalty to Anna or Trisha. Shouldn't two truths for three trollops give me a good enough grade? Or should I bring in more bimbos to bring it above a D?

"Everything okay?"

"I should go."

"So soon?"

"I wish I could stay."

"We do this again?"

2:54 p.m.

Rain rests her head on my heart, her sweet surrender some solace for not meeting Trisha for one last tryst before her man lands tomorrow.

My pouty little princess has been through a lot lately. She needs me.

I am, after all, a man of morals.

"I sorry I not come to your show last night baby ko."

"It's okay," I reply, rubbing my ruby reassuringly.

"*No* baby ko!" she cries. "It *not* okay, because Friday I drink too much and yesterday I feel sorry for myself. I should always be at your shows baby ko."

"Things happen," I console. "Don't beat yourself up."

"You forgive me?" she asks, heaving her head to make certain I see her anguishing eyes. How could I help but try to soothe such suffering?

"Of course."

"Thank you mahal ko. Ikaw lang sapat na."

"Ikaw lang sapat na."

"Promise?" she purrs, puddly peepers pleading for phallicular forgiveness.

"Promise."

"Always?"

"Always."

I summon my strength for the cockular comforting of my crumpet.

3:49 p.m.

I'm positive this planet still fosters fairy tale affairs, flames for whom romance richens with the turning of time, even as entropy tugs her tits to her tummy and his nuts towards his knees. Alas such loyalty my hardened heart will never know, for like Sexyphus I am serving a greater good than a lifelong love, and though my burden may be mammoth, I shall not shirk it.

"What you think about baby ko?"

"Nothing."

"You look like you think."

Threshing through my thoughts, my pensiveness found my paws pausing their post-coital caresses, my breath growing broody as I contemplated my path. "It's nothing," I reply.

"It not nothing," she whines.

"Don't worry your pretty little head about it."

"Okay baby ko."

I shut my eyes and search her silky skin for the fervor it once fired in me, being too moral a man to let my loss of love for her muddy the mood. Pushing to make the passion palpable, I imagine Anna's minge and Trisha's two and a half tits. It works wonders. Like a method actor pushed into porn by poverty, His Girthiness heads the charade.

"Mmm *baby* ko! *Again?*"

Monday, February 10, 2014, 6:03 p.m.

Dad: **Sounds like you really got it going on over there son. Now, I can't say I've removed your mother's misgivings, but I may have at least convinced her that voicing them isn't gonna change your need** to make your own mistakes. She has some nutty notion that they'll be serving roast dog at the wedding? I'm not sure where she'd get such an idea, your mother isn't typically prone to such xenophobic notions. Maybe you could try and put this silly fear of hers to rest? I know how her worries make you feel son, as I never liked being worried about when I was your age either, nor did I like being told what to do with my life. When I was not much younger than you they wanted to send me to Vietnam. Now, my daddy wanted me to go, said it was my duty to kith, kin and country and it would make a man out of me, but my mamma, she kept on crying and saying I was gonna get blown to bits and turned to rice fertilizer. Now, of course I was not ready to return to the compost cycle, but I'd be lying if I told you I knew much about what was going on over there, as I was engaged in a lot of, how you say, extracurricular activities at the time. I did know that I wasn't gonna go just because some fat cats wanted war, so I left Virginia and ran off to a commune in the Sierra Nevada. That was where I discovered my calling son. You see, when I got there they had just one smelly old outhouse that saw more use than a Times Square crack whore during the Christmas rush. (Don't ask me how I know them to be busy that time of year. Let's just say it was a dark time in my life and before I met your mother.) I wracked my head over our poop processing problem and how to approach it in a both aesthetically pleasing and environmentally responsible manner. After a couple weeks of careful contemplation, several consultations with the commune elders, and a moment of doobie induced insight, I set at last to erecting my log walled ode to the daily dump. By the time I left that patchouli perfumed outpost I had erected not one, but three of these shrines to regularity. In the years since my edifices have populated the northwest from the redwoods to the San Juan islands, helping thousands in their most private of moments. When I get to feeling small I remind myself how many poops have plopped in my colon cathedrals. I think that's how singing is for you. It makes you feel big because it warms a place in people's hearts. I just want you to know I'm tickled pink about it.

Me: **Thanks dad. Maybe you ought to give mom some credit. I don't think I can go through with the wedding. This girl has me on such a pedestal that if I jumped I'd break my neck. It's overwhelming. I'm as smothered as a little girl's first kitten. I hope you haven't bought tickets for April yet.**

On the walk home I buy three liters of lager and a durian for my love dove.

10:07 p.m.

"I sleepy baby ko," my darling whispers dreamily, emphasizing so with a sigh as she heaves her head onto my heart.

Soon my sweet will sleep and I'll slip away into the warmth of a night still new, leaving my love safe with the Sandman as I go forth to bring goodness to a world wider than our apartment's walls. "Okay baby ko. You can go to bed then."

"You join me?" she asks, lifting loving eyes to behold my handsomeness.

"I'm not sleepy," I reply.

"Not for *sleep* baby ko."

The minge is a maiden's built in crystal ball, wising his wandering even as her hamster wheel whirls in worship of his wiener. Guessing at my plowing of greener pasture, her cooter is committing counter-subterfuge by endeavoring to drain me before another cunny can.

To subvert her slit, I must tango to its tune.

11:01 p.m.

My performance was so persuasive that my fake orgasm nearly turned real, like Pinocchio.

With my darling adrift in dreamland, I don fresh duds, fleeing the flat with a giddy gait and a mammalian musk.

11:22 p.m.

"Hiiiiii Jooohn."

"Hey there."

"You want a Pale Pilsen?" Anna purrs, captioning the question with a lusty lip bite. "Or something stronger?"

"Jim Beam."

"Ah, you are homesick again?"

"Nah, bourbon is more a state of mind than a place," I say, smittening her my smirk. "Bourbon ascribes to a moral flexibility that other liquors can only aspire to."

"What you mean moral flexibility?"

"Don't worry your pretty little head about it."

What's that dear reader? What *do* I mean by moral flexibility?

My morals are made of a spring steel that stands staunch against forgoing good times simply to satisfy scruples I can't even clarify, blessing me with an ability to maxify merriment that would make the average Joe beyond jealous.

How, then, are your morals mightier than mine? Some highfalutin hogwash about the golden rule?

I lavish upon lassies the same lust I'd like requited. The golden rule to a T.

Some Christly monogamy cockamamie?

Last I heard, Jesus' love was free, like mine.

I am the second cumming of Jizzus.

Tuesday, February 11, 2014, 2:11 a.m.

"I don't like this," Anna whines.

"Don't like what?"

"I don't like being the other *girl*," she laments, leveling me with a look that says I should have seen through any claims to the contrary. "My friends always ask me if I meet someone. Now I do, but I cannot tell them, because I am your secret. Why you still with Rain?"

"Um…" I mumble, her peepers imploring me to wrong this right. "Uh… I don't know," I admit.

"If you are going to break her heart, then why not just do it? The longer you wait, the more it hurt her."

She's right. Remaining with Rain is only postponing her pain. "I know," I sigh.

"*Please*," she pleads. "I want to *be* with you."

"But I'm a heartbreaker."

"So you've broken *hearts!*" she bewails, tears torrenting in trails. "How you know it not different for *us?*"

"I don't."

"Can we just *try* John. *Please?*"

"Let me think about it."

"You know you not happy with her."

"I just… I just need time to think."

"So you will pick me?" she pleads, snuffing back sniffles, puddly peepers imploring me to prattle sweet syrupy reassurances as I attest them with tender touches, warming her from her woe before punctuating my compassion with the pounding of my penis.

"Yes," I relent, giving up on negotiation.

At long last her waterworks wane. I couldn't possibly portray the following frenzy. Fame, even in provincial pinches, foments a feminine fervor that your typical fella's tepid fluffing of his frigid flame will never come near.

11:43 p.m.

I've been too big-hearted, too giving for my girl's own good.

You let a lass swallow your sword and she noshes on nut butter tonight only to beg for more in the morning, but teach her to nibble her own nani and she lunches for a lifetime all on her ownsome. This is the epiphany that pushes us towards conservatism over time, the wisdom that welfare weakens the will to work and when instituted by the state is a slippery slope to candlelight dinners of dog meat.

"Baby ko, everything o*kay?*" my crumpet enquires, sensing something's wrong and making her syllables extra syrupy to showcase that she cares more than any mortal competitor can.

"Yeah, everything's *fine,*" I grumble.

"You seem different tonight baby ko."

"Oh? *Do I?*"

"Yes," she whines, putting on her pout. "What you think about?"

"What does it *matter?*"

"Baby ko, why you *mad?*" she asks, clutching my thigh in request of comforting, peepers imploring me to hush her hamster with my hammer.

"Why must you know what I *think?*" I shout, pushing her paw off my pants and getting up to give my rage room for release. "What is so fucking important about my *thoughts?* Do you really think I'd *tell* you? Do you really think you'd even under*stand* them?"

"Baby ko? I don't understand. What is *happening?*"

"Nothing!"

"Why you *mad?*"

"Because you question every crinkle that furrows my face! I can't walk out the door without twenty Goddamned questions! You smother me!"

She reaches out to tug me to her, as forlorn as the last puppy left in a parking lot giveaway. "Baby ko, *please.* Sit *down.*"

"Just forget it," I shout, shedding the moaning minx once more.

"Forget *what* baby ko? What you *mean?*" God, those eyes! Those suffering saucers of dizzy dreams dashed!

"I mean *this! Us!* I can't fucking *do* this! I can't assure you everything's gonna be rainbows and unicorn farts every time you get in a funk, because it's *not* sugartits, it's *not.* Look around. There's a whole lot of shit out there, and I ain't so far above it as you think. I'm not your Goddamned savior. I'm just a drunk, selfish asshole."

"Don't *say* that baby ko!" she cries, her kisser quivering on the cusp of inconsolable sobs.

"It's said."

"You are *not* selfish! You are so sweet to *me.*"

"I'm not sweet."

"But *why* baby ko? I *love you.*"

Two tears charge my cheeks in sympathy for her suffering. Perplexed by their presence on such a paragon of perfection, they develop an identity crisis.

"Baby ko?… *Baby* ko?… Why you don't say you *love* me baby ko?"

My look could loop the world and still have the steam to make it to Maui.

"Don't you *love* me?"

"I *did.*"

"What you mean *did* baby ko?"

"I mean it's *over.*"

"But *baby* ko! You are my one and *only!* We are always and for*ever*, re*member* baby ko?"

Like a movie set machine gun of the soul, my baby blues blast her with emotional blanks. "I can't be that for you Rain. I can't be the foundation for your emotional house of cards. I won't be a good father or husband. I only care about singing, drinking and fucking. We got swept up in a fantasy, and that's all it was."

She collapses on the couch in whimpers and wails. Were I weaker I'd hold her to my heart, and as her head heaved to behold my baby blues, I'd find her lips locked to mine, peepers pleading me to ploink her one last time. Tomorrow morning we'd awaken entwined, and the wedding would follow not far behind.

Her pain is a plowing of the psyche's soil, an essential suffering if new seeds are to be sown. Not wanting to impede the process, I pack up my possessions.

I am, after all, a man of morals.

She watches me woefully as I dally at the door to bid her goodbye, the gut wrench of her grief leaving me at a loss for several endless seconds. "You go now baby ko?" she snivels through the snot flowing from her nose, the film turning into tendrils as her mouth opens in a moan.

"Yeah."

"Take care always, okay baby ko?"

"You too."

21

Sexyphus

Wednesday, February 12, 2014, 12:17 a.m.

As I come up to The Club the texts turn up:
Please come back baby ko
I try harder
I really really love you
I don't know what I do without you
No one can take your place
Mahal kita lagi
Ikaw lang sapat na
Please baby ko

Sending her sorries and swallowing my pride, I turn my phone off and step inside. Anna reads the tea leaves faster than a Bangkok stunt vagina can shoot a ping pong ball through a ring of fire.

"You tell her?" Anna asks, stopping restocking to put all her energy into empathy.

"Yeah."

"She okay?"

"No."

"*You* okay?"

"*Fuuuuck!*" I exclaim, running my hands through my hair over the annoyance of her nurturing. "I'll be a lot better with a Jim Beam and a Pale Pilsen," I reply, awarding her a way to help me through my hardship.

"You *sure* you okay?"

"Can you do me a favor Anna?"

"Yes?"

"Grab my fucking drinks."

1:47 a.m.

"Thank you for pick me," Anna sighs, nuzzling her nose sleepily into my side.

"Nothing to thank."

"This mean you my boyfriend?"

"Yeah." I am Sexyphus, the second cumming of Jizzus, your prince from the promised land come to cut the shackles of shame you've worn for giving your gift without the gracing of God, but you can brand me boyfriend if it fits your fancy.

"Mmmmm I so happy I have you."

"We have each other."

"Mmmmm yes baby ko, each other."

Baby ko! Oh Rain, may you meet the king who'll crown you the queen I couldn't, not a string of studs to pluck your petals until the wall leaves you wilted.

"I say something wrong?"

"Don't worry about it."

"I think I say something wrong."

"Rain called me baby ko."

"So what I call you then?"

"Just John."

"Mmmm okay just John."

9:12 a.m.

Certain as the sun sets, it rises reborn.

For every love lost, another forms afresh.

I cannot alter this order.

"Good morning John."

"Good morning doll."

"I love you."

"I love you too."

Do I? So waffling that word. Ideally denoting an unbreakable bond, it too often tells of an electric lust that fritters itself in a flurry of pheromones, leaving only bitterness behind. So what *do* I mean when I murmur of amour?

I burn to feel the butterflies bursting her bosom as it heaves against my heart, her claws clutching me close in fear of losing my love, jealousy driving her to drain my dingis daily, lest another nymph do the deed in her stead. But would my lascivity last should her butterflies fail to flutter, her jealousy fail to flow? Alas this could not be so, for just as her own passion is a product of other cuties coveting my cock, my cupidity comes from the licentiousness thus elicited. Like a mercurial maiden my prurience is provisional. Who could rebuke my balance as I find my femininity?

But if it *is* love, then where is this sentimental Rubicon crossed? When does like become love?

A love is declared by deed, and only one deed will do.

A pre-breakfast boning. Proof that the sun has not soured what the night had nurtured.

In the evening you go out, gussied up and giddy, intent on tapping a ten. With every beer and rebuff your standards stumble, until closing time comes and you lug home a land whale, only by daylight to curse the hooch for this corpulent cooch, who opens her eyes, smiling as she smothers you with a smooch. As your morning breath meets her morbid melange, you're as mortified as a mutt who'd dozed by a dumpster only to awaken in a wok.

Yes, it is those mushy morning moments that loosen love from its counterfeit cousins. Love doesn't disappear at dawn, perfunctorily promising to call. Love touches you tenderly, morning breath and all. Only love will lay you before coffee confers it composure, murmuring monosyllables that make monkeys look eloquent. Love will-

Thursday, February 13, 2014, 3:49 p.m.

Dad: **Shit son, I've been wondering if that would happen, but I wasn't gonna say anything cause I believe in letting people make their own mistakes, a philosophy that has caused your mother and I to come to heads a time or two over the rearing of you youngsters. I won't rub your nose in it either, for I believe in letting people contemplate the aroma of their own decisions at their own pace. Shit, you think I never fell prey to a maiden's passion, only to find spending time with her as smothering as slathering oneself in bacon grease and playing with a litter of puppies? Believe it or not son, but your mother, bless her worry wart heart, was not my first. Why, I made quite a few hearts melt in my day. Back at that commune in the Sierra Nevada there was this girl Anabel, real southern peach. She liked to watch me work, and it was during the construction of my second log cabin shithouse that her emerald green eyes locked onto my sinewy muscles as I sawed and wrestled my logs into place. She would just sit there in the grass, watching me, offering me sweet tea and lemonade and making sure I never went hungry. After a week or so of this she showed up one day in a paisley dress, flowers braided into her hair. She asked me if I was hungry, so I said sure I'm famished. She beckoned me to sit down on the grass beside her. Now, as far as I could tell she hadn't brought anything along but herself and that dress, but in spite of the confusion about the whereabouts of this picnic I was promised, I sat down beside her anyway. I asked her what's for lunch. She just smiled and bit her lip alluringly, so I did what any red blooded lad would've done, and kissed her. Minutes went by in that kiss before she finally says she's not wearing panties, so naturally I pull up her dress for a** peek. It was then I saw a sight that still comes to me unbidden at flower shops and fruit stands, often eliciting an embarrassing bulge. Braided into her bush was a bouquet of May flowers. In the middle of her garden, parting those sweet lips like an apple in the mouth of a roast pig, was a strawberry. Now, the look on my face was the look Neil Armstrong would have had had he discovered the moon to be made out of cheese, but she just smiled like this was normal and asked if I was hungry. That outhouse was delayed weeks because of that girl, and by the time it was finally finished the two of us were engaged. But the bliss passed as fast as the peak of an acid trip, which means I suppose it felt like a long time but it wasn't. During the erection of the third and final shithouse I built at that commune her incessant attentions began to wear me down. I yearned for time alone with my logs. Now, I was one prize stud, but that girl's appetite would overwhelm the energizer bunny on a coke binge. I couldn't sit down to read a book or roll a doobie without her shoving her Sparkle Montgomery in my face. (I never did figure out where that nickname came from.) By the time the outhouse was finished I was fed up. I snuck off one day while she was occupied in that very same shitter I'd been building when her eyes first met mine. Quick as I was engaged I was disengaged, and that was the end of my time in the commune. I guess what I mean to say is I know how you feel son. I'm sure how I felt with her eyes on me while I built that last shitter was a lot like how you've felt at your shows lately with this girl's eyes on you. Don't worry son, there's other peaches in the pie. It sounds like you've stuck your face in a pretty tasty one too.

Me: Well dad, I went through with it and broke the girl's heart. Otherwise things are good I guess. Seeing a different girl, but I don't see things ending much differently than they did with Rain, so don't tell mom. Band is doing well. Not much else to report. Sorry you lost the bet to mom.

Removing the remorse Rain has whinged all over my wall to make room for new rubies to worship my whiteness, I pop off for a pre-show pint.

185

22

The Second Cumming

Wednesday, February 26, 2014, 2:07 p.m.

Your eyes do not deceive you dear reader, I have once more transported you past tedium to titillation, lest my descent into domesticity seem a sleazy sequel to my relationship with Rain. (Any further leaps forward will not be noted, even omissions of a month or more.)

"Meet me at the Balut stand?" Trisha asks, letting me read the rest from her lusty leer.

"Yes," I reply, looking over at my love busy stocking the bar. I should bid her goodbye with a quick little kiss and a promise of penis, lest I leave her languishing in unsurety through her shift. It's the right thing to do and I am, if I am anything, a man of morals. "Five minutes?"

"Make it ten," she says. "Say goodbye to Anna."

"You know about that?"

"Everybody knows John."

4:44 p.m.

"John, I have something to tell you," Trisha sighs, all of a suddenly solemn.

"Yeah?" I reply, a flutter of foreboding in my belly.

"I'm leaving."

The dread in my depths heaves into my heart, leaving me at a loss for a tick of eternity. "You're... you're... you're *leaving?*"

"Yes."

"Where are you *going?*

"California."

"Cali*fornia?* Why the *fuck* would you want to go *there?*"

"Mark lives in California. My fiancée visa came through."

"You never thought to tell me that you're en*gaged?*" That maybe I *might* want to know?

"What we have is special! I didn't want to ruin that."

"Not special enough apparently."

"John, *please!*"

"Fuck!... When do you leave?"

"Monday."

I let that settle for what seems like a century, but is actually only a minute at most. "I'll miss you," I mumble.

"I'll miss you too, and what we do together, but everything will work out."

"Yeah... sure."

"Maybe this is not the end John. Not for forever. I have a feeling we will see each other again."

"Yeah? A titty intuition?"

"Just a feeling our paths will cross again," she says, ignoring the note of venom in my voice. "But first they must part."

I weigh her words, taking slight solace in all the sluts giddy to gulp His Girthiness, the new depths of depravity I'll descend to for distraction. "Davao won't be the same without you."

"The city will go on."

187

"The band won't be as good."

"The band will get along. It is you the girls come to see," she whispers, craning forward to caption her consolations with a kiss. "The future is but a wish. Be here with me."

8:13 p.m.

"Do you believe in fate?" Trisha asks.

"Not really... I think we're just fumbling through life."

"So then what is the point?"

"Like the meaning of life?"

"If you want to call it that."

"To squeeze what pleasure we can from our fumbles."

She furrows her face, taking a moment to muddle my meaning. "But what *drives* our fumbles John?"

"Butterflies flapping their wings in Africa, steam from cows pissing on flat rocks in Oklahoma, solar storms... you know, a cosmos of coincidences colluding to crush us."

"Sound's like fate."

"So what's this? Us here?"

"Fate."

"And your fiancé?"

"Also fate."

"*Both* of us?"

"I lucky girl."

Thursday, February 27, 2014, 1:07 a.m.

"Mmm John, finally we alone," Anna lilts as the door latches.

"Mm hmm," I murmur, letting out a long exaggerated yawn. "It'll be nice to lie down and cuddle."

"Cuddle?" she coos, petting me through my pants. "Is that a name for what we do?"

"Yeah, you know, just hold each other tenderly."

"You don't need to be tender John."

Words are worthless. In the blink of a boner my beauty is bare and pawing at my pants. I must muster my mojo. A flaccid phallus can be fatal to a floozy's sense of self. I am, after all, a man of morals.

I am Sexyphus, the second cumming of Jizzus.

1:41 a.m.

My cock caricatures a carrot long forgotten in the fridge.

"How come it like this?" Anna whines.

"I must've drank too much."

"But you only have three beer."

"Was that it?"

"Yes, three beer at the bar."

"Huh. Guess he's tired."

"But we sleep lots last night. We not even make love this morning. You in hurry get to practice."

"Oh… maybe he's stressed."

"Stressed?"

"Like performance anxiety or stage fright. Maybe you're putting too much pressure on him."

"Maybe you have, how you say? Where you need those pills to make love?"

"Erectile dysfunction?"

"I worry about you baby ko."

"I'm sure it will resolve itself," I reassure, smittening her a smirk to quiet her concern. "Maybe I can do something for *you*."

"What you do?"

"You'll see."

2:07 a.m.

Even the most cunnilingually cunning cannot shield a Sheila from the shame a weary wiener weaves.

"He still not excited," Anna complains. "Usually when you kiss me there he get excited."

"Give it til tomorrow. Sleep on it."

"On *top* of it?" she asks, furrowing her face in confusion. "That *help?*"

10:01 a.m.

Trisha and I tumble through overgrown grass, crushing fallen fruit as we cavort beneath the cover of time-contorted trees.

But a gust from the ground hangs an apple as alluring as Eve's forbidden fruit. Getting up to grab it, Trisha takes a taste before brushing it across her beaver and laying it to my lips for a bite of ambrosia.

"Lie down," she lilts, tossing the apple aside. "I have a surprise for you."

Squatting so her squiz is so close to my kisser I can breath her bouquet, she lets go a flow of liquid gold. It tastes like... champagne.

I jerk awake. Anna is saying something.

"Hmm?"

"I think you okay baby ko!"

"Oh... yeah."

"He happy this morning!" she squeals, tugging my tool with the stumbling but instinctual technique of a farm maiden milking her very first cow.

2:06 p.m.

Dad: **Shucks son, sounds like you've opened Pandora's clambox and found the aroma rather fishy. Good on ya. There comes a time in** the life of any lad worth his salt when the lure between a lass's legs is no longer enough to hold him on the hook. I think you might have reached that juncture. I know it's hard to see the good in it now, disillusioned as you are about ever finding a woman who won't make you want to take a permanent fishing vacation, but what this experience will give you is discernment. 'You'll never get what you want if you don't know what you're looking for.' Sure, we've all heard that tired truism, and now that we've said it let's tuck it back in, it's sleepy. What's more important son, is to remember that you'll never get what you need if you blindly take whatever comes. What's important is not to know exactly what you want, but to be able to weigh the worth of what crosses your path, cause chances are when you finally find that lucky lady there's gonna be something special about her you didn't know you were looking for, and you wouldn't have noticed it if you didn't have your eyes peeled. This may sound easy son, but you have to remember that our genes come to us from times of true scarcity, times when you could not afford to refuse low hanging fruit, a wounded deer, or a brainless beauty, whose love is liable to blind you of better options. Now we have an overwhelming abundance of empty options. Look around America. This country is crowded with men and women wolfing their way into a brain-fogged obesity, only to demand deliverance from cancer when it claims them. Now, I could have gone to war like those trigger happy fatcats wanted me to, but I cast that option aside faster than a house flipper tearing out tacky wallpaper. Had I gone and been lucky enough to come back, who knows whether I'd have discovered my log cabin composting shithouse dream or not, but the point is that the journey began not with a clear vision of what I wanted to create, but with a firm refusal to go forward under falsehoods. I think that's what this trip is all about for you. Learning to say no, I don't want that. Thank you but no thanks. In a society so full of superficially different GMO corn products, a society driven not by our mutual best interests, but through the thought control of a vampiric elite keen to keep us trapped on a treadmill of drudgery and donuts, this skill is invaluable. I'm tickled pink you're figuring it out.

PS. I don't know what your plans are as far as returning to America or work goes, but if you find yourself needing employment and want to work with your pops, I got plenty of projects coming up on Orcas.

Me: **Thanks for the offer dad, we'll see. Gonna stick it out here a little longer. Not sure if I'll go back to serving. Hope you and mom are well.**

To my slight surprise, a note from Annetta: **Not engaged anymore huh? Diddle too many groupies? I've always said you liked the idea of love more than it's practicalities. You can be so giving of affection, but you get distracted. It's not that you intend to cheat, it's just that you can't resist a girl who shares your favorite interest: you. I'm not saying you're totally selfish. Indeed, John my dear bunnyfish, you are to vaginas what Santa Claus is to chimneys. Now that it's over will you stay over there or will you turn your sleigh back home? My chimney could use a sweep...**

Me: **Oh Annetta, my dearest friend with benetits, soon my sleigh balls will be bouncing their jolly way back to your bosom. But before I leave I must clean a few soot spots from my suit.**

23

Leaving Elysium

Sunday, March 2, 2014, 4:54 p.m.

"I'll miss you," Trisha murmurs.

"I'll miss you too."

"You are king of the stage John. Never forget that."

"I guess so," I reply, dangerously near depression, or what I imagine the emotion to be. You see, I have a mental switch that makes me run from routine before I bury myself in bourbon. Though I believe this button to be inborn in all of us, the coercion to conform to civilized society's codes of comportment prevents its pushing, and so with age it atrophies, leaving a soul crushing acceptance of middle-class mediocrity.

"You don't feel like king of the stage?"

"It's just not gonna be the same without you," I sigh. "I think I might leave Davao. Maybe I'll even go home."

"Where is home?"

"Washington State. Olympia."

"Where is that?"

"Northwest corner of the country. Close to Canada."

"Ah. We will not be so far apart, no?"

"Not so far."

"You tell the band yet?"

"No."

"Miguel?"

"No."

"Anna?"

"No. I'm better at sudden separations than drawn out goodbyes."

"Then promise me this is not goodbye."

"What the hell *else* is it?"

"This is *now* John, and now is all we have, all we *ever* have. Why worry about tomorrow if you cannot taste or touch it?" As if to whisper sweet words too tender for open air, she leans in to my ear only to lick its lobe, hand slipping south to settle on my rising rod. "Mmm. *Again?*"

"Mm hmm."

"He like me."

"Yeah… I-" I pause, pining to portray the champagne shower with which she'd drenched me in my dreams, but unsure if I should.

"Yes John? I think you want to tell me something."

I tell her.

"Mmm John, I have this dream too."

"Yeah?"

"Yes, but in mine you pee on me."

"We don't have an orchard, but we do have a shower."

Monday, March 3, 2014, 12:57 a.m.

Our sidewalk kiss is worth its weight in words.

"I have to go now."

"I wish you'd stay."

"I will always carry you with me John. Wherever I go and whatever I do, you will hold a place in my heart."

"As will you Trisha, in mine."

"I dream I see you again, somewhere far from here."

"Maybe someday."

"Yes John. Someday."

With one last bittersweet embrace, she slips away, tears welling as her outline wanes.

Turning around in resignation, I find myself facing Anna's pint-sized pique.

"So *this* why you tired for me!" Anna exclaims, pelting me with her purse, impassioned from such palpable peer approval of her paramour. "It not enough for you to have me every morning and night! You have to have her in between *too?*"

Have I not exceeded expectation? Shouldn't our own duplicitous pairing provide me a pass to pound other poon, an unspoken double standard that's simply part of the package in loving such a legend as my superlative self? "What did you ex*pect?*"

Expect is the spouse of assume. Their children, aspect and exhume, are disappointments. Aspect can only analyze a piece of the picture. Exhume is always digging through yesterday's dirt. The whole family is a dysfunctional mess if you ask me.

"What I expect? You are my *boyfriend!* I expect you not *cheat!*"

"And how the fuck do you think *we* got together?"

"But that different."

"*How?* Because it was with *you* it was okay? How the hell is *that* different?"

I can all but hear her hamster wheel redlining under the load. "Because… because it feel real between us, like true love."

Amazing abilities that bugger has. We've reached that timeless tiff where a lad's logic and a female's forgery of it compete to put their partner in their place (or subconsciously, for the female, to prove her paramour hardened to her histrionics, and therefore worthy of her warmth). "True love? Are you *shitting* me? All I am is trophy white meat to you. You don't love *me.* You love what I repre*sent.* You love that everyone wants me, that all the girls stare at me but you get to take me home. You knew what you were getting when you opened your greedy little gash and wrested me from Rain."

Too much too fast. The overwrought rodent whirled off its wheel and knocked its noggin. *"Please* John," she cries, sobbing inconsolably. "Don't *be* like this."

"Like *what? Honest?* I can't take your begging. I can't take your fucking emotions right now."

"John... I..."

"WHAT!?"

"Can I come up?" she enquires, her hamster wearily remounting its wheel.

"No! You *can't* come up! Go *home!* Go *drink!* Go find another sorry soul and surrender your sadness to the their body's embrace! Just *don't* come *up!*"

"But I leave some things in room."

Of course she did. It's instinctive for a strumpet to lay reminders around her paramour's place, both to bring her to mind, to tell trespassing trollops he's taken, and as a last ditch to land him alone should he leave her, one whack to weaponize her woe to receive cockular consolation and a few more months of his misery. "Oh, fine, whatever," I grumble. "But you can't stay."

In solemn silence we slink through the fluorescent flicker to room 113, where our flame flowered only to expire in its infancy. Quick as the door closes she casts herself upon me, coating me in kisses to relight our love.

"What are you *doing?*" I shout, shaking free from her frenzy.

"We have fight, now we make up."

My jaw drops like a lead weight. "You saw me kissing another girl, and you *still* want to kiss me?"

"But that not mean anything."

"It was *us* that didn't mean anything," I declare, delivering the doozy with a double dollop of indifference.

"You mean it," she mumbles, her hamster finally defeated.

"Yeah."

"Maybe I go then."

"That would be best."

In a deadened daze she collects her clothes and assorted sundries, saying not a word the while. "Goodbye John," she says, turning toward me in the doorway, a lone tear tumbling to land on her lip, a pearl depicting the petal I'd plucked from her feminine flower, a salty symbol of the sweetness an unwed lassie loses a tittle at a time with every affair until the carousel casts her away at the wall, coldhearted and clutching a clowder of cats with what's left of her love.

"Goodbye Anna," I reply, watching her turn away to hide her weeping, leaving my life in a sniffly-snuffly pitter-patter of dream-shattered despair.

12:21 p.m.

"Good afternoon Miguel."

"Good afternoon John. What you do with your pack? You are moving hotels today? You know it is Monday. You have day off. What you do here so early?"

"I... I need to talk to you."

"Is not drugs I hope?" he asks, eyeing me oddly. "You not look so good John. Look like you spend all night snorting coke off whore's ass."

"It's not drugs."

"Ah, good, it is woman, no? You sleep with wrong man's wife and now you need protection? I know people can maybe help. Are you thinking more *reactive* or *proactive* approach?"

"It's not that."

"Good! So what is problem? You are my star John! Talk to me. Maybe is money? I can probably help with that too. How you feel about older women?"

"I'm leaving Davao."

"You *leave*? Where you *go*?"

"Home."

"Why you go home? What is so good about home? I thought you run away from home?"

"I... I dunno. I just need to go," I sigh.

"If you are unhappy here John, I understand," he sympathizes, patting my shoulder paternally. "But maybe we can figure out how to make you happy?"

"I don't think I can be here. Not anymore."

"Is because Trisha is gone, da? You want me find pretty new keyboard

197

player to replace her? You want girl with big tits, I find you. Small tits, I find you. Ladyboy, I find you. Hermaphrodite maybe little harder to find, but I try for you. Whatever my star wants."

"Sounds nice," I sigh. "But I'm over it."

"You take big bites of life John. Maybe you bite too much? Maybe you just need to slow down?"

"Exactly. Away from all this."

"Maybe you just need new girl? This is no problem John! Is like shooting titties in a barrel. Hey, I have idea to solve your money problems and girl problems! We sell raffle tickets for date with you."

"Ugh."

"No? Of course, we only let pretty girls buy tickets. You want we rig it so your favorite girl get date with you. That way everybody wins, da? Except maybe the girls that don't."

"I couldn't do that with Anna watching."

"Oh... Anna. You tell her you leave?"

"I broke up with her last night."

"Ah! So *this* is problem. You want me fire her?"

"*Fire* her?"

"Yes, if it is hard to look at her while you sing then I fire her."

"No. She needs the job more than me."

"Maybe so John, but that not how business works. She easy replace, but you not so much."

"I'm going. I'm sorry Miguel."

Setting aside his persona to appraise me, he can tell I'm as tattered as a bar floozy's beer koozie. "I see in your face you mean it."

"I do."

"When you go?"

"I fly to Manila this afternoon. Tomorrow home."

"We need drink John. Is sad day for club."

As I stare at the wall letting my eyes lose focus he hurries upstairs, returning with two tumblers and a bottle of scotch old enough to sip itself.

"I buy duty free on business trip," he says, answering the unspoken question mark on my mug. "Save for special occasions like bribing officials to ignore a certain singer's lack of work permit. You like scotch?"

"It has its charm."

He pours three fingers in each, giving me my glass and raising his for a toast. "A cheers to my star. He will be missed."

Scotch is thinking man's whiskey. An oxymoron obviously, as whiskey's wont is to return men to their native tongue of expletives and fisticuffs. The firewater's confusion comes from the nuanced notes of swamp monster sweat that make it the quintessence of acquired taste, the holy grail a gourmand spends a lifetime learning to love. Unlike lesser libations meant merely for making merry or numbing the ennui of existence, the purpose of this potion is to parade one's pretensions through the parlance of its palate, an aim at odds with a proper plastering.

"I'm glad you're not mad."

"Why I be mad?"

"Because I didn't give you notice."

"Notice?"

"Two weeks to find someone new."

"Does death give two weeks John?"

"No."

"Does wife give two weeks before fuck other man?"

"No."

"So don't worry! You are no worse than death or cheating wife."

"Uh, thanks?"

"I kid you John. Cheers."

"Cheers." touching tumblers, we savor a sip and a moment of remembrance. "Can I ask you something Miguel?"

"Of course John."

"Why do you speak English with a Russian accent?"

Consulting a skosh of scotch, his eyes turn upwards as he mines the mists of memory. "When I was younger I had Russian associate. Good guy Petrov. He work on the, uh… security side of things. Was too bad what happened to him."

"What happened?" I ask, cocking an eyebrow in curiosity.

"Is very dark. You don't want to know."

"You've got me curious."

"He take business trip to Thailand to acquire… some things. Was always ladies' man, Petrov, very smooth and mysterious, but he come back from this trip shaken all the way to his, uh… mojo. After that I never see him sober again. Not once. He still ladies' man when he can stand, but now when he talk to a girl he squeeze her crotch before get her alone. You'd be surprised how many girls not like that." Miguel pauses, sips.

"So he got arrested?"

"No."

"Beaten to death?"

"No… one day he grab wrong girl. Her brother, he tattoo artist. He act friendly to Petrov, buying him drinks and being very buddy-buddy. When Petrov pass out in corner he take him to tattoo parlor. He wake up taped to chair, needle making smiley face on his, uh… little man. When I see him next day his face, his neck, his arms all covered in tattoos of cocks and balls. Was very sad. That was last time I saw him. I think after that he finally crawl through bottle to other side."

9:03 p.m.

"What a dump mate," Luke states, showcasing his country's superior capacity for social commentary.

"I dunno," I shrug, surveying the drinkers, diners and doxies dolled up to be dicked for a couple dollars, the entrepreneurial nippers waving their wares in the faces of foreigners, the technicolor tide of tricycles dragging down Adriatico. "It has a beauty to it."

"Maybe I need more of these to see it," he replies, swigging his Red Horse. "What the-"

"What is it?"

"Under the table mate. I think the pork got out of the kitchen."

A pint-sized puss pleading for a pittance.

"The cycle of life," I muse, picking a piece of pork off my plate and tossing it to the teensy tramp.

10:34 p.m.

Dad: **Well son, it sounds like you're perched on a precipice preparing to plummet into the unknown, or rather, back to the known, which can be just as mysterious. That's great. Remember how I left that commune in the Sierra Nevada? Well, the Vietnam war was still going, so I was still on the lamb. A friend of mine had given me directions to a commune in the redwoods where I could hide out until the agent orange blew over and the napalm settled. (That these chemicals make very poor fertilizers is perhaps one of the most shameful legacies of that war for America.) After a few days of hitchhiking and a few close calls, I was welcomed there with open arms and open... let's just say that the girls were very hospitable. You see son, you gotta understand that this was during those delightful years around the summer of love, a magical moment in time when love's electricity flowed freely from man to woman, and not so much back and forth as round and round and multiplying in the process. Now, I emphasize flowed freely because the queermosexual cancer of Aids had not yet made condoms so common. Now, if you think condoms were created to stop the spread of VD, then I dare say you've been deceived. No son, the purpose of condoms is to stop the electrical loop of love that flows from man to woman to be grounded into the Earth and given back to man as he sows and harvests its soils, leaving him in a state of spiritual constipation. The sexual revolution was not a denial of love, but an embracing of it, a building bubbling buzzing worldwide worship of the one in the all and the all in the one. Now, just as I was proactively recovering from my disengagement, I was also back to work, making my model 2.0, if you will, the composting log cabin** shithouse. I discovered that by notching the logs like Lincoln logs you could stack and restack them to your heart's content. These shithouses were designed to be moved every couple of years, leaving behind one of the best manure piles on God's green earth. There's just one little thing you gotta understand though, the log cabin composting shithouse is a lot like life, in that you get out of it what you put in. If you think you can give it the poorly digested remnants of the average American diet (emphasis on the die and not the T, as the American diet is conducive neither to longevity nor testosterone production) and still end up with an organic gardener's wet dream, you'll be sorely mistaken. We had the good stuff though, boy did we! When we fertilized the soil with our first batch those vegetables went gangbusters. I've been sort of thinking about this trip you've embarked upon as your own proverbial log cabin composting shithouse of the soul. You won't know what you're fermenting until you pick up and move your logs, which is what going home is, in your case. Only with a new perspective, or in your case old perspective reexamined, will you be able to look back at the mulch you've left upon your mind. I've got a feeling it's gonna be pretty good stuff.

Me: Interesting analogy. Hopping on a flight tomorrow. See you soon.

Annetta: Oh John, that must be the most romantic thing you've ever told me. But then, that's not saying much. Let me know when your sleigh touches down at Sea-Tac. I might be able to pick you up.

Me: I'll be in Tuesday night. Should be through customs by 7:00 PM. Can you make it?

Tuesday, March 4, 2014, 3:45 p.m.

There is a time out of time in a place out of place, where a fluorescent flicker razzles circadian rhythms and melts the mind into globs of gravy.

Business travelers and vacationers stressing out about relaxing will divide layovers into three concurrent times, all wrong:

1. Time where they came from. (Showing a perverse preoccupation with the past.)

2. Time at the airport. (The layover is limbo and does not deserve its own hour. Having tugged a time for you out of the ether, I have only included it to mollify my editor, whose anal-compulsive fetish for consistency has been tested to the limits by the plasticity of my prose.)

3. Time where they're going. (Showing excessive fretting over the future.)

The proper way to divide layover time is as follows:

1. Beer time.

2. Boarding time.

Between beers, I take advantage of a free internet cafe.

Annetta: **Done. I switched shifts just for you, so you owe me sexual favors LOL. Although I might make you double up on condoms now that you have tropical super syphilis. Get some sleep on the flight. I'm gonna need a ride for that ride...**

Me: **See you tonight, or tomorrow, or whenever the hell it is. This international date line is confusing. I fly out Tuesday night (a few hours from now), going the opposite direction of the sun, arriving in Seattle earlier Tuesday night than I leave Taipei, so I guess that'll make me a time traveler. But don't you worry doll, for their isn't enough circadian confusion in this wide old world to take the dip from my dipstick. See you soon.**

I guess I should message my brother River: **Gonna be back in town Tuesday night. Can I crash at your place?**

24

The Wanderer's Woes

7:02 p.m.

Our lips lock as if our paths had never parted, as if my trek were torn from the river of time like an oxbow lake, taping departure to return.

"How was your trip?"

"Good."

"Just *good?*" she goads, starting her steel steed with a lusty leer.

"Mostly good," I mumble, my gift for gab halved by a headache I picked up on the plane. "Just a lot to process I guess."

"You could give it to me raw, if you want."

"I *do* want."

"You know what I *meant!*" she squeals, awarding me a playful punch for my perversity.

"I know what you *think* you meant."

"Aw, it's cute. You're afraid I won't sleep with you now that you have tropical super syphilis."

"Eh," I shrug.

"Jeez John, where's your witty comeback?"

"In my pants."

"I wouldn't call his spitting witty, unless that's a euphemism for infectious. Thirsty?"

"Parched."

"I bet I have some water back here somewhere…" she says, turning around to forage the floor.

"Whoa! Watch the road there lady!"

"So! You gonna tell me some stories?" she asks, correcting her course as she hands me a quart.

"What sort of stories? I wouldn't want to distract you from driving."

"I dunno. Your broken engagement sounds like a good story. The band sounds like a good story. Whatever you want to tell me."

"Roses are red. Violets are blue. I have two lips. I'd like to plant my bulbs in you."

"That was a poem."

"I wrote it just for you."

"Come on John, give up the goods."

"Alright," I grumble, recounting my quest as candidly as I can without a condom cutting the electric loop of love between the two of us and Terra.

9:43 p.m.

"You sure you're okay?"

"I'm fine."

"You don't usually have trouble going twice. Oooooh! Maybe you picked up an exotic tropical disease!"

Oh shit.

"What's up?" she asks, reading the fear on my face. "You *did* get vaccinated, *didn't* you?"

"Um."

"Like, as a *child?*"

"My parents are hippies."

"Before your trip?"

"When? You saw how quickly I left."

"Oh, right."

"I ate dirt as a child. That count?"

"Probably against food poisoning. You get food poisoning over there?"

"Not once."

"There you go. But no vaccines? *Ever?*"

"I got a tetanus shot once."

"Oh… you had a good run at least. It's been a blast knowing you. I bet you're tired. Where you wanna go? Hospice?"

"Worried I'm contagious?" I ask, giving her the ghost of a grin.

"Nah, but I got my shots," she says, slapping the inside of her elbow for emphasis.

"Good for you."

"Don't look so *worried!*"

"I'm not worried."

"John, your face is playing teeter totter with terror. What's up?"

"Nothing," I grumble. "Just a long flight."

"Come on John, I *know* you. Something's up."

"Just been through a lot lately."

"So you made a couple girls incapable of ever loving again. So what?"

"You put it so nicely."

"So where you want to go?" she asks, slipping me a sly smile. "We could go back to *my* place."

"You moved out?"

"*Finally.*"

"So why'd we do it in the car?"

"Well, we can't have *sex* there with my roommates in the other room, but it looks like you're not up for that anyway. Let's get food first. I'm famished."

10:32 p.m.

"Tuna melt," the waitress states, placing Annetta's plate. "Mother and child," she snarks, smirking at her smartness as she sets my meal before me, unashamedly showing off the sort of technicolor tattoo sleeve that advertises all orifices open to Mr. Right Now. I don't mention that the smirk, manly mug that it makes, does not give the same glory to her once feminine face.

"Is it wrong to put a fried egg on a chicken sandwich?" I ask Annetta.

She shrugs. "Since when did you care about right and wrong?"

"I've always cared."

"Since when?"

"Always. My morals are just more flexible than most people's."

"*Flex*ible?"

"Yeah, morals are like bodies, they need to be stretched so they don't get stiff."

"Maybe you're just projecting your mother-daughter fantasy onto your sandwich."

"Speaking of which, what's your mom doing tonight?"

"*Gross!*"

"So did you learn to psychoanalyze like that at college?" I ask, captioning the question with a bite of my burger, finding it an insipid shadow of the meal in my memory.

"Is it okay? You look like you don't like it."

"I dunno, it tastes less flavorful than I remember."

"You've been in Asia John. You're probably totally addicted to MSG now."

"Yeah… maybe. You ever try a fertilized duck egg?" I enquire, causing the corpulent couple across the aisle to dart us dirty looks.

Annetta swallows, oddly aroused by my culinary courage. "That's popular over there?"

"Yeah."

"Just recently fertilized? Or…"

"Embryonic." Landing on a lull in the couple's conversation, the word finds their mouths slackening from milkshake straws as their faces pale, as if having heart attacks whilst sucking pencil shaped penises.

Wednesday, March 5, 2014, 5:44 p.m.

"Well if it isn't my homeless brother," River says, offering me a hand shattering shake, a declaration of dominance from a brother whose rebellion against the bohemian has led him to wed his worth to the manipulation of money, a pseudo jewery that jades him to the majesty of myself. "Come in."

"I'm back."

"I thought you'd be here yesterday."

"I crashed at a friend's place."

"You should have called."

"Oh... sorry."

"Hungry?"

"Yeah." Sort of. I should probably eat, but my stomach feels like a black market abortion performed on a man by mistake. I could probably swallow soup.

"How about we go out?"

"Sure."

"What the fuck's your shirt mean?"

It's a white T-shirt Rain bought me to honor my membership in the master race. "I dunno, it was from some Filipino mall parking lot daytime soap celebrity appearance. That," I say, pointing at a logo above the actor's face, "is the drug company that sponsored the event."

"How did you end up with the normal name?" River chuckles. "Though, as a Realtor River is a fantastic first name, conjures peaceful pictures of cozy cottages by babbling brooks, so I can't complain. But *you're* the weirdest one of us. Where they get off naming you John?"

"Maybe dad forgot to get stoned that day."

"I don't think that's something dad forgets."

7:58 p.m.

The cliché that the worst culture shock occurs upon homecoming carries a trifle of truth, but it misses the mark. It's not shock that rattles the rambler when returning to native turf, but a failure to relate his revelations to indoctrinated dolts, who reply to his parable with platitudes.

Touring hometown taverns to reconnect to his compatriots, he for the first time fathoms how far western floozies have fallen, having known naught but their nastiness til the time of his trip. Bantering with some bimbo on the barstool beside him, his quest is compared to her holiday in Hawaii, as if her week in the waves quaffing piña coladas and boffing beach bums she'll exclude from her cock count could in curiosity compare to his derring-do.

The codes of his own culture burden the backpacker, for the mental muscle that manages mores had barely been used abroad, as the natives had not oft impugned his faux pas, preferring him to present a caricature of his own countrymen over attempting to assimilate. Craving deeper connection than fleeting friendships with other foreigners, the wayfarer fell in love with a local, a dalliance doomed in its idealism to burn too bright to abide, a chip in the chimera leaving her pedestal in pieces, our drifter disillusioned.

Heading home heartbroken, the tramp feels, like an astronaut returning to terra firma, the crushing weight of his culture, and must appoint a professional to temper the transition.

At my entrance Jay removes a wedge of lime from his lips, tossing it in the trash and leaving his mouth slack. "Well holy shit, look who the cat dragged in. When did you get back?"

"Last night."

"What the hell brought you home? Last pictures I saw some cutie was hanging off you smiling like she wanted to whiten Asia with your wee ones. Running away from the wedding, or just run out of money?"

"Neither."

"Then what the hell? You know what to expect here," he chuckles. "You miss nagging? Is that it? Did being treated so well make you suspicious?"

"Just got burnt out."

"Have a close call with a ladyboy or something?" Ed asks, turning from the TV.

"Nope. All anatomical tests came back negative for nuts."

"Well, you can't be too sure. I'm told the surgeries are pretty convincing these days. You see much of that measles outbreak over there?"

"Um… measles outbreak?"

"You've gotten your shots, right?" Jay asks.

"Uh."

"Well?"

"No."

"Aw, come on John, *really?*"

"That's it," Ed chides. "Bleach down the bar."

"Whatever. Who gets measles anymore anyway?"

"*You* maybe."

"I feel okay," I lie, my bowels burbling in disagreement with the declaration.

"You need some whiskey?" Jay asks. "That should kill anything you brought back."

"Never heard of that remedy," Ed says.

"Sure, old family remedy. Mom gave us hot toddies when we were sick. Puts your white blood cells in the fighting spirit. Have a Makers on me bud. It's good to have you back."

"I remember having the measles," Ed recollects, a note of nostalgia foretelling a tall tale. "It wasn't so bad as everyone makes it out, as I recall. I was in the third grade when the neighbor kids came down with it, and my mom thought we were at a good age to get it over with, so she went and invited little Chuck to come spit in our breakfast cereal. We didn't get to leave that table until we'd slurped every last drop of milk. Chuck got to stay and watch too. I think it was mom's way of punishing us for the wedgies we'd give him. That was how we got the chicken pox too, come to think of it. Let's see… it was like a bad flu with a full body rash. Hmm." His eyes turn upwards as he strokes his stubble, clearing cranial cobwebs and boosting his bullshit mill to max. "There were other symptoms that gave it its own unique feel, like diarrhea. That got real bad after the rash showed up. By the time it was over I'd thrown away a dozen pairs of underwear. I had a nasty dry cough, wracking spasms like a lung cancer patient on a smoke break. That was the worst at the end. The strangest symptom of all was that food lost it's flavor. It was like I was tasting in black and white."

"That's not strange," Jay says. "They hadn't yet brought color to flavors when you were a kid. How's the whiskey John? Still taste brown? Or is it more of a gray flavor?"

"Um... brown," I reply, sensing intestinal trouble.

"You sure?"

"Yeah," I say, clenching my cheeks as I slip from my stool. "Back in a minute."

To make it crystal clear how dire this dash is, in the pecking order of places I'd put my posterior, The Flipper's facilities are between a pride parade porta potty and a leper colony Sani-Can.

"You sure you're alright?" Ed asks at my return. "That was too long for a piss. No offense Jay, but I'd sprint home sooner than I'd sit my ass on that toilet."

"Me too," Jay agrees.

"I'm fine," I reply. "Besides, wouldn't I have a rash?"

"Nah," Ed dismisses. "That doesn't show up til halfway through. How long've you been feeling symptoms?"

"Who said I was feeling symptoms?"

"Suit yourself. Denial won't prepare you for what's coming. If I were you I'd be stock piling chicken soup and toilet paper. I'd be on the couch with a couple dozen movies ready to ride out the storm."

Oh God.

"Aww come on," Jay says. "You're scaring him. He's probably just jet lagged."

"Jet lag don't cause the shits," Ed says.

"So he ate some spoiled dog meat before flying home, so what? He'll be alright. Whiskey kills parasites."

Imagining myself not so lucky next time as to make it to the men's room, I down my drink and stand up. "I'm off," I croak.

"Not sticking around for karaoke?" Jay enquires.

"No."

"Stock up on chicken soup," Ed advises.

25

Patient Zero

Saturday, March 8, 2014, 10:31 a.m.

The days drag on in a delirium of hot toddies and toilet dashes.

"You need to see a doctor," River declares, eyeing me as if I were cancer of his couch.

"I'm fine," I croak.

"You look like shit."

"Maybe you should compost me. That's what dad does with shit," I reply, mustering a memento of my signature smirk to mend the mood.

"Christ, I don't know how you can find humor in this."

"There's humor in everything River, if you look with the right lens." (At the risk of reiterating what you likely wisened at once, you must understand that in rebellion for being raised on the fruits of his family's feces, my big brother is unbemused by the humor in life's hardships.)

"Yeah? And I suppose the rash on your forehead is funny too?"

"Funny looking." Cough.

"Jesus Christ John! It's like your deviance grew too big for your brain and found itself on your face. What the fuck did you bring back?"

"Measles maybe. That's my working hypothesis."

"Who the hell gets the measles anymore? And how do you know enough to even *guess* that?"

"There-" A dry cough convulses me. "There's an outbreak-" Cough. "Over there."

"In the Philippines?"

"So I hear."

"Fuuuuck," he exclaims, tugging his jelled back hair into horns.

"Straight laced guy like you must have got your shots, right?"

"Uh… shots…" he mumbles, turning white as a Klan wedding. "Mom and dad were against those, huh?"

"Yeah."

"Then no."

"Shit… I'm sorry-" Cough. "On the bright side, by the time you get sick I'll be better, so I'll be able to bring you Gatorade and pho and stuff."

"Fuuuuuuuuuck!"

"Don't worry-" Cough. "It's not that bad."

"FUUUUUUUUUCK!"

"Can we pause this conversation?" Cough. "I'm about to shit myself."

Sunday, March 9, 2014, 3:37 p.m.

We've reached an impasse.

"I'm taking you to the hospital," River states, impatiently pacing the wood floor in front of me.

"Why?"

"Why? *WHY!?* Have you *looked* at yourself lately?"

"I'm a bit red."

"A BIT RED?" he roars. "You look like you bathed in poison oak!"

Cough. "No need to be dramatic."

"Oh! *I'm* being *dramatic!* Calmly declared by the unemployed alcoholic casually dying on my designer couch. *I'm* being *dramatic.*"

"I'll be alright." Cough.

"I want to hear that from a doctor."

"What the hell can *they* do?" Cough. "Inform me I'm in fact a carrier of contagion? Tell me to drink lots of liquids and send me a big bill?"

"You need to get *tested!*" he fumes, flailing his fists to punctuate the point, looking like Hitler rehearsing for a rally in his living room. "The community needs to know if they've been e*xposed! I* need to know if *I've* been exposed!"

Monday, March 10, 2014, 2:14 p.m.

Suckered by the Satanic faith of feminism into the cold bosom of bureaucracy, the harpy from the health department appears to have popped from one of those demographically diverse job fair employment pamphlets full of fresh young faces assuming ivory smiles to sell themselves their own slavery. Sans synthetic smile, she sits across the table with pen and paper prepared to neuter my narrative, professional propriety so impenetrable that Casanova reincarnate could not breach her barrier with a bottle of bubbly, a bouquet of roses, and a loaner boner from Ron Jeremy.

"When did you first feel symptoms?"

I am not being hyperbolic when I call this an inquisition.

"Tuesday afternoon," I reply, watching her inscribe my answer with the forced formality females affect when role-playing as professionals.

"What time?"

"I couldn't tell you exactly. I was in a plane over the Pacific." Cough. "It was four or five hours before I landed at Sea-Tac."

"And when were you at Sea-Tac?"

"6:30 to 7:00 p.m." Cough.

"Can you give me the flight number?"

"Uh, yeah, I've got the boarding pass somewhere," I say, getting up to grab it.

"I just need it before I leave. How did you get home from the airport?"

"My friend Annetta picked me up."

"Does she know you have the measles?"

"Yeah."

"Do you know if she's been vaccinated?"

"She has." Cough.

"Anywhere else you went in public on Tuesday?"

"I went to King Muhammad's Leaf, the diner."

"And when were you there?"

"A little after ten til a little before eleven."

"Where else have you gone in public while you've been sick?"

I muster all facts fit for print. The park with Annetta on Wednesday, then going to dinner with River and drinking at the Flipper. I furnish her the flight number and other potentially pertinent points, including Annetta's number. Being on a roll and Thursday having been dreadfully dull, as I couldn't manage much more than to stumble to the store for bourbon and broth, I accouter the account with a trek around town, hobnobbing with every hobo around. After that I cruised out to Evergreen State College, combing the campus for nuggets of knowledge that might have weathered the war between facts and feelings.

When given the chance to spend government money, one is wise not to waste it.

"This Wednesday should be your last contagious day, so Thursday you'll be free to go out in public again," she states, primly placing her files in a folder and tucking it into her messenger bag.

"Will this be on the news?"

"As a matter of public health, yes. Of course, neither your name nor your photo will be used."

Such uncanny control to her career cuntery. A lesser lad would bow before her withering womanhood, but I want to pop the cork on the carnal creature hiding behind her disagreeable demeanor.

"Could they?" Cough.

"Sorry?"

"I always wanted to be famous." Cough. "Could they use my name and photo if I signed a waiver?"

"They can't legally do that. It's for your own protection."

"That doesn't sound right. I don't think you can legally deny a man the right to his story. Could you look into it?"

"I doubt the answer would change."

Maybe a more direct tack might crack her prematurely shrewish shell, uncovering her camouflaged femininity or divulging her medusean depths. "Well that sucks. You wanna go on a date?"

"Ex*cuse* me?"

"A date." Cough. "Once I'm out of quarantine, of course."

Her mask holds. Amazing. "It would be unprofessional for me to accept a date with you."

"Suit yourself. I thought you might like the chance to go out with someone famous. Or soon to be anyway, if rather anonymously."

"I think I've got all I need John. Here's my card if you think of anything else."

Has this witch of a woman been so cuntified by college that she doesn't detect the majesty behind the measles? "Is this the number I should call for our date?"

"There is no date."

"There could be."

"Please don't call for that."

"You prefer sushi or steak?"

"Have a nice day John."

"You a vegetarian?" Cough. "It's not a deal breaker if you are. We'll just skip dinner and go straight to whiskey and bad decisions."

Saturday, March 15, 2014, 7:09 p.m.

"Well holy shit!" bellows bartender Jay, greeting me with a grin. "They let you out of quarantine?"

"Sure did."

"You're cleared for public places?"

"It only lasts a *week* Jay," Ed pipes in.

"Can't be too careful. They might fumigate us for harboring a biological terrorist. What'll you have?"

"Jim Beam."

"Neat?"

"Better make it a hot toddy."

"That was quite the list of places you frequented."

"Sorry about that."

"Are you *kidding?*" Jay asks, warming my glass with hot water. "We haven't gotten that much exposure since that junkie died on the toilet. We're gonna milk it for all it's worth. Did you see the specials?"

The marker board lists two specials. The 'Measles Boy': a hot toddy with Jim Beam and honey liquor instead of honey. The 'Patient Zero': A shot of equal parts Jose Cuervo and Jagermeister with a dash of Tabasco. "Huh," I reply, pondering the latter. "Interesting."

"Here bud, I made you a Measles Boy, on the house. Good to see you feeling healthy. Karaoke's not the same without you."

"Thanks."

"You seen the news?"

"About me? A bit. I'm kinda miffed they won't use my name."

"They're expecting cases to start popping up over the next few days. Up to a couple dozen here in Olympia, with all that running around you did. They think it might turn into a multi state thing too, with you being contagious at the airport."

"You ask me it's overblown," Ed declares. "When I was a kid measles would blow through town every once in a while, leaving a dusting of skin flakes so thick you'd think it was a Jeffrey Dahmer Christmas special, and nobody made a big deal out of it. Nowadays if you get it you make the news faster than a teacher sleeping with a twelve year old. Hardly seems fair to us old timers who suffered through it without a sensationalist media's sympathy."

"You didn't make the news for fucking your teachers?" Jay asks.

"Nope. It was don't ask, don't tell back then. Matter of fact, I had a buddy whose father was so worried he'd turn out queer that he paid his son's high school French teacher to give him private lessons in the language of love.

She'd come over twice a week with a bottle of bubbly and they'd go upstairs and close the drapes. Word never got around about *that*. My buddy didn't even let *me* know about it til after the statutory limitations kicked in, for her sake. What *did* get around was girly gossip about his tongue's new tricks." He leans in, as if to tell a tidbit too tantalizing for unauthorized ears. "Why, this one time he got caught under the bleachers by the custodian, Betty Lou splayed open to his lips like a wishbone. After that everyone called him muff diving Dave." At that Ed nods sagely and sips his suds.

"You don't see that kind of dedication to education anymore," Jay laments.

"You keep up with him?" I enquire.

"Well I did, til he died of throat cancer a few years back."

26

Faithfully Friends

Sunday, March 16, 2014, 7:29 p.m.

Girls, capricious creatures that they are, are only sentimental so long as their last lay with a lover was electric. Being the emotionally stronger sex, men are capable of conjuring the tiniest tenderness from the testiest trollop after love is long lost to the call of the carousel. Should you wish a wench to pine for your power as she flicks her flower, rather than cringing her minge at your memory, then you must leave the lass begging for more boner, doing this deed without apparent premeditation. Not all men are made so magnanimous, but we all ought to aim for it.

"You owe me," Annetta coos, a grin growing from muff to mouth.

"I owe you?"

"A ride from the airport is worth at least *two* lays John. I only got *one*. Plus, there's *interest* now."

"*Interest?*" You must understand that though I'm as eager as ever, my still delicate constitution concerns me. I don't dare deliver the least bit less than the dicking she's been dreaming of, lest her memory be marred.

"There's no panties under this dress."

'Was a strawberry...'

Muddled by the mental mix of father eating fruit from a fanny and myself doing the same from Annetta's nani, my flag hangs at half mast, my jaw slack.

"You okay John?"

"Yeah, I was just thinking of strawberries."

"Is that a euphemism?"

"No."

"Oh, I thought maybe that was what you called a girls…"

"Hoohoo?"

"I was thinking tatas, actually," she coos, craning forward to force her pair upon me, breath hot and heavy but an inch from my ear. "You want dessert?" she whispers, the warmth of her words going straight to my stiffy.

"Dessert?" I parrot, still fantasizing of fruit in inappropriate places. "What's for dessert?"

"*Me* dummy. Would you give her a kiss?"

"A kiss?"

"Mm hmm. *Interest,* John, *interest.*"

Tuesday, March 18, 2014, 7:46 p.m.

"You see the latest?" Jay asks, removing a rack of glassware from the wash.

"Maybe. What's the latest?"

He pauses before putting the washed glasses away, giving a proud grin. "You've started a nationwide outbreak."

"Nationwide?" I parrot, trying to taste the word's weight but failing to feel it.

"Yeah, there's half a dozen cases around the country traced to yours, not to forget the dozen here in Washington, half of which are in Olympia. Looks like our karaoke star's finally making the big time."

For several breaths my heart beats with the giddies of greatness, til it occurs I'm an unaccredited poster boy for the breakdown of natural immunity by medicine, a case for the cocktails of chemicals that mediocratize the masses by leaving the weak once weeded instead languishing in half lives of drug

221

dependent debility until succumbing to cancerbetes, all part of the plan to supplant belief in a higher being with submission to Science, a dogma designed by Luciferian elites to glue shut the God-shaped holes in our hearts, undermining the codes of western culture by praising the perversions that prevent us from pair bonding, bringing down birthrates as the march of machinery makes our masters more than mere mortals and the rest of us no longer necessary for their lengthening lives of luxury. "Except those CDC fuckers won't let those media fuckers use my name."

"You can't get everything," Jay shrugs.

"But how'm I gonna get a movie deal if no one knows my name? I can sit down at a bar and watch a news story about the outbreak, but the person on the stool next to me will never know it's my fault. How'm I gonna get any publicititty?"

"Pub*licititty?*" Jay asks, turning up an eyebrow.

"You know, when fame gets you laid."

"Oh, I thought you tripped over a syllable."

"If you ask me fame is passed out too frivolously these days," Ed remarks. "When I was young, you wanted to be famous you had to be *good* at something, had to *merit* your fame, had to put in blood, sweat, doobies and acid for it. Now all it takes is a spot on a reality TV show, and from then on your life is talk shows and tabloids. Is that what you want? Fame for fame's sake? No pride in paying your dues?"

"I get drunk for the sake of it."

"Well that's different," Ed grumbles. "Inebriation, unlike fame, has its own inherent value."

"If it gets me laid, that's value right there. Besides, I suffered through eight days of misery, I figure that's dues enough."

"I suffered through those eight days too. All I got was invited over to watch cartoons with Betty Ann and her kid brother Buck."

"I wish I could help you John," Jay says. "But that lady from the health department told me not to give out your name."

"She did?"

"Sorry bud."

"It's alright."

"Maybe you should write a book."

"Yeah?"

"Yeah, people love that true confessional shit. You gotta come up with a good title though. Nobody judges anything by its content anymore." Jay sucks a lime wedge, peering prophetically past his patrons to my forthcoming fame. "How about 'Drink, Lay, Infect'."

Wednesday, March 19, 2014, 10:31 p.m.

Assuming society hasn't sissified him with soy or chemically castrated him with plastic particles, pubescence finds a boy god granted the gift of a lion's libido, a strength that stays with him long past his prime and even through the test of her talking. In contrast to our cocksurety, a trollop portrays her passions as capriciously compelled by heavenly hands and those 'feelings' she's so fond of blithering about. Yet when met with the majesty of a man like myself, a broad's libido becomes a runaway snowblow, her passion overpowering the very king who'd kindled it.

"I can't help feeling like I've violated the children," I remark, recalling a furtive fondling of budding breasts in this very vicinity as I pull my pants up. "These playground tubes should be places of innocent childhood discovery."

"This is a new side of you," Annetta murmurs. "I've never known you to worry about the mess your penis makes. The measles bring this out?"

"It brought out a lot of feelings Annetta. It was a terrible terrible time, full of long restless nights wondering what dastardly deeds I'd done to deserve such despair. Without your minge on my mind I might not have made it though the misery."

"That's sweet, I think. You hear something?"

"No."

"Shh."

Wafting in the wind come the cries of a crush richer in beauty than brains.

"Hey babe," the bonehead booms. "Let's swing. When's the last time you

223

swung on a swing?"

"It's been, like, for*ever* Joe," she coos, bewitched by his brawny imbecility.

"Let's go," I whisper. "I think they're gonna do it on the swing set."

"Let's stay."

"I didn't know you were such a voyeur."

"Listening to a couple swing?"

"*Now* they're swinging. Ten minutes all bets, and probably pants, are off."

"Not everyone's as dirty as you John."

"People don't go to parks at night just to swing."

"You hear something babe?" the clod enquires.

"No, what is it Joe?" the prom princess replies.

"I thought I heard something."

"Wow, really specific," I mutter. "Lets-"

"Shh," Annetta whispers, putting her pointer finger to my lips and trailing it to my tallywhacker. Pooh poohing my pleas for prudence, my lion springs to life.

"Now? With them-"

"Shh," Annetta repeats, pulling off my pants and saddling herself on my sword, the world washing away as our ecstasy echoes off the walls of our plastic womb.

"Oh my *God!*" the skirt squeals, returning me to terra firma. "Let's go. People are like, *literally* doing it in that tube."

"Damn, that was my idea babe."

"*What?*" Annetta asks. "How *else* were we supposed to get rid of them?"

11:12 p.m.

"Mmmmm," Annetta murmurs. "I've never felt like this before."

"Like what?" I whisper, heart hammering with hope, an I love you too tucked under the tip of my tongue.

"So sexually open," she purrs.

"Yeah, that was something," I mumble, wishing her words could warm me, feeling the fool for holding hope in a harlot so committed to the carousel.

"I wouldn't have done that with anyone else."

"Yeah?"

"Mm hmm."

"If you're so comfortable, how come we never do it in your bed?"

"You know I don't feel comfortable with my roommates in the other room."

"But you feel comfortable with strangers hearing us fuck in a plastic tube?"

"That's different."

"How the hell is *that* different?"

"Because I don't *know* the strangers!" she cries. "I don't have to walk out to pee and see them looking at me like they know what I just did! I wish you'd just *accept* that!"

"I don't get it," I groan.

"Please don't try to understand it," she pleads. "What we just did was a big step for me."

Wednesday, April 14, 2014, 8:03 p.m.

"I'm glad my roommates are gone," Annetta murmurs, her nose nestled into the nook of my neck, her free hand's fingers figure eighting around my rib cage.

"It's novel doing it in a bed for once."

She bends her head back to behold me, her Persian tan purple under the light of her lava lamp. "You know you like the places we go."

"In a thrillingly compromising sort of way."

"There's just something about you."

"That makes you want to be arrested for public indecency?"

Her fingers frolic from my chest to my chub, middle and index fingers miming a march. "When I'm with you, I feel like our bodies are treasure maps."

"Quests over," I quip, giving her pooper a pinch. "I found the booty."

"Goof."

"You're the one who got the goof off."

"John?"

"Yeah?"

"Why'd you come home so suddenly? You had all your vices at your fingertips."

"My fingers got bored."

"Come on John, I'm serious."

"It was so easy over there," I sigh. "Everybody wanted to be my lover, but I never really connected with them. I couldn't tell if they wanted me for me, or for a taste of America, so I left." Or more accurately, I came home when the one cutie who kenned me moved to America, but I don't bother bringing that up, as Annetta prides herself on her perception, and now is too tender a time to give her competition.

"*I* like you for you," she purrs, nuzzling sleepily into my side. "Even if you are the most depraved person I know. I thought maybe you missed me."

"I did miss you."

"Good. I missed you."

Warming in her words, a pregnant pause finds me slipping towards sleep. "I love you," I mumble.

"I love you too," she lilts.

The weight of what we'd whispered wakes me from the woozy cusp of unconsciousness, stirring my stomach into a flurry of flutters, my heart a hammer of hooves, my tongue trembling to make her mine. "Be mine," I beg.

The softness of her surrender turns into tension, and I wise before she words it I'd made a mistake. "I can't."

My tummy is a flock of monarch butterflies dying in a Monsanto corn field. "Why not?"

"I don't know *how* to be," she bemoans. "There are too many expec*tations*. Too many unspoken *rules*. It's *terrifying*."

"We're together all the time anyway," I plead.

"But fidelity's not your strong point."

"It could be."

"Let's not ruin this with commitments."

"How do you know it wouldn't perfect it?"

"Only free things are perfect John. If we commit, then we put a price on our passion. You want to put a price on something priceless?"

"I just want *you*," I whine, feeling defenseless for having held out my heart.

"You have me here right now. Isn't that *enough?* Isn't that what *matters?*"

"No," I grumble, getting up to go. "It's *not*."

"What are you doing?"

"I'm leaving."

"Stay," she pleads, reaching out an arm to tug me back towards the bed.

"I need a drink," I declare, pushing away her paw, feeling too fully the helplessness of holding the larger love, the love a lass instinctively understands should be held by her, but is too overwhelmed with options for the possibility of something better not to harry her hamster. Had I really thought I could thwart the tug of Satan's tide? Had I assumed I could save her flower from falling petal by petal as she flits from peter to peter, propelled by propaganda towards the false empowerment of promiscuity?

"I have cider in the fridge."

"At the bar," I assert, pulling up my boxers, forevermore leaving our love to the mists of memory. "I need company as degenerate as my own."

"Please," she pleads. "Just because we're not together doesn't mean I'm not yours tonight."

"It does now."

8:46 p.m.

Not all who are lost are wandering.

"You look down," Jay observes. "You feeling guilty or something?"

"About the outbreak?"

"You got something *else* to feel guilty about?"

"Nah," I reply, looking longingly at the last drops of my drink, stirring it with my straw so the ice cubes clink. "It's all grown up now. It doesn't need me anymore."

"What is it, your *child?*" Jay chortles, head shaking at the sheer oddness of it all. "It's crazy man. I'd be feeling pretty special if I were you. Can you imagine how much the CDC has spent? Tens of millions of dollars! Over four hundred people now! And that's not including the cases in Canada or Mexico tied to yours. You're going international! You're famous!"

"So what?"

"So it's gotta make you feel pretty important."

"Not really," I reply, glaring at my glass. "What good is fame without fortune or recognition? It's like being an emperor without a harem."

"Sort of like a president."

"Something like that," I grumble. "Why do presidents always have ugly old wives? I want to see a president with a hot young trophy wife."

"For aesth*etics?*" Jay asks, furrowing his face to say he doesn't follow me. "What's it *matter?*"

"What's it *matter?*" I repeat, bunching my brows to say it ought to be obvious. "If a man can't bring beauty to his bedroom, how can he hope to uplift our great land? I mean, if you can't trust a man's penis, what part of him *can* you trust?"

"Oh I don't know," Jay counters, our faces now stuck in stalemate. "His *handshake?*"

"No way," I dismiss, shaking my head. "A handshake is just a polite surrogate. Why do you think we trust firm ones?"

Jay's face falls over several seconds into the sort of deep disgust only time can treat. "You just ruined handshakes for me John."

"Sorry," I shrug.

"My girlfriend's a cute little thing," Jay muses, having apparently made peace with a whole life of handshakes. "Maybe *I* should run for president."

"Yeah? And what would your platform be?"

"Daddy issues," Jay replies, giving his grandest grin. "I'd reach out to the good people of this great nation and give their daddy issues a *niiiice* little rump squeeze. They'd fill out their ballots with butterflies."

"That's *it?*"

"*Every*body's got daddy issues."

11:33 p.m.

What cruel fortune that finds me fallen so far from king of The Club, the euphoria of my fans replaced with the perfunctory applause of these fragile flowers who quaff from Pabst cans while communicating in eye rolls and virtue signals. In a ritual of repentance for the collective crimes of the evil white ancestors whose rapaciousness made possible their Darwinian dead end, they scar their skin with tacky tattoos, puncturing it with piercings that plink like wind chimes when they walk, hacking their hair til they look like post-traumatic pigeons, as if aspiring to an independent poverty their parents could not provide.

I can blame nobody but myself for my suffering. What kind of bonehead leaves behind the blooming beauty of foreign floozies gagging to gobble their first white willy for the world weary wilt of western witches?

Belly burbling with brashness, I stop at the stage's edge, turning around to retake the microphone. "Don't you hipster fucks know who I am?" I castigate the crowd of cucks and cunts. "I'm Goddamned patient zero! I'm one of the most famous fuckers in this country right now and nobody knows my Goddamned name! I don't go out of my way to be unique. I *drip* unique. I have more unique in my left nut than all of you pasty pissants combined. I'm a hard-drinking, hard-living, hard-fucking force of Goddamned nature! I doubt the lot of you has two original thoughts to rub together."

As silent as a DDT spring. Tough crowd.

Exit stage left?

I slam my whiskey and slink out into the alley. I shouldn't have left the Philippines. I shouldn't have begged Annetta to be mine. I should have learned to play guitar instead of wasting so much time in karaoke bars. I shouldn't have lived so long with Sarah. I shouldn't have said that in there. I-

27

Time Turns

Monday, April 6, 2015, 8:09 a.m.

"Feeling up to working today son?" dad asks, turning his head to the side to assess me, somehow staying between the lines without looking.

"Of course."

"Your legs are alright?"

"Yeah, they're fine. I'll let you know if they're not."

"Feel free to take a break whenever you need to son. It's a helluva thing what those fellas did to ya in that alley, sucker punching you and breaking your legs while you were unconscious. I guess that guy was sore about you getting him sick, so he went and confused results with intentions, as if you'd come home *wanting* to give him measles. It's an unfortunate fact of life that you'll meet many people who think small, folks who think good and evil fit in tidy little boxes. I tell ya son, these are the people to watch out for. Don't get me wrong, you should love all of God's creatures, and do your best to help those in need, but that doesn't mean you have to trust them unconditionally. It was this small, black and white thinking that nearly ruined us when you were a teenager. They didn't see the healthiest, most prized vegetable patch in Thurston County. No sirree! You see son, someone had connected the dots between my log cabin composting crappers and our perennially prized produce patch. That USDA inspector had a serious medical condition son, a stick so far up his ass it gave him a lump in his throat. His eyes were too shaded by fear and hatred to see the cycle of life. He couldn't see the red in the tomatoes or the green in the broccoli, no sir! He only saw the black of evil, as if the Devil himself had planted that produce patch. You see son, that sorry soul had failed to fathom the potential of poop. You give poop time and it transcends its stinky start to become one of the world's finest fertilizers. The inspector only saw poop, as if we'd been out there with our pants down, shitting on the shallots and wiping up with the watercress.

"Now, traumatic experiences bear striking similarities of potential to poop. The foolish lock up that experiential fecal matter in airtight mind boxes, so it won't infect the rest of their head. As their mind becomes stuffed with these boxes, their supposedly safe thoughts have less and less room to pass by without jostling them, until pretty soon they're one cranial quake away from a mental shit tsunami. This is where the term 'going postal' comes from son. You see, thinking in boxes is a job hazard in the postal profession, but the analogy applies to any mass murder, as they're all precipitated by a cranial quake, cerebral shit storm. A wise man sees his emotional shit for what it is, throwing it on a mental compost pile. In time, that experiential poop produces topsoil, from which the richest mind flora may flourish.

"Now, I've got a sneaking suspicion that the men who beat you were not wise men. Remember that that has nothing to do with you. Their failure to transform life's lemons into lemonade is nobody's fault but their own. But you see, it's people who have trouble processing their own mind poop that fling it at others. I just hope you haven't boxed up the shit they flung at you. I hope you're raking it over that cranial compost pile of yours until your mind flora flourishes."

"I'm alright dad, just a bit of a limp."

"I'm sure you are son, and I know you're the sort to view this experience holistically." He pauses ponderously, pulling a joint from his jacket and a lighter from his left pant's pocket, almost cremating his mustache as he pulls his first puff, surrendering to serenity as he exhales a smoke ring. "You want some of this son? Might help with your legs."

"I'm alright dad. It's too early."

"You sure son? It's all organic, even the papers."

"I'm good."

"Well alright, just let me know if you change your mind. I find it to help with the creative process. You know, if it wasn't for the humble doobie I might not have had the inspiration to erect that first log cabin composting crapper." He pulls another puff, simultaneously staring at and through the road ahead, as if verging on a vision he's many times touched but never quite caught. "Say, did you hear about that Silicon valley CEO that died in a freak golden shower accident a couple months back?"

"I don't watch the news."

"Well, who can blame you? I don't either. Must've been strange to flip on the TV or open the newspaper and see yourself as the unnamed instigator of the country's most overblown panic. I tell ya son, it was a joke to an old fart like me. When I was a kid, measles was just something you got. It came and threw a little party inside you and after a week or so it was gone. In our infinite wisdom we declared war on it. Don't get me wrong, I have nothing *against* the eradication of measles, my problem is the means *used*. We, like it or not, are part of the cycle of compost – or cycle of life – whichever you want to call it, it's just two sides of the same coin. Well, vaccines are dead viruses swimming in a soup of mercury, aluminum, formaldehyde, and other chemicals commonly considered unsafe for consumption. Not only do these chemicals hasten the ending of the life part of the cycle, they also corrupt the compost, and therefore, the subsequent life cycle. But you see son, not only does the corporamerican conformaceutical complex not make a dime off the dirt from which mother nature's medicines grow, their interests are actively at odds. That's why I always have a little talk with my customers, ensure they understand that the composting log cabin shithouse is just one part of a balanced life, that inputs are as important to outputs as the process in between-"

"Dad, weren't you gonna tell me about the CEO?"

"I was getting there son."

"You were sidetracked." Waiting for dad to make a point is a real diatribulation.

"Well, that's getting into semantics now, isn't it? Where was I? Oh, right. You see, the dire problem facing the cycle of life is that not only are we adding chemicals to the life part of the cycle, no sir! We've been chemically crippling the compost cycle too. I don't like it. Not one stinking bit."

"So what happened to the CEO?"

"The CEO?"

"The one that died."

"Oh, strange story that. Guy's in the shower with his young Oriental wife when she starts peeing on his leg. Apparently she was daydreaming about an unfulfilled fantasy or something. Now, in my humble opinion there are two kinds of people when it comes to peeing in the shower: the more enlightened kind who do it if they feel like it and those who irrationally think that, though urine is relatively sterile, it should be treated like toxic waste. I'm guessing that this CEO, probably as a result of his aseptic suburban childhood, was one of the latter."

"So she pissed on his leg? That *killed* him?"

"No son, what killed him was his fear of the compost cycle, and how that fear manifested itself when he saw that golden flow streaming down his leg. What should've made the fella honored to have a wife so willing to share herself, caused him to jump back in shock. After tripping over the tub's edge, his head came down on the toilet, snapping his neck."

"Holy shit."

"Yeah, what a crappy way to go out. Now, the reason I bring up the story is that it's his widow we're working for."

"No shit?"

"No fooling son."

"And she wants a log cabin composting *shithouse?*"

"Oh son, we're building her *so* much more than *just* a shithouse. We're helping in her recovery, facilitating a return to simplicity, rebuilding her relationship with nature one log at a time. You see, most buildings are moats against nature, sterile walls to keep *us* in and *it* out. I like to think of my

233

structures as more of a bridge to span the gap. Not only will there be a shithouse, but also a shower house with both solar hot water and wood-heated hot water, where she may pee whenever it tickles her fancy. We're gonna build her the finest hobbit house this side of Middle Earth, a haven for her to rest her tired eyes when the world wears her out. Last but not least, we're gonna erect her a studio out of recycled wine bottles, so as to facilitate the mind expansion of her artistic endeavors."

"Glass bottles? In the *walls?*"

"Sure! Course you gotta have mortar between them just like with bricks. That's where the cob comes in. She's quite the gal son. Inherits one of the biggest fortunes in silicon valley and she just wants to live off the grid. I think you're gonna like her."

"Is it a painting studio?"

"No, she said she plays an instrument, but I can't recall which one. You're gonna *love* the property she picked. Old abandoned orchard out by Doe Bay. She said something funny when I went to look at the job. I was pulling out my portfolio to show her some photos of a real deluxe log cabin composting shithouse I built out on Waldron island. She'd barely taken a glance at the first couple of photos when she says she's got a feeling I'm the one for the job. Now, she was scratching herself below her breast as she said that, so maybe she was just too preoccupied with an itch to really look, but she had this glow. It was like she was looking through my skin into my soul. Now, I love your mother dearly but a man still looks. If he doesn't look its time to pick out his casket, or my personal favorite, a tree. Did I tell you that son? When I die – which is decades away, don't you worry – I want to be buried under a Ginkgo tree. That tree hasn't changed since the dinosaurs. I can hardly think of a better assistant in my transition. No casket between William Walter Woods and the compost cycle, no sir. Where was I?"

Terminally rambling. "The girl."

"Oh right. Woowee! That girl is built like a brick shithouse!"

"You said she was scratching under her breast?"

"Yeah, I tried to offer her some of your mom's beeswax and tee tree oil cream, but she said it would pass in time. I asked if she had a rash, but she just smiled and said in her pretty little Philippine accent that she couldn't explain it and not to worry, so I let it go."

Holy shit.

Dad relights his joint, sending a smoke ring past my confounded face as he peers out the passenger window at Cascade lake, bouncing his brain waves off its sun-dappled surface. "Beautiful day," he declares.

"Can I ask you a question dad?" I enquire, hoping to hold down the hope hammering in my heart.

"Sure son, shoot."

"Where'd I get my name John from?"

"I never told you that story?"

"No."

"Well, I had this dream right before you were born that you and I were at some sort of Asian girly bar. You're in your diapers putting two dollar bills in these girls' panties. They're loving you, though whether because you're a cute little kid or because you're handing out twos instead of ones I can't tell. After a while one of the girls takes a fancy to you, so she picks you up and takes you off to a back room. You've got this big grin like you're pooping yourself. I told your mom about the dream and she says, 'you dreamed our child was a *John?*' So I said, 'that's *it!* Let's call him *John!*' Course we didn't know you were gonna be a boy or if you'd have a predilection for prostitutes, but then you were and the name stuck."

"That's it?"

"Sure! Seemed as good a reason as any. I ever tell you why your middle name is Thomas?"

Acknowledgments

For being my first beta readers I would like to thank Gail Ochoa and my brother Forrest Dick, both of whom made the mistake of offering me encouragement. For pointing out stylistic mistakes and sending me back to the drawing board I would like to thank Eilis Keely. For beta reading a later draft I would like to thank Donald Burpee, Greg Sellentin, and Hannah Enich, all of whom either genuinely enjoyed it or are too amiable to admit how deeply it disturbed them.

For not feeding me the factory food that perpetuates the poverty of the American mind and sends millions to the meat grinder of the medical machine I would like to thank my mother, who not only helped me repel the food-pyramid programming, but also made possible my first brush with fame by not having me innoculated, a fifteen minutes for which I must also thank the tiny army of invaders that not only left me immune to measles without need of a needle packed with poisonous preservatives, but also immunized me against the fearmongering of the media and their manufactured public opinion.

Last but not least, I would like to thank the real Rain, who reaffirmed my faith in femininity and earned a broken heart for her trouble.

About the Author

Born on September 5, 1985 outside of Olympia, Washington, Gordon Dick floundered through his first third of a century with only his animal urges, contrarianism, and his mother's assurance he's special to guide him. Despite this lack of direction, he still found the time to get his BA in liberal arts from The Evergreen State College, get food poisoning on four continents, dabble in the import/export business, and learn how to operate both a shovel and a cocktail shaker. He once held a baby sloth. Thanks to this novel, he is now as employable as your average ex con. Buying this book saves him from a lifetime of manual labor.

www.privilegepress.com

https://twitter.com/PrivilegePress